Clara drew in a deep breath, hoping it would help her think, but she could still feel Roger's arms around her.

Still feel how he'd kissed the top of her head. At that moment, she'd wanted to wrap her arms around him and hold on. Just hold on.

That made no sense.

All it did was frustrate her even more. Spinning back around to face her friend, Clara held up one finger. "I awoke to discover he'd kidnapped my child right from under my nose."

Suzanne set her pen in the holder and rose from her chair. "He did not kidnap your child. He took her downstairs and fed her breakfast."

"Without my knowledge."

Suzanne let out an exasperated sounding sigh. "Roger hasn't been able to do anything right in your eyes since we stepped foot in England."

Clara opened her mouth, but closed it again when she couldn't come up with a reply.

"Your daughter lights up when she sees him, even your dog adores him, but you can't find a single thing to like about him. Not one." Suzanne shook her head.

"I just want our lives to be normal again," Clara said. That won't happen living in a marquess's home. Nor being hugged by him. Even if it felt so amazing. So real.

Author Note

Thank you for picking up the second book in the Southern Belles in London series. I've had fun writing this series about young women being transported halfway around the world, where they find their heroes.

Research for each and every book I write is always interesting, but during Clara and Roger's story, I discovered that the International Exhibition of 1862 took place in London from May to November. It was a sensational event that attracted millions of visitors and had exhibits from countries around the world. One of the exhibits that drew great excitement was a "refrigerator" that made ice. That invention would have been of great interest to Roger, so I had to find a way to make mention of it.

I hope you enjoy Clara and Roger's journey of getting to know each other and, ultimately, admitting that they both do deserve the love they'd found together.

LAURI ROBINSON

—

The Making of His Marchioness

HARLEQUIN
HISTORICAL

HARLEQUIN®
HISTORICAL™

Recycling programs
for this product may
not exist in your area.

ISBN-13: 978-1-335-72368-0

The Making of His Marchioness

Copyright © 2023 by Lauri Robinson

For questions and comments about the quality of this book,
please contact us at CustomerService@Harlequin.com.

Harlequin Enterprises ULC
22 Adelaide St. West, 41st Floor
Toronto, Ontario M5H 4E3, Canada
www.Harlequin.com

Printed in U.S.A.

A lover of fairy tales and history, **Lauri Robinson** can't imagine a better profession than penning happily-ever-after stories about men and women in days gone past. Her favorite settings include World War II, the roaring twenties and the Old West. Lauri and her husband raised three sons in their rural Minnesota home and are now getting their just rewards by spoiling their grandchildren. Visit her at laurirobinson.blogspot.com, Facebook.com/lauri.robinson1 or Twitter.com/laurir.

Books by Lauri Robinson

Harlequin Historical

Diary of a War Bride
A Family for the Titanic Survivor
The Captain's Christmas Homecoming

Southern Belles in London

The Return of His Promised Duchess
The Making of His Marchioness

The Osterlund Saga

Marriage or Ruin for the Heiress
The Heiress and the Baby Boom

Twins of the Twenties

Scandal at the Speakeasy
A Proposal for the Unwed Mother

Sisters of the Roaring Twenties

The Flapper's Fake Fiancé
The Flapper's Baby Scandal
The Flapper's Scandalous Elopement

Visit the Author Profile page
at Harlequin.com for more titles.

To my amazing editor, Carly, who has been my editor since my second book with Harlequin. This is now my fiftieth book, and my gratitude for all you've done is endless.

Chapter One

1862

It took nearly all her strength for Clara Walton to walk up the sloped bank at the wharf from where they'd just disembarked the ship that had brought them from America to England. She held on tighter to her daughter in her arms and focused on putting one foot in front of the other. Annabelle would be there to meet them. It would be wonderful to see her lifelong friend. To thank her for sending someone to find them and bring them here to stay with her until the war ended.

A safe place, where Abigail, who was only a year and a half old, could sleep in a real bed and have plenty to eat.

All of that should make Clara happy, but she couldn't find it. Happiness. How could she? She'd left her home, the last tangible bits that held memories of her family. Of her husband and the life that they'd made together.

Other than her daughter. Abigail was her everything. All she had, and that was the reason she was here. In

England, along with Suzanne and Sammy, the dog who had been walking beside her but paused to wait while she stopped to catch her breath.

Suzanne, her dearest friend who had agreed that coming here was what they had to do, paused, too.

'Here,' Suzanne said, holding out her arms. 'Let me carry Abigail for a little while.'

Because her arms were trembling, making her fearful that they might give out at any moment, Clara released her daughter to her friend. 'Thank you.' She didn't have the energy to say more, but thought about all they'd been through, and how walking up this small hill should be easy, not taxing.

Taxing had been the death of her husband, immediately followed by the death of her father and in-laws the night that the entire town she'd gown up in had been burned to the ground. Taxing had been trying to live through a war, scrounging for food every day and having to keep Abigail and Sammy quiet inside the root cellar whenever soldiers had been nearby. Taxing had been having to climb up the rope ladder hanging over the side of the large ship that had brought them to England. *The Lady of the Sea* hadn't been able to cross the Union blockade, therefore it had been a smaller, blockade runner steamship that had sailed them from the shore out to the large ship.

Taxing had been the long sea voyage in a rocking, rolling ship.

Clara would never have considered leaving with Captain Harris and his sailors, if not for the letter he'd given her. From Annabelle. Stating that she'd heard about the burning of Hampton, their home town, and asking that Clara please send a return note with the sea captain, letting her know how they were all doing.

She'd been prepared to write that note, but the captain had explained that he'd been commissioned to return them all to England if he felt they were in danger. The closeness of the cannon fire, their living conditions, their appearances, had all been more than Clara could deny. She'd had nothing to justify remaining on the farm. Even to herself. Therefore, she'd conceded and left her home. Her country.

She still questioned if she'd done the right thing, however, she was extremely grateful to be off the ship. The constant rocking and moving had sapped her of her last bits of resolve.

'That's the coach,' Suzanne said. 'And there's Captain Harris.'

Clara saw the elegant black coach at the top of the hill and the tall, older man standing beside it, and pushed herself to start walking again. She'd rest tonight, once they were reunited with Annabelle. Rest and eat. Now that their trip was over, she'd be able to eat and keep the food down.

By the time she reached the top of the hill, she was so winded, so weak, she didn't dare take Abigail from Suzanne. The short distance to the coach felt like miles, and once they arrived on the road near the coach, she willed herself to not wobble as Captain Harris introduced them to a man standing next to him.

A tall, smartly dressed man with bright green eyes.

'Mrs Walton, Miss Bishop, allow me to introduce you to—'

'Where's Annabelle?' she asked, looking past both men, but not seeing her friend. Or any other woman. Just men and wagons and traffic and buildings.

'Roger Hardgroves, at your service,' the green-eyed man said. 'It's my pleasure to meet both of you. I hope your voyage to England was uneventful.'

The voyage was little more than a blur to Clara. She shook her head at the man and asked Captain Harris, 'Is Annabelle here?'

The captain looked towards the other man.

'I am prepared to oversee your travels—'

'Oversee our travels?' Clara asked, interrupting the green-eyed man while trying to gather her mind. Everything was so foggy. She just wanted this trip to be over. It had to be over. Her head was throbbing and she couldn't blink away the flashes of light in her eyes.

'Yes.' The man waved at a coachman who moved towards the coach door. 'We can leave immediately.'

'Leave for Annabelle's home?' she asked hopefully.

'No—'

'That's where we need to go,' she said. 'To Annabelle's home.'

'My apologies, but that's not possible at the moment. I have—'

'Not possible?' Despite her exhaustion, or perhaps due to it, Clara felt a surge of anger. All she wanted was a bit of normalcy. To know where she was going to sleep each and every night. To know that Abigail would have enough to eat each and every day. 'We have travelled halfway around the world under the impression that we'd be united with Annabelle upon arrival.'

'I understand that, but—'

'I don't mean to be rude,' Clara interrupted, 'but we will not be going anywhere with you.' She would not be obliged to another stranger. Couldn't be right now. She just didn't have it in her. 'We will wait right here until it is possible to go to Annabelle's home.' Hoping for an ally, she looked at the captain. 'Perhaps you could help us with that, Captain Harris?'

Roger's patience was wearing as thin as a morning fog before it gives away to the sun, and the smile on his face was slipping. He'd become known as the most eligible bachelor in London—though personally, he didn't appreciate the infamy since he had no plans of changing his bachelorhood—because Roger Hardgroves, the fourth Marquess of Clairmount, had a way with women. He could have them eating out of his hand within minutes. That, however, was English women. American women were apparently different.

Very different.

He'd seen that via his best friend, Drew, Andrew Charles Barkly, the Duke of Mansfield, who had married an American—Annabelle, the friend that Clara Walton was intent upon being reunited with.

Their reunion would happen as soon as possible, and he would tell her that, if she'd let him. With the wind tugging at the brown and gold hair she had pulled back into a loose knot, her dark brown eyes narrowed into slits and her lips pursed into a pucker, she'd interrupted him every time he'd opened his mouth.

The dog beside her was just as obstinate. Solid black, of good size, and hunched, Roger had the distinct feeling any wrong move and the dog would launch forward and sink inch-long canine teeth into his thigh.

'Excuse me, ma'am,' Tristan Harris said, looking apologetic, 'but it was the— It was Mr Hardgroves who commissioned me to bring you to England. I assure you that you are in good hands with him.'

Roger was glad that the ship captain had noticed that he'd avoided using his title during introductions. Annabelle had been against titles and he assumed her friends would be, too.

Tristan's answer did not impress Clara. 'Good hands?' she asked.

'Yes, ma'am,' Tristan replied.

The heavy fog that had settled over the saltwater of the harbour during the night had completely dissipated, giving way for the sun to warm the air and make the scents of the harbour stronger. The sun also brought life to the seashore. Gulls now crowed and called out, signalling others as if a feast lined the shore rather than a morsel or two, and traffic, freight wagons, flat beds, and carriages, full and empty, were beginning to roll up and down the roadway.

Unabashed that traffic had to swerve around her, Clara stood there, glaring at him, with both hands on her hips. 'Why did he want us brought here?' she asked the captain, rather than him.

If he hadn't already been steadfast in his reasons for

remaining a bachelor, Clara Walton would have done the trick. Everything about her reminded him of exactly why he'd chosen the life he had. Women simply were not worth the trouble. And they were trouble. From the cradle to the grave, they did little more than make a man's life far more complicated than it needed to be. 'Because Annabelle requested that you be found,' Roger said, 'and I agreed to commission Tristan—Captain Harris—to find you and bring you to England if necessary.'

'Why?'

He understood that the Civil War was tearing her country apart, and that she'd just sailed across the ocean, arrived in England upon one of his ships, but couldn't she understand he was simply trying to help?

That wouldn't be so difficult. Not nearly as difficult as she was being. Furthermore, she had to comprehend that she couldn't go on living the way she had been back in America.

Early this morning, Tristan had told him that she'd been found, along with her young daughter, dog, and friend, living in small earth cellar. A literal hole in the ground, because her farm had been ravished by soldiers. The captain had also said that her husband and other family members had all perished, leaving no one to look after them.

'As a favour for a friend,' Roger replied. 'Annabelle was afraid that you and Miss Bishop were in dire circumstances. From what Captain Harris told me, she was correct. Therefore, he followed my request and brought you here, and I will now provide transportation and housing until all of you can be reunited.'

Roger watched the expressions cross her face. How she blinked and glanced from him to her friend and Captain Harris. Even wearing mended and worn clothes, her attractiveness could turn heads. The Good Lord had a sense of humour in creating women the way he had. Giving them all sorts of things to attract men and then giving them hearts of stone.

His mother had shown him how hard a woman's heart could be years ago, when she'd cared more about what she wanted than what he'd needed.

Done trying to convince Clara, because they all could get run over if they didn't move out of the street, Roger turned his attention to her friend. 'Miss Bishop.' The blonde woman standing near the edge of the street where his coach was waiting and holding the child in her arms had given out silent looks of compassion while Clara had been interrupting his every word. Therefore, he hoped she had more sense than Clara. 'The coachman will assist you and the child into the coach.'

'No!' Clara lurched forward to stop the other woman from moving, but lost her footing and stumbled.

Acting fast, Roger closed the space between them and caught her around the waist before she fell to the ground.

She gasped and attempted to right herself, but couldn't seem to get her feet beneath her.

He held her firmly, giving her time to find her footing. She was trembling and little more than skin and bones. He could feel her rib bones through the thread-bare material of her dress. 'Easy,' he said.

She blew out a breath. 'I'm fine. Fine.'

Though she had straightened herself, she was still trembling, and he didn't release her. 'We need to get out of the street before we get run over.'

She let out a little moan sound, but nodded.

Slowly, he guided her towards the coach. 'The sooner we start our journey, the sooner you'll be reunited with Annabelle.' That was a lie. Drew and Annabelle had been called to Scotland last week due to the illness of one of Drew's aunts, and he hadn't heard when they'd return.

At the coach door, she turned weary, dark brown eyes up at him. 'How do we know you're really Annabelle's friend?'

He could tell her that if by some unrealistic cause he was ever in the mind to kidnap someone—if that's what she thought he was attempting to do—it wouldn't be the odd bevy of misfits filling his coach. However, he could understand her concern, and though he didn't want to bring up sad memories it was the only way he knew to convince her. 'Annabelle assisted your father at his livery for years.' He knew that from how Annabelle had helped Drew's old horse. 'That is true, is it not?'

Clara stared at him, but said nothing.

'That is true, is it not?' he repeated.

Placing a foot onto the coach step, she said, 'Yes.'

She was still unsteady, and he kept a hold of her waist until she was inside the coach. He then turned, bid a farewell to Tristan, and climbed inside the coach himself.

Roger took a seat on the empty bench and nodded to Jacob, his groom, to close the door. No one said a word, and he figured that Clara was still processing the fact that he did know Annabelle and wasn't trying to kidnap them.

A moment later, the coach lurched forward, then soon settled into a smooth ride—as smoothly as the wheels could move over the cobblestone road that led them away from the wharf—and Roger imagined this could very well become the longest journey of his life.

Running a hand through his hair, he glanced out the window at the sun-filled blue sky. In that, he should be thankful. April was a finicky month for weather and it could be raining, which would elongate the trip. His best guess was that the trip would take five, maybe six days.

He could have chosen to take these companions that he was saddled with to his family's home here in Southampton, but that would have meant staying with his grandfather and possibly his mother. They—mainly his mother—were the reason why he maintained a small townhouse to stay at when he had business to conduct in town. The townhouse was too small for hosting guests, which was how he liked it. He'd never likened to the idea of being a host to any manner of guests.

He not only lived alone and liked it, he normally travelled alone. On horseback. Smokey, his grey gelding, was tied to the back of the coach. Later, after they stopped for a midday meal, he'd ride, which would give the women more room.

As well as the dog.

The black dog sat on his haunches between the women, and even though they were all skinny enough that there was plenty of room, Roger felt sorry for the dog and patted the seat beside him.

Evidently the dog understood the command, because he jumped off the seat between the women and leaped up beside him.

Clara's brown eyes still held apprehension as she reached over and took the sleeping child from Miss Bishop.

Roger had an eye for beautiful women, and Clara was striking. Several long strands of brown and gold hair had come loose from her bun, and her features were dainty, elegant. So were her lips. A unique glow, that he couldn't ascertain came from the sun shining in through the coach window or not, overtook her features as she looked down at the child in her arms. Carefully, she repositioned the sleeping child so that the little head was resting in the crook of her arm.

'Captain Harris had mentioned that you would take us to Annabelle,' Miss Bishop said softly. 'Clara may have been taking care of Abigail when he said that.'

Suzanne Bishop was as thin as Clara, but she didn't look quite as worn out. She had more colour in her face, which made him frown slightly as he turned his attention to Clara again.

She avoided his gaze by turning to look out the window.

Roger had yet to explain why he was their escort,

mainly because he hadn't had a chance. 'Annabelle is currently in Scotland.'

Clara's head snapped back in his direction. 'Scotland? Then why aren't we in Scotland?'

'Because Annabelle is merely visiting family in Scotland.'

'Family?'

He nodded. 'Her husband's family.'

'Husband?' Suzanne asked, eyes wide with surprise and hosting a grin.

'Annabelle is married?' Clara asked. 'To whom?' Her eyes widened even more. 'You?'

A shiver rippled his entire torso at the mere idea of marriage. That was an agreement that he'd never enter. He liked his carefree life. It was simple, and that was the one thing that women weren't. Furthermore, the one thing that his mother wanted from him was for him to get married, therefore, he wouldn't. His mother claimed marriage was one way he could honour his father, by having an heir to carry on the family name, title, and legacy. To him, that was ironic, considering the way she'd given up the family name and her title of marchioness by remarrying shortly after his father had died.

'No, not me,' Roger replied. 'Annabelle is married to my very good friend, Drew. Andrew Barkly.'

'When did she get married?' Suzanne asked, clearly not as sceptical of the news as Clara.

'Last year,' he replied, watching as the women glanced at each other. 'A few months after she arrived in England.' At one time, Drew had sworn off marriage too, but had changed his mind upon meeting Annabelle.

Roger vowed that would not happen to him. Nothing would change his mind about marriage, because nothing would change his mind about giving his mother what she wanted.

'Where are you taking us?' Clara asked.

The sigh in his chest was so heavy it was painful. Still, he held it in. If there was any other option, he'd have taken it, but there wasn't, therefore he admitted, 'To my home.'

'Your home?' Clara shook her head. 'No. Absolutely not.'

'Do you have an address that you'd prefer I took you to? Someone you know here in England who would welcome you to stay with them?' he asked. 'I'll take you there instead.' Gladly, he added only for himself.

She glared at him.

'No, Mr Hardgroves,' Miss Bishop said. 'We have nowhere else to go.'

He knew that and gave her a nod. 'My given name is Roger. Feel free to use it.'

'Thank you. I am Suzanne. This is Clara and little Abigail.' She then pointed to the dog who had lain down beside him, taking up a fair share of the seat space. 'That is Sammy.'

Roger had known their names from Annabelle's list and months of searching, except for the dog. Notwithstanding his not so sterling reputation when it came to the ladies, he wasn't heartless, and his stomach clenched at the sadness on Clara's face as she looked out the window again.

'I promise you will all be safe in my company,' he

said. 'It will take a few days to get to my home, and I assure you that I'll make the journey as comfortable as possible.'

Clara let out a *humph* sound.

'Thank you,' Suzanne said, with a somewhat apologetic glance towards Clara. 'It will be good to be done travelling, and wonderful to see Annabelle. Is she well?'

'Yes. I saw her and her husband three weeks ago, and they were both doing well.'

He and Drew had been best friends since they'd been small boys and were as close as brothers. In fact, Roger felt as if Drew was his only family, and therefore, he'd used every resource at his disposal, including the ships, captains, and sailors in his employ, to gain information about the people on the list Annabelle had created of people from her home town in Virginia. He'd crossed names off that list, one by one, and had delivered sad news to Drew with each one. The final three names on the list were Clara and Abigail Walton and Suzanne Bishop. The two women and child had seemed to have disappeared. Last month, he'd informed Drew and Annabelle that he'd commissioned Tristan to not return to Southampton until he either had the women with him, or had proof of their whereabouts, or gravesites, which is what Roger had expected, considering the outcomes of the other names on the list.

It appeared as if Lady Luck was still his friend. Annabelle was sure to be ecstatic. Drew would be, too.

In time, he was sure that Clara would be thankful, too. She just needed time to adjust to all the changes. He held a great sense of compassion for all she'd been through, and Suzanne, and even if Drew hadn't been his best friend, he would have been compelled to assist them.

Looking at Clara, he said, 'Champion is one of Drew's horses—an old horse, who had been ailing. Annabelle helped him with a mint ointment that she'd learned from your father. He must have been very knowledgeable.'

'He was,' she replied.

'You have my condolences for all you have lost,' he said. 'You both do.'

'Thank you,' Suzanne replied.

Clara didn't want condolences. She closed her eyes, tried to block out the tall man wearing his fancy frock-coat and ruffled white shirt sitting across from her. Block out the fact that her home was thousands of miles away, on the other side of the world. Not only the home she'd once shared with her father, but also the one she and Mark had lived in since their marriage three years ago. Sometimes, if she tried hard enough, she could remember being happy. Remember eating regularly and wearing clothes that didn't have holes in them. Remember crawling into bed at night and snuggling up next to the warmth and comfort of her husband.

All she'd ever wanted had been her own home and a family. To be a wife and mother. Mark had given her that and they had been happy. He wouldn't recognise their farm now. None of it. Soldiers had ransacked it, taken everything worth taking and even things that weren't. There had been so many nights when she'd been certain that the house would be set afire, like the barn had been months ago.

Destroyed or not, it had been her home and she dreamed of the day when the war would be over. Then she would find a way to rebuild the barn and fix the house, so Abigail would have a home again.

The ache and pain inside Clara grew. The war had taken everything.

Mark, her father, her town, her home, the very country where she'd been born and raised.

Swallowing the bitter taste in her mouth, Clara opened her eyes and looked down at her sleeping daughter. She was still so dizzy that everything was blurred. Even Abigail, but Clara knew how beautiful her daughter was, and how precious. Abigail had only been three months old when Mark had left to fight for the Union. That was almost a year ago now. Eight months since they'd received word that Mark had died in battle. That very night, the town of Hampton had been marched upon by the Confederacy and burned.

'How old is your daughter?' Mr Hardgroves asked.

Clara didn't want to answer him. Didn't want to be sitting across from him in a coach travelling across England. Yet, she was here and the ugly truth was that they'd had nowhere else to go. They'd had nothing left to eat, nothing left to hunt or scrounge. The constant regiments camped near the farm had cleared the area of game and the ongoing cannon fire had kept them all inside for days on end, eating the last bits of the food she'd put up before… She shoved aside the haunting memories. 'She's fifteen months old.'

'We'll stop at a coach inn and eat in a couple of hours, but if she needs something in the meantime, Jacob put a basket of foodstuff in the box beneath your seat.'

Clara kept her gaze on Abigail, who was sound asleep. A great wave of embarrassment over how she'd lost her temper, lost her very last bits of composure in front of this man, who truly was being kind, washed over her. What sort of example had she set for her daughter with that behaviour? Not a very high one, and she'd always prided herself on her behaviour, her manners. The fact that she didn't want kindness right now was an excuse and not a very good one.

He'd proven that he knew Annabelle, but the ultimate truth was that she had to accept his kindness for Abigail's sake. And she had to mind her own temperament, set a better example for her daughter. Even though it was hard to be so far away from all she'd ever known.

'Thank you,' Clara replied. It had been a hellish thing, not having enough food to feed her daughter. 'She might be hungry when she wakes up.'

'Then we'll get her something out from under the seat,' he said. 'And we'll get something for this guy, too.'

Clara's heart clenched, knowing without looking that he was referring to the dog. Sammy was nothing like the roly-poly pup that Mark had brought home before he'd left for the war so she and Abigail wouldn't be alone while he'd been gone. Her eyes burned, but it was as if she'd cried out all her tears, because only one formed and trickled down her cheek. Sammy was so skinny, yet so devoted to them. Especially Abigail. The two were inseparable.

'I sent a messenger to Mansfield,' Mr Hardgroves said, 'this morning, as soon as I'd learned of your arrival. That is Drew and Annabelle's home. Upon their return, she'll know where you are, and I assure you, she'll be very happy to learn to news.'

Clara nodded. The three of them had been friends for years, and she and Suzanne had missed Annabelle greatly since Arlo Smith, Annabelle's father, had sent her to England when the war had broken out.

Hearing that Annabelle was married had left Clara with mixed emotions. She'd hoped that Annabelle had planned on returning to Virginia. That they all could return together.

'Excuse me, Mr Hardgroves,' Suzanne said. 'Captain Harris said that you'd been looking for other people that Annabelle knew.'

Clara turned her gaze to the window again, watched as they rolled past cobblestone cottages with stone wall fences and iron gates glimmering in the bright sunshine. She couldn't remember much of anything that Captain Harris had said. The ship ride had made her too sick. The rocking of the coach was making her feel ill all over again.

'That is correct,' he answered Suzanne.

'Did you learn anything about her father? His name was Arlo Smith.'

'Yes, I did.'

Clara turned her attention to him. 'We heard he'd been burned while fighting the fire, but nothing more.'

He nodded. 'He had, but has made a full recovery.'

'How do you know that?' Clara asked.

'Because he has moved here, to England, and lives not far from Drew and Annabelle.'

Happiness and hope sprang forth inside Clara. 'We can go there. We can stay with him.'

'Unfortunately, no,' Roger said, 'He and his wife travelled to Scotland with Drew and Annabelle.'

'His wife?'

'Yes, Cecilia, she came from America with him.'

'Oh, Clara,' Suzanne said, laying a hand on her arm. 'They are both alive. And married, isn't that wonderful?'

It was, but she was still focused on something else. 'Do you know for sure that Arlo isn't home? That any of them aren't home?'

'I'm sorry to disappoint you, but yes, I know none of them are home,' Roger answered.

Clara tried to find appreciation in all this man had done and was doing for them, but she was disappointed. She wanted to see a familiar face. Wanted a place to rest. She was tired of being sick. Tired of everything.

The anger she'd had inside her for months, mixed with a great amount of sadness, twisted her stomach. It was all so unfair. So egregious. And wrong. So wrong that so much had been taken away from so many, leaving people helpless. Completely helpless. That's what she felt, helpless, and hated it.

It angered her, too. Her daughter needed things. Food and clothes and a safe place to live. If Roger Hardgroves could provide that, she'd accept it and appreciate it, until Annabelle returned.

Because she had no other choice.

Clara sucked in air, told herself to breathe, but it was impossible. The lump in her throat blocked the air. Smothering a sob as much as she could, she set her gaze on the window again, but whatever was rolling past was nothing but a blur.

She had no choice, but she didn't want to live anywhere but on the farm that she and Mark had turned into a home for their family. Together, they had dreamed of doing so many things as they grew old together.

What if she forgot all that while she was here? All their dreams and plans. What if she couldn't hold on to her dream of rebuilding the farm?

She couldn't give that up, too.

Just couldn't.

That was something that Abigail needed, too. A place to remember her father.

Her head throbbed harder and hurt. Hurt as badly as her heart. She leaned against the side of the coach and closed her eyes. Tried not to think about the man sitting across from her. The one with thick black hair and sideburns, and eyes as green as a hayfield before it turns golden brown. The one who was petting Sammy, letting the dog sleep with his head on his thigh.

Chapter Two

Clara tried to open her eyes but couldn't lift her lids. Panic welled inside her and she tried harder, but it was as if they were pasted shut. There was also something pulling her downward, back to sleep, and it was strong, much stronger than her.

'Take a sip, Clara, just as sip.'

She couldn't. Couldn't eat or drink anything. It would come right back up.

'It's just water. Take a sip,' the voice coaxed.

The voice was vaguely familiar, but the fear of her stomach revolting was more familiar. That's all it had done since boarding the ship. Nothing had stayed down, yet she was thirsty. Very thirsty. She parted her lips as the voice requested, felt the moisture enter her mouth, trickle down her throat, but then the force pulling her downward won.

That happened again and again. Her eyes wouldn't open, but someone dribbled water in her mouth. It scared her that she couldn't open her eyes, made her question what she couldn't see, couldn't hear. She had to open her eyes. Had to wake up, and tried harder. 'Abi—'

'Abigail is fine,' the voice said. 'She's sleeping. Sammy is with her. So is Suzanne.'

Suzanne. Bless her, and Sammy. Dear, sweet Sammy. He would alert them to anything out of the ordinary. That meant she could sleep a little longer.

But the voice wouldn't let her sleep, not for long, it kept telling her to take a sip and water kept trickling into her mouth, down her throat. It was all as much of a nightmare as an oddly comforting dream.

Roger had spent nights in bedrooms with women in the past, but never with a widow, and never as a nurse-maid. Widows were always looking for their next husband, something he would never be to anyone. As far as being a nursemaid, he wasn't overly confident he was being a good one because he had no experience at that whatsoever, but he wasn't about to let Clara Walton die.

When Abigail had awoken in the carriage, but Clara hadn't, both he and Suzanne had assumed that Clara had simply been exhausted from all they'd been through. Between the two of them and Sammy, they'd kept Abigail entertained and let Clara sleep. However, when they'd arrived at the inn to eat at midday, and Clara couldn't be roused, he'd known it was more than exhaustion.

Upon his demand, the inn's proprietor had summoned the local doctor, who claimed that Clara's body didn't have enough fluid and that she'd perish if they couldn't get her to drink.

That had been hours ago. It was nearly midnight and she still hadn't woken enough to drink any significant amount. He'd been spooning water into her mouth at regular intervals and was doubting how much good it was doing.

The lamplight in the small rented room reflected off her still form. Perhaps he was a blackguard. All he'd seen was her attractiveness upon meeting her, even while arguing with her, when in reality, he should have paid attention to her pallor, her sunken eyes, and he should have taken into consideration that anyone who hadn't eaten properly for months and then travelled across the ocean, could easily have become seasick. So sick that anything she'd taken in had come back up.

Suzanne had stated that Clara hadn't eaten much while on the ship, but had also said that Clara never ate much, that she always took small portions so Abigail and Sammy could have more.

Roger disapproved of women who thought along those lines. How they claimed that what they were doing was for the benefit of others, yet they never considered how those very actions affected the other people. It wasn't always a benefit. He knew. He was the product of such a woman.

What Clara didn't understand was that by making the choice not to eat enough, she was putting Abigail in danger of not having a parent. He didn't know much about children, which is why he chose to sit with Clara, dribble water in her mouth, while Suzanne watched over Abigail. Suzanne and Sammy that is. The little girl and dog were never far apart. The dog made sure of that, and with the dog at her side, Abigail chattered and giggled and toddled about as if the world was a wonderful place.

Perhaps to her it was, and he hoped it would continue to be, because she would still have her mother, the one parent she did have.

In order for that to be, Clara had to drink, eat, and gain her strength.

Once again, Roger coaxed her to part her lips, dribbled a spoonful of water into her mouth and lifted her chin to assure the water made its way down her throat.

Then, he set the glass and spoon on the table to wait for the next interval.

He'd never been good at waiting. It held too many memories. He hated waiting as badly as he hated the sea.

Despite owning a prosperous shipping conglomerate and managing another large shipping company for his grandfather, which he would one day inherit, he hated sailing. The sea was moody, unpredictable, and fickle. At one moment she could be bright, gorgeous, and giving, then, within the beat of a heart, she could turn dark, ugly, and unforgiving. Like women. That's what he compared the sea to. No matter how beautiful she looked, how loving and welcoming she appeared, she could change a man's life in the blink of an eye.

That was exactly why he hired men to sail his ships, and why he was very cautious of the women he chose to spend time with, for he did enjoy a woman's companionship in some ways, but he never attached himself to one. Nor would he.

There was no reason, no benefit for him to attach himself to anyone. His needs were met by willing companions who were just as happy to part sheets as they had been to climb between them.

He had a good life. A happy life, and would return to it as soon as this trip was over.

As soon as Clara was well enough to travel, he'd take them to Clairmount, let his servants take care of them and he'd go to London, to his townhouse and await word from Drew there.

He picked up the glass and spoon again, and coaxed Clara to part her lips, dribbled water between them, and lifted her chin.

He continued those same actions throughout the night, sitting on the side of the bed, and thinking how he wouldn't let her die. Not after she'd come this far. Not after all she'd been through. She had fight in her. He'd seen that at the docks and would see it again. He'd make sure of that.

It was in the wee hours of the morning, just as dawn was breaking, that he set down the glass and spoon and turned up the flame of the lamp on the table, questioning if he'd seen her lashes flutter.

His breath stalled as he heard her sigh, and the beating of his heart kicked up a notch as her eyes opened, closed, and opened again.

She stared at him blankly, then a tiny frown formed between her brows, as if she was overly puzzled.

He had no doubt that she was puzzled, and knew the moment recognition hit by the accusation that filled her eyes.

He smiled, because that was the fight he wanted to see again. 'Hello,' he said. 'First, let me assure you that nothing clandestine is happening. You've been ill and I've been assigned to tend to you. Abigail is fine—she's sleeping in another room with Suzanne and Sammy.'

Her eyes fluttered shut for a moment, then opened again. 'Assigned by whom?'

'Dr Purdy,' he answered, which was a lie. The doctor had suggested the inn owner's wife see to Clara. With six rooms to rent and several patrons to feed, Roger had ascertained that the owner's wife already had enough on her hands and had volunteered himself for nursing duty. It had been him or the inn owner, who clearly let his wife do all the work. 'He'll be around to see you in the morning.' Roger picked up the glass that he'd recently refilled from the pitcher. 'You need to drink as much as possible.'

She shook her head.

He nodded.

'It won't settle,' she said quietly.

He slipped his other hand beneath her neck to lift her head and held the glass near her lips. 'Don't take a lot, just a sip or two.'

She refused at first, but then took a drink, a tiny one, and closed her eyes. 'You've been giving me water.'

'Yes, I have.' He laid her head back down and set the glass on the table.

'Why?'

'Because you need it.' The covers were up to her shoulders, but he could see the movement of her hands under the blanket, rubbing her stomach. 'There now.' He laid his hand atop the covers, over her hands. 'Don't think about your stomach. You don't want to make yourself sick. Suzanne and Abigail will want to see you as soon as they wake up. Sammy, too.'

She opened her eyes and looked towards the window beside the bed. 'How long have we been here?'

Her voice was no longer harsh and high-pitched as it had been this morning; instead it was soft, low, and very enchanting. He'd grown used to Annabelle's American accent, and Clara's was very much like it. There was something about that Southern twang that had a lilt and a song to it that tickled his insides in an endearing way. However, there was also sadness in her voice. In fact, she sounded more despondent than when they'd been arguing about leaving Southampton with him. He would never have imagined the woman quarrelling with him had been so extremely ill.

'We arrived midday,' he answered. 'How about another sip of water?'

She shook her head.

He picked up the glass. 'Don't think of your stomach. Just take a sip.'

'Even little sips don't like staying down.'

'Well, I've spooned almost two glassfuls into you, and it's all stayed down.'

Her eyes were wide when she turned, looked at him. 'Two glassfuls?'

'Yes, but you still need more.'

Her eyes fluttered shut again, and because there was still fear inside him that she'd never wake up, he had to bite the inside of his cheek to keep from telling her to not fall back to sleep. Instead, he said, 'Come now, just another swallow.'

The tiniest hint of a smile curled the very corners of her lips. 'Are you always so obstinate?'

'Are you?' he asked in return. Then instantly chided himself. Considering her current condition and her past situations, he truly could understand her stubbornness.

Her smile grew a bit more before she bit her lips together to hide it and then nodded. 'I'll have another sip of water.'

She tried to lift her head and he slid his hand behind her neck, aided her, and held the glass as she took not one, but two sips.

As he set the glass on the table, he mentally measured the amount, as he'd been doing for hours.

'I do appreciate your kindness,' she said.

Her tone was meek, submissive, and he decided that he liked when she'd been arguing with him better and would appreciate when she was well enough to do that again.

'But?' she said.

He grinned to himself, glad to know that her spunk was still there.

She pinched her lips together, a clear sign that she knew what he was thinking, and then shook her head and sighed. 'I can imagine that Annabelle didn't like you very well when you first met.'

'Why would you say that?' he asked, grinning, because that was true.

'Because I know Annabelle.'

He nodded and wondered if he should tell her that Annabelle was married to a duke and that she was now a duchess. Annabelle had been so dead set against anything to do with peerage when she'd arrived in England that she and Drew had almost not got married because of it.

Titles of nobility had frustrated her, and she'd most certainly told him that without mincing words. He assumed it must be that way for her friends as well. It did seem odd, considering the women he normally encountered were generally seeking a titled man in order to obtain a title for themselves.

Ultimately, though, he'd chosen not to tell them about Annabelle's title, or his, because Clara had found enough to argue about with him this morning and he hadn't wanted to give her more fodder.

'She didn't, did she?' Clara asked.

A chuckle rumbled in his chest over how accusatory her expression looked. 'You do know her well.'

'I do. We've been best friends since childhood.'

'As I have been with Drew, her husband. Yes, you could say that Annabelle and I didn't get off on the best foot.' He was known for cajoling women, getting them to tell him secrets of the *ton* or other bits of information for a variety of reasons, but this was different. He couldn't say exactly how, but he didn't want to trick Clara into liking him for his benefit, which is what he usually did. Perhaps it was because she was different than most women he knew. 'The same could be said for you and I. That we got off on the wrong foot.'

Her gaze wasn't condemning, but it was direct, and remained locked on him as she said, 'I loved my husband very much, but have never been overly fond of a man telling me what to do.'

'Did he tell you what to do?'

She gave a slight one-shoulder shrug. 'He attempted at times.'

Roger gave a slight head nod while holding back a grin. 'So noted, I should have asked you to accompany me rather than telling you, for I too know what it's like to have someone telling you what to do. However, I must also defend my actions. I would do anything for Drew, as he would for me. When he asked me to find information about Annabelle's family and friends, I dedicated myself to doing just that. Apart from Arlo and Cecilia, you, Abigail, and Suzanne are the only good news I've been able to provide.'

'Because no one else is left.' There wasn't sarcasm in her voice, just honesty. 'They were all in the same dire position as Suzanne and I. The few who weren't, who had money enough to survive, left.' She sighed. 'We, the entire town, were looked upon as Unionists. Many residents of Hampton had opposed leaving the union. Not everyone—some men from Hampton had chosen to fight for the South, but more had chosen to fight for the North. That's why the Confederate Army burned the town, to keep the Union Army from forming a stronghold there.'

He knew the ins and outs of the war being fought abroad, and, as an outsider, had not chosen either side as the right or wrong one. Nor would he. It was a sad state of affairs for all involved. 'War is difficult to understand, even at times to those fighting it.' He picked up the glass of water and raised a brow.

The shake of her head wasn't a no, it was more of a

humorous reaction to his action, as if it was signalling that the two of them were at war, or at least in a battle.

Which is exactly how he meant it. He would battle with her to drink until she was well. Lifting a brow, he nodded.

She sighed and gave in to his request with a nod.

He helped raise her head again, held the glass, and made a mental measurement as he set the glass down on the table afterwards. She'd taken in more that time. A good solid drink.

'I have a feeling that you are used to giving orders and having them followed,' she said.

'I can't deny that I expect my orders to be followed.'

'Then who were you referring to when you said you knew what it was like to have someone telling you what to do?'

He bit the inside of his cheek, contemplating his answer. In the end, he went with the truth. 'My mother.'

Clara's smile grew tender. 'Children are taught to mind to their parents.'

'They are,' he agreed. 'But grown men have minds of their own.'

She nodded. 'What is it that your mother wants you to do, and you are so opposed to?'

'Marriage.'

'She doesn't approve of your choice?'

He laughed. 'She doesn't approve of my opposition to getting married.'

'Opposition?'

Like other women, she most likely wouldn't understand, yet he said, 'Yes. I have no desire to entire an arrangement that ultimately leads to grief.'

Clara glanced at the window, and the sadness that filled her face was like getting kicked in the stomach. His intention hadn't been to remind her of her husband's death, and he wasn't sure what to say or do now that he had done just that.

'You don't need to sit here with me all night,' she said quietly.

He looked towards the window, at the faint light that was penetrating the glass, and explained, 'I already have. That is dawn breaking, not dusk.'

The look on her face reminded him of her daughter. Abigail was an adorable little girl, with a grin that made him want to smile every time he looked at her. She was a little chatterbox, though she, and apparently Sammy, were the only ones who knew what she was saying. Her tiny head was covered with hair the same shade of browns and golds as Clara's, and her eyes were like her mother's, too. A deep dark brown.

Children were foreign to him. He'd never spent any amount of time around them, but after spending a good portion of the day travelling with Abigail, he could see why people liked them.

He could see why people liked dogs, too. Ones like Sammy. The inn owner had said the dog needed to stay outside, and between the sadness on Abigail's face and Sammy's, when the two had heard the man shout 'Out!' Roger had nearly lost control of his usual cool temperament.

He'd been carrying a limp Clara at the time, and at that moment, had known one thing for sure. Abigail and Sammy would not be separated. The inn owner had agreed to that request within his next breath.

'Dawn?' Clara asked.

He nodded.

Clara could have shaken her head in disbelief, but she knew what he said was true. Dawn was breaking. It was breaking inside her, too. An awakening of knowing this man had sat beside her bed for hours, dribbling water into her mouth and saving her life. She was convinced of that. The darkness that kept pulling her down was more than sleep. That was a frightening thought, yet very real.

Tears burned the back of her eyes at the idea of Abigail not having either parent.

She questioned her good sense as she lifted a hand out from beneath the covers and laid it upon his knee, but she had to express her gratefulness to him. 'Thank you, Mr Hardgroves, for…for all you've done.'

His smile curled up the sides of his mouth and caused wrinkles along the sides of his eyes as he softly patted her hand. 'You are most welcome, but, please, call me Roger.' He picked up the glass of water. 'And how about another sip?'

She felt something she hadn't felt in years. A warm blush flooded over her face and she looked the other way. Her hand on his knee felt overly warm, too, and she lifted it off, slid it back beneath the cover.

Thunderation, but what he must think of her. First, she'd argued nonstop, then… She couldn't even remember the coach ride or how she'd got into this bed, and now she'd been much too forward, not only by touching his knee, but in talking about marriage with him.

Despair washed over her, but she quickly pushed it aside. That, she was used to. Despair had been a constant companion for a long time. She'd fought it off until she'd finally decided that it was simply a part of her life now.

Her head was no longer pounding as it had been for days. Still cautious, though, because it could easily return, she swallowed hard and planted her hands on the mattress in order to push herself upwards. 'I think I'll sit up.'

'Here then, let me help you.' He set down the glass and helped her sit up in the bed, then piled the pillows against the headboard and helped her scoot back against them.

She didn't like needing his aid, but her weakened state left her trembling and exhausted. Determined to not let that last long, she clutched the glass when he handed it to her and took several small sips, testing each one as the liquid hit her stomach. It was strange how she could feel that. Feel the water in her stomach. It was also strange to not instantly feel nauseous.

Almost as strange as the quickening of her pulse at his nearness. Her body and emotions were out of sorts, from being sick for so long no doubt. Along with travelling across the ocean to an entirely different world. It was needless to think that sitting in a room alone, with a strange man could also cause such reactions. That was a given, and something she needed to rectify as soon as possible.

Cradling the glass with both hands, she set it in her lap. 'I'm sorry. I knew I was seasick on the ship. I tried to keep drinking and eating, but very little...' She shook her head, embarrassed to share how she'd heaved up everything she'd tried to eat or drink.

'That's not unusual,' he said kindly. 'You were already weak, so it took a toll on you. I told the innkeeper to have chicken broth ready for you in the morning. You'll need to take it slow, but soon you'll be able to eat a full meal.'

A few sips of water were one thing, eating an entire meal was another, and that filled her with anxiety. It had been so long since she'd eaten much of anything, she was certain that her stomach would revolt.

He laid a hand on her leg. 'There now, don't worry. Don't think about your stomach. Trust me, not thinking about it will help.' His smile made his eyes shimmer as he continued, 'You should have seen Abigail earlier. After finishing her bowl of stew, she sat back in her chair and patted her stomach like an old man.'

Clara wished she had seen that, and smiled at the image. But then bit her lips together when they began to tremble. All she could hope was that Abigail would never remember how scarce food had been for them the past several months.

'When we lose something that we take for granted, it's hard to believe that we didn't appreciate it more,' he said.

She knew how true that was, and she knew that when dreams fail, or are stolen, taken away with no hope of ever returning, they leave a reality that is empty. So empty it affects everything. She missed Mark, but it was more than him. She missed knowing there was someone strong at her side, that if she couldn't lift it, couldn't open it, couldn't move it, that someone else was there who could do it. They seemed like odd things to miss, but they were real things. There were other things, too. So many things that she'd taken for granted and would never have again.

Suzanne had been with her since the night of the fire, and between the two of them, they had managed, but it wasn't the same.

Nothing would ever be the same again.

Roger was right when he said marriage led to grief. She was full of it, and would be for ever.

Lifting the glass, she took another drink to give herself something else to think about. Sunlight was starting to filter into the corners of the room. Small, holding nothing more than the bed and the table beside it, the room didn't even host a chair, which is why he sat on the edge of the bed. The one window was on the wall that the bed was pushed up against, and the door was only a couple of feet away from the foot of the bed.

He took the glass and filled it from the pitcher on the table. 'I remember being seasick once, couldn't keep anything down.'

Curious if he was telling the truth or simply attempting to make her feel better, she asked, 'When?'

'Years ago. I was a small boy and was on one of my father's ships. I became sick. Very seasick and refused to even try to eat. My father carried me up onto the deck of the ship, had me stare at the horizon, exactly where the sea met the sky, and told me to focus on how that line was straight. How it never moved, how the waves didn't affect it whatsoever, and while doing so, he broke off small pieces of a biscuit and had me suck on them. He told me that if I had to think about eating, then I needed to think about how good the biscuit tasted, how it dissolved in my mouth, but not about swallowing or my stomach. Which, if you think about it, is how we normally think about eating. About how food tastes, not how it lands in our stomachs. Before long, I'd forgotten all about being sick and by the end of the day, I was roaming the ship from bow to stern.'

'It sounds like you have a very wise father.'

'I did. He died shortly after we'd taken that trip.'

Saddened for his loss, she said, 'I'm sorry.'

'Thank you, but it was many, many years ago.'

'I'm sorry that I delayed our travels today.'

He shrugged. 'No harm was done. We don't have a set schedule to follow.'

'But it is a setback,' she said.

'I believe we've all weathered worse setbacks than a travel delay.'

'Yes, we have,' she agreed.

'I know this is difficult for you, Clara. Being ill, having to trust someone you don't know, but you must know that Annabelle wouldn't have asked for my help if she didn't trust me.'

She did not know this man, but did know that Annabelle would never have sent someone to collect them that they couldn't trust, and that alone was a comfort.

'You are right, Mr Hardgroves. I apologise for my behaviour at the docks. I was just—'

'Roger,' he said. 'And how about we forget our first meeting and concentrate on you getting well.' He gestured to the glass.

'How long did it take before you and Annabelle became friends?'

'Not long.' He winked at her. 'Once she figured out that I wasn't the blackguard she thought I was.' Giving her knee a pat over the covers, he stood. 'I'm going to check if the inn's cook is in the kitchen yet. Get her started on the chicken broth.'

In a matter of a couple of steps, he was gone, yet Clara continued to stare at the closed door. He was a man of means; that was obvious from his clothing, coach, and manners. In some ways, he reminded her of the rich English lords who would moor their ships near Hampton. She'd seen many for they often had rented horses and buggies from her father, wanting to see the countryside. He spoke like those lords had, too. Very precise, and with an accent in which each syllable was distinctly pronounced.

However, he wasn't as standoffish as those men had been. They'd often had servants with them, who had treated the lords as if they were royalty, and expected everyone else to, too.

A smile touched the corners of her mouth, remembering how she and Annabelle had laughed over how some of those men had behaved, and how the two of them had mimicked some of their actions.

They'd had such fun together back then, and seeing her would be wonderful.

Her wandering mind stayed with Annabelle, wondering how she had met Roger, and her husband, Drew, and many other things. It appeared that now that her brain was clear and working, it was attempting to catch up for all the days that she'd been surrounded by a fog.

It ended up that she had two full days to catch up on all her thinking, because Roger insisted that they would not begin their travels again until she was eating enough to endure the trip.

She accepted the challenge, because she knew she was too weak to argue. Furthermore, she wanted to gain her strength so she wasn't a burden to anyone. Including him.

Dr Purdy was an interesting man. His eyes were forever watering, and he spoke with a slur that made her question if he'd been indulging in spirits prior to his visits.

She was thankful that Roger was in the room whenever the doctor was present because between Dr Purdy's English accent and his slur, she had a hard time understanding him.

Roger would repeat what the doctor said for her, and at times, she wondered if it was so she would understand what the doctor had said, or if it was so Roger could repeat that it was doctor's orders that she empty her plate or drink a second glass of water.

He was forever pointing out those things.

He was forever doing other things, too, like reading to Abigail from a large book of children's stories.

Abigail and Sammy were completely smitten with him. Understandably, Abigail had never had someone who would let her ride on their shoulders or toss her in the air and catch her, and Sammy had never had someone throw sticks or give him a treat after he'd sat or lain down or rolled over.

She and Suzanne had always been too busy scrounging their next meal, cutting wood to burn in the parlour stove they'd hauled into the root cellar, or numerous other chores that they'd needed to complete in order to stay safe and hidden.

Clara didn't mind admitting that she was glad to not be living that life any longer, but she had no idea what the future had in store for them in England. Other than it was a future that she didn't want. She had to return to Virginia, to the farm, and rebuild it so Abigail could know her father through what he had provided for them prior to his death.

Roger had sent his groom, Jacob, to the nearby village, and he had returned with a coach full of items. New dresses for both she and Suzanne, two each, and new underclothes, and new shoes. There were also dresses for Abigail, and material for swaddling, and shoes. Abigail had never had shoes and was still getting used to them.

Clara was getting used to her new shoes, too. They fit perfectly and were made of soft leather, with thick, solid soles. That's what she was trying to get used to—not having holes in the soles of her shoes.

It felt good, but nothing on earth had felt as good as the hot bath that she'd had that first morning after waking up at the inn. It had been so long since she'd soaked in hot water, she'd nearly fallen asleep in the bathtub.

Would have if Suzanne hadn't entered the room with new clothing for her to put on after her bath. A pretty yellow and white dress, complete set of new, crisp, underclothes, including socks, and the new shoes.

She was worried as to how she would repay Roger for all the purchases. They were all things that had been needed, but she had no financial means whatsoever. That was something she would need to figure out right away. She would also need money for her and Abigail to return home.

Suzanne suggested that perhaps Annabelle had given Roger money to buy the things they needed. Clara doubted that. Roger appeared to be a man of means himself. He was also insightful, considering the paper, pens, and messenger bag that he'd had Jacob purchase for Suzanne.

Suzanne had great aspirations of becoming a writer and had been chronicling the incidents and events that had happened since the beginning of the war, believing it would make an interesting historical book for generations to come.

The two of them were very different in that aspect. Suzanne wanted to remember, to keep track of everything that had happened, while Clara wanted to forget it all.

Chapter Three

Clara had made remarkable progress in regaining her strength. She was now eating full meals and keeping them down. Although they were awfully small meals. Little Abigail ate nearly as much.

Progress was progress, though, and Roger was grateful her illness was behind them.

He was glad to get back on the road, too. Of all the women who had floated through his life, not a one had affected him the way Clara did.

His gaze was on the door of the inn, where Clara, with Abigail in her arms and Sammy at her side, exited the building. He couldn't define exactly what happened inside him whenever he saw the two of them together like they were right now—well, three of them, counting the dog—but it was something. Something unique that was triggered inside him. That *triggering* had started right after he'd spent the night by her side, and it caused other unexpected and unwanted thoughts to live inside his mind.

Numerous ones, all related to Clara.

Their gazes met, and the connection he felt to her caused a warmth to spread through him that was indescribable.

What would have become of them if Tristan and his sailors hadn't found them, hadn't hauled them to England? He had no idea, nor did he like contemplating the various outcomes that crossed his mind.

He tried not to be too concerned over that. Just as he tried to not appear to be too concerned over them. He reminded himself that he was merely a middleman in this entire escapade. Once Drew and Annabelle returned home, his promise, and his commitment to this bevvy of companions would be over.

That thought was like a stab in the gut, one that he chose to ignore.

As she'd started to do recently, Abigail held her arms out for him to take her from Clara. The little girl had got used to him the past couple of days, and him to her. After that first night, he'd let Suzanne see to Clara's needs while he kept an eye on Abigail, which turned out to be easier than he'd imagined.

The way her little eyes lit up was adorable, as were some of the expressions she made, as if seeing things for the very first time in her life. Many things were firsts, considering the life she had been living, and he was glad to be witnessing them with her. The baby skin of her chubby little cheeks glowed with good health, and her hair was as fine as spun gold and formed tiny ringlets that stuck out from beneath the pale pink bonnet that matched her new dress.

He took Abigail and gently tossed her in the air,

laughing at her giggles, before settling her in one arm. Like her mother, Abigail had benefitted from their stay at the inn.

Over the years, Roger had spent a significant amount of time at the card table, betting on horses, and other such games and events of chance and skill, and had learned how to never let his emotions show. In all aspects of his life, however, it was as if he didn't have control over anything when it came to Abigail, or her mother.

Abigail's giggles made him laugh, and Clara… well, she made him smile. He couldn't help it.

'It looks like it'll be a nice day for travelling,' Clara said, somewhat shyly as they walked towards the coach.

He paused long enough to glance up at the blue sky, feel the sunshine on his face. 'That it does, but as I said at breakfast, if you feel yourself getting motion sick we'll stop and rest.'

Her dark brown eyes held streaks of gold as she looked him. 'Thank you, but I'm sure we will be fine.'

No longer pale, her cheeks shone with a peachy tone, as did her lips, reminding him of just what a pretty woman she was. Not that he needed the reminder. Seeing her every day, practically all day, had done a fine job of embedding her image in his mind.

Her thick, golden-brown hair was pinned up and fluffed around her face in a way that many women wore their hair. Yet on her, it was enchanting. A few loose tendrils fluttered in the breeze, and he had a hard time pulling his eyes off her.

'Nonetheless,' he said. 'Just knock on the roof and Jacob will stop the coach.'

A frown of puzzlement formed between her fine brows. 'Are you not riding with us?'

He nodded to where Smokey stood, saddled and ready to depart. 'I'll ride.' There was nothing perplexing about that. He doubted that he knew a man who would rather ride in a coach than a saddle, yet he felt a bit confounded by a sense floating inside him. Quite contrary to all his thoughts about riding in the saddle, were thoughts about riding in the carriage so he wouldn't be separated from her. For the life of him, he couldn't figure out where that came from. He'd never before worried about being separated from anyone.

'That will give you all more room,' Roger said.

'There's plenty of room for you, too,' she said, with a tiny grin, 'but I understand why you'd want to ride.'

'It has nothing to do with the company,' he said.

Her laugh was soft. 'I didn't say it did.' She patted the side of her thigh, then pointed to the open coach door. Sammy immediately followed her command, and as the dog jumped inside, Clara held her hands out for her daughter.

Roger continued to hold Abigail with one arm and held out his other hand to escort Clara into the coach. He understood that she'd been doing for herself her entire life, whereas most of the women he knew had been waited on their entire lives. However, she deserved to be treated like a lady, for she was more of one than others he'd known. From the moment she'd started feeling better, he'd seen subtle changes in her, not just her health, but in her confidence and conviction. She was now the one assuring Suzanne all would be fine and how they'd needed to leave America.

She also insisted that she would return home as soon as possible. He wasn't overly sure if that was a smart thing for her to do, and made a note to discuss it with Drew. Perhaps Annabelle would have some influence on Clara and her desire to return.

'Thank you,' she said, taking his hand and stepping into the carriage.

Once she was inside, he handed over Abigail. 'Just tap on the roof,' he repeated.

'I will if needed,' she said, while taking a seat across from where Suzanne was sitting with Sammy on the bench beside her.

'Promise?' he asked.

A hint of pink rose in her cheeks. 'I promise.'

'I'm going to hold you to that,' he said, then gave both women a nod and shut the coach door.

It would be good to put some distance between him and her. In fact, it was needed. It was not like him to become smitten with anyone, at any time. Not that he was admitting that he was smitten, but he was feeling something. That something included being a bit too overly concerned about Clara, and he needed to get it out of his system.

Women of any kind were not in his future, especially a widow with a child. That hit too close to home. In his experience, widows with children were only looking for one thing. A father for their children. That's what his mother had been doing when she remarried shortly after his father had died. He hadn't needed a new father as a child, and wouldn't do that to someone else's child.

His mother would really think she'd won then. She wanted him to marry, have children, and would believe that he had succumbed to her wishes. He'd decided years ago to never succumb to what she thought he needed.

Clara told herself that she was relieved that Roger was riding on his horse rather than in the coach. For good reason. She was grateful to him for all he'd done for them and continued to do, but she couldn't come to depend upon him. That wouldn't be right, and there was no way she could feel any sort of attraction to him in any— She swallowed a groan, forcing herself to not go down that line of thinking any further.

She was a widow! Should still be wearing widow's weeds. If things were different, that is. As it was, she'd not been able to afford to buy black material since Mark's death.

Still couldn't afford it.

Not that she needed to be dressed in black and wearing an armband or veil to be reminded that her husband was dead and that she was in mourning. Her heart told her that every single day, and no man, no matter how kind or decent, would change that.

It's just that Roger was such a gentleman, and so kind and caring. As well as generous.

She should have told him that the dresses he'd purchased for her were too pretty, too colourful for a widow to be wearing. One was bright yellow, the other one a pretty pale green colour.

Ultimately, she hadn't told him that, because her sensible side told her that her old dress was barely serviceable and so threadbare that it shouldn't be worn in public. Roger had to have been embarrassed to be seen with women dressed in such worn-out clothing, but was simply too much a gentleman to say anything, or to hurt anyone's feelings.

She shook her head and silently told herself to get her mind off Roger. Completely, one hundred percent off him. She would not think about him.

Not at all.

She huffed out a breath. Mark was the only man who had ever evoked these kinds of feelings inside her, and that was the way it would stay.

What she felt when Roger looked at her wasn't desire. It was… She muffled a moan.

'Are you not feeling well?' Suzanne, sitting on the opposite bench, leaned across the open centre with concern in her furrowed brows.

'No, I'm fine,' Clara replied, settling Abigail on the seat beside her.

Suzanne eyed her closely.

Clara felt her cheeks grow warm, not wanting Suzanne to know what she'd been thinking about. 'Honestly. I'm fine.'

'You certainly look fine,' Suzanne said. 'Better than you have in months.' She sat back in her seat and sighed. 'Can you believe this? I never dreamed of seeing England, but here we are, riding in a fine coach across the lush, green English countryside on a bright and sunny spring day. It's a genuine adventure.'

Clara hadn't been looking for an adventure, but with the way the sun was shining as bright and glorious as she'd ever seen outside the window, it did feel quite like one.

A wave of frustration washed over her, mixing in with all the other feelings that were already enough to overwhelm any given person. Even if this felt like an adventure, that wasn't what she needed, or wanted. She needed to find a tangible way to make money, enough money for them to return to America.

She glanced at Abigail, playing with the little wooden thaumatrope that Roger had given her. There was a colourful bird painted on one of the wooden discs and a gold birdcage painted on the other. When the ropes that were attached to the discs were twisted tightly, then released, the discs would swirl so fast it looked like the bird was in the birdcage. Abigail couldn't twist the ropes to make the discs spin, but was still enthralled with her first store-bought toy.

There was no one in this world that Clara loved more than her daughter, and her only hope of giving Abigail the life she deserved was to return to the farm. Show her daughter the home her father had bought for them, the apple trees he'd planted behind the house, and so many other things.

Rubbing her daughter's leg, Clara glanced towards the window while asking Suzanne, 'Do you think Annabelle well return to America with us?'

'I doubt it.'

'Why do you doubt it?'

Suzanne set aside her diary. 'Because there is no

reason for her to return. There is nothing there for her. Even her father and Cecilia are here, in England.'

'Yes, but it's her home.'

'It was. Now her home is here, with her husband.' Suzanne drew in a breath so deep her shoulders lifted up beside her neck. 'I'm anxious to meet him, aren't you? Annabelle's husband, Drew.' Letting out a sigh, Suzanne continued, 'I imagine he'll be handsome, and of course he'll be as much as a gentleman as Roger.'

Something inside Clara bristled. She was trying hard not to think about him. 'Why do you think that?'

'Because they are best friends. Roger wouldn't be best friends with a rake.'

'We don't know that. Roger might be a rake for all we know.'

Suzanne laughed. 'Yes, we do.' Shaking her head, she added, 'Just because you don't want to like him doesn't mean he's unlikeable.'

Clara pinched her lips together. 'I didn't say he's unlikeable, nor did I say that I don't like him. I was merely asking why you think Annabelle's husband will be like Roger.'

'Because that is what I think, just like I think Roger is very likeable. In fact, I think he is charming, and so do Abigail and Sammy.'

Roger was charming. There was no denying that, and any other thought in Clara's mind flew out of her head as if her thought was the little bird and her mind the gold cage on Abigail's toy when Roger appeared next to the window of the coach.

'Hello,' he called through the open window, from the back of his fine-looking grey horse.

Abigail scrambled onto Clara's lap and grinned out the window, while Sammy, who had been sleeping next to Suzanne, sat up and barked.

Suzanne grinned as if she'd somehow manufactured all of that to happen to prove the point she had just made.

No proof had been needed. Clara had already known that Abigail and Sammy liked Roger, and to be perfectly honest, she didn't mind that. She wanted her daughter to be happy and it was clear that Roger made her happy. However, she did feel the need to be cautious, because Roger wouldn't be in their lives very long.

She drew in a deep breath, hoping to calm her racing heart and pulled up a smile. Which wasn't overly hard. He was grinning, and when he did that, a dimple appeared in his right cheek. Already a fine-looking man, it merely increased how easy it was to look upon him. And that increased how easy it was to like him.

That was the real problem.

Roger Hardgroves was a very easy man to like.

Too easy.

That of course was Clara's opinion.

And that itself was a potential issue.

Travelling with him, being in such close proximity, was another issue. One she was going to have to find a solution to. Quickly.

Days later, Roger sat with his back against a tree, chewing on a blade of grass and watching as Abigail and

Sammy chased after a high-hopping, long-legged frog. Neither child nor dog looked any worse for wear due to having been travelling for over a week, longer if their time on the ship was taken into consideration. However, Abigail's blue and white ruffled dress might end up with some green grass stains before the chase ended with the way she kept tumbling onto the new spring grass.

Each time she stumbled, Sammy would stop his chase, wait until she clambered to her feet, and then with the dog sniffing out the frog, or perhaps a different, yet identical one, the chase was on again.

Roger shifted his gaze to where Clara descended the coach steps, having cleaned and packed away the dishes and leftover foodstuff from the meal they'd stopped to consume along the side of the road. Nearly a week ago, after they'd left the first inn, Clara had initiated and insisted upon a pattern of sorts. She'd told Jacob, and everyone else, that she would see to the midday meals, both the arranging of them from the inns where they found lodging each night and in serving them along the way.

Jacob had looked to Roger for advice, or permission, to allow her request to be fulfilled, and Roger had given it. He'd explained to Jacob that Clara wasn't used to being waited on and that she felt a need to do her fair share during their travels.

She hadn't told him that; he'd surmised it for himself. She was meticulous in every detail, and pride literally shone on her face when she loaded up the provisions that she'd acquired for them each morning. That pride was there again when not a single morsel went to waste.

Taking the final step onto the ground, she continued to hold up the hem of the yellow dress with one hand, making sure to not let the material catch on the metal of the coach step, while closing the coach door with her other hand.

She wiped the palms of her hands together as she glanced towards where Abigail and Sammy were frolicking, then smiling, she smoothed her hands over the material covering her stomach as she began walking in his direction.

The buttercup colour of the dress was fitting for her, made her look like a walking ray of sunshine. Her health had rebounded this week, even while travelling. She'd been pretty before, but now, he'd describe her as radiant, for beauty simply radiated off her.

He watched her approach the tree and stood before she arrived.

'There's no need to get up on my account,' she said.

Her smile was always gentle, or perhaps the right description would be faint—a mere glimmer of a smile. Almost as if she was afraid to smile and did so only out of politeness.

Roger tucked away that thought as he acknowledged her comment with a simple nod. He considered informing her that every man should stand when she approached, out of respect if nothing else. However, he'd discovered she wasn't as used to the rules of propriety as him—at least some of them, that is. 'Would you care to take a short walk along the bank of the stream?'

Her smile momentarily disappeared as she glanced to where Suzanne was perched on a fallen log closer to the stream, writing. Unable to utilise a pen and ink-well while travelling, Suzanne never let any chance of getting pen to paper go unused.

'Perhaps Suzanne would enjoy a walk,' Clara said.

Roger knew what was happening. Clara had been attempting to divert his attention to Suzanne since they'd left the inn after her illness days ago. Suzanne was fine looking and pleasant to be around, would most likely make a fine companion, or wife, if a man was looking, but that's where his confusion over Clara's behaviour lay. He wasn't looking for a companion or wife and she knew that. He'd told her about his aversion to marriage.

'I believe Suzanne is quite engrossed in her writing at the moment,' he said.

'Yes, but she still might like taking a walk,' Clara replied.

Roger held in a sigh. 'May I ask you a question?'

'Of course,' Clara answered.

'Why do you feel the need to divert my attention onto Suzanne?'

'Why—I—' She huffed out a breath, clearly miffed at his straightforwardness.

He bit back a grin at the blush that rose up over her cheeks. 'You what?'

'I am not trying to divert anything,' she said.

'You aren't?'

'No. That's plain silly. I merely thought that if you wanted to take a walk, and didn't want to walk by yourself, that Suzanne might like to accompany you.'

She could be telling the truth, and he could just be reading more into her actions than he should be. Truth be, he wasn't overly sure of a whole lot anymore. Because of her. There had been women whom he'd looked forward to seeing over the years, but none compared to how he looked forward to seeing her each morning.

He knew enough to know that was a reason he needed to stay away from her. Therefore, he'd continued to ride Smokey every day, preferring that to the coach, and he kept his distance from her when they stopped at road-side inns each evening in time for a meal and to sleep.

Or to try to sleep. It seemed he did a whole lot more tossing and turning than sleeping. She was on his mind both day and night. Despite his night-time musings, where he would tell himself that he was no more inter-ested in her than any other woman, come morning, his heart would skip irregularly as soon as he'd catch sight of her, as if it had been awaiting such an event.

He went so far as to tell himself that it was Abigail that he was excited to see each morning. Making that little girl smile brought great joy to him, to his heart.

Clara, however, not only affected his heart, she af-fected his mind.

That had never happened to him before. He'd always been very sure of what he wanted and what he didn't, and nothing, not a single person had ever changed his mind.

He wouldn't change his mind now, either. Giving a slight bow, he said, 'Very well. If you'll excuse me.'

She caught his arm as he turned to walk away. 'Wait… I… I…'

'It's all right, Clara,' he said. 'Forgive me for com-ing to the wrong conclusion.'

'You didn't,' she said. 'I was trying to…' She sighed. 'Keep my distance.'

'Why?'

She looked at him and shook her head even as a smile emerged. 'Because you are too nice.'

He chuckled. 'I don't believe anyone has accused me of being too nice before.'

'Well, you are, and I…' Her gaze went to where Abigail and Sammy frolicked in the grass.

A pang struck him. 'You don't want anyone to be nice to you?'

She shrugged, and then shook her head as if she didn't know how to answer.

Roger knew she'd been through hell and back and silently applauded her strength of character. The desire to hug her, to tell her that things were different now, was great, but he wasn't certain that she'd appreciate that. Therefore, he merely gave her shoulder a gentle squeeze.

Clara had to plant her feet hard against the ground to fight the draw inside her to lean against Roger. The desire to be held by his strong arms nearly overwhelmed her. She knew the strength that could be found in a hug, but also had to remember that she'd never have that again. Not from any man. By even wanting that, she was being disloyal to Mark.

She couldn't do that.

She'd tried keeping her distance from Roger while travelling, but it wasn't working. If anything, she'd become more comfortable around him the last few days.

That was wrong.

She should feel uncomfortable around him. Should feel uncomfortable around any other man for the rest of her life. She had known Mark for as long as she could remember and they'd shared the same dreams. That of living on a farm, raising crops to sell at the food store and elsewhere.

He'd given her the other thing that she'd wanted, too. A family.

It had just been her and her father. Her mother had died before she could remember, and she'd wanted more. Wanted a family with a father and a mother, and children. Lots of children.

They had both wanted that, too, and had been overjoyed when she'd become pregnant.

Their love had produced Abigail, and just because Mark had died, didn't mean her love for him had. Nor should it ever.

She had to keep that love alive, for Abigail.

Not doing that was frightening. She had to honour his memory. That was another fear. Her memories of him. They seemed to be fading, becoming little more than echoes of what they used to be. While at the farm, she'd thought about him all the time, but here, her mind wandered to so many other things that she'd found herself searching for memories that used to come with ease.

Abigail's giggle as she ran with Sammy floated on the air, and Clara's already bruised and battered heart cracked a little bit more. It was such a sad thing, an awful thing, to think that her daughter would never know her father. Never have a father.

The emptiness she'd felt inside ever since the death

of her own father made her think that maybe she should be glad that Abigail couldn't remember Mark, because then she'd never know the pain of losing him. But that wasn't right, either.

It was just all so hard. Losing her father and Mark at the same time had been like being stabbed in the heart twice over. If not for Abigail, she wasn't sure that she would have survived that time in her life. But she had, and she had to make sure that Abigail had the best life possible, despite the war and the losses it had caused.

Roger was looking at her, probably wondering why she was standing there, staring at him without saying a word. Clara's throat swelled, making it even more impossible for her to speak. The things he stirred inside her were just too raw and ran too deep to mention them to anyone.

The compassion on his face, the way he was looking at her, as if he was about to embrace her, scared her, and she stepped backwards, off the blanket. 'It…it must be about time to leave.'

Roger grinned slightly, then nodded. 'I'll go help Jacob hook the horses back up to the carriage. We won't stop again, and it'll be late when we arrive tonight. Very late.'

Clara bit her lips together, but curiosity, or perhaps another fear that had been growing inside her the past few days, won out. He'd explained earlier that he'd sent a messenger to his property, informing the servants to have the house ready for guests. Having never had servants, she was nervous about that. 'How many servants do you have?'

He was thoughtful for a moment, then shrugged. 'I'm not sure.'

'How can you not be sure?'

'Because others oversee the hiring and management of staff, but don't worry—they are good people. You'll all be well taken care of by them.'

This time she kept her mouth closed, stopped herself from proclaiming that she didn't want to be taken care of by anyone. All she wanted was for her life to regain some sense of normalcy.

Chapter Four

Hours later, with the aid of a big three-quarter moon, Clara got her first glimpse of Roger's home. It was not simply a house. With round turrets on each of the corners, the massive structure grew larger as the carriage rolled closer. Perhaps the largest building she'd ever seen, it was as close to a palace as she could imagine.

Lamps lit several windows on the lower floor and several flickering lanterns sat upon a large stone wall that extended out from the edges of the building, lighting the pathway to the front door.

'I knew this was going to be an adventure,' Suzanne said, her head out the carriage window, staring at the house. 'This place has to be centuries old.'

Clara was staring out the window next to her seat and silently agreed that the place had to be old. Very old, but beautifully maintained, and it was also massive. It was too dark to determine if the building was built of stone or bricks, or a combination of materials, including wood that created the ornate shutters on the rows of windows on the second and third floors, and of course the turrets. She lost count of the number of chimneys as the carriage travelled closer.

Having arrived before them, Roger opened the door from the outside as the carriage rolled to a stop. After letting Sammy leap out, he leaned his head inside. 'Hand me Abigail.'

The golden moonlight was like a whisper on his face, soft yet bright enough to highlight his dark hair, his shimmering emerald eyes and his smile.

Wrapped in a blanket, Abigail had been asleep for hours. Clara lifted her daughter off the seat and handed her to Roger.

It wasn't until after she'd released Abigail to him, that Clara questioned herself on how easily she'd come to trust him and the fact she held no qualms about putting her daughter in his care. He was strong and trustworthy; she knew that, yet, she should be more cautious.

He laid Abigail against one of his shoulders, and as Clara took the hand that he offered to aid her down the carriage steps, their gazes met. The thing that happened inside her reminded her that she indeed needed to be more than cautious for several reasons.

Although he'd ridden his horse the entire trip, she'd felt a connection to him growing stronger every day. Whenever their eyes had met, even from afar, she'd felt a stirring inside her, in ways and places that should never be stirred, and though she'd tried, she was not able to ignore it, or make it stop.

'Welcome to Clairmount,' he said.

She quickly stepped down onto the ground and held her arms out to take Abigail. Once her daughter was back in her arms, she quickly moved away from him. 'Thank you.'

He assisted Suzanne out of the carriage, and Clara's heart thudded as he walked towards her again. She took a slight sidestep to keep a larger distance between them, but mainly managed to slightly twist her ankle. Not enough to hurt, but enough that he noticed and took a hold of her elbow.

'Are you all right?' he asked.

'Yes. Fine.' She kept her gaze straight ahead, on the tall double doors that were behind four people standing on the top of the wide set of stairs leading to the house. She felt out of sorts, and wanted to blame it on being tired, but it went deeper than being worn out from travelling, and wanting normality back in her life.

Or maybe that is exactly why.

This—this palace—was as far from normal as things could get.

'You will be shown to your room as soon as I introduce you to the staff,' Roger said, using his hold to guide her up the steps. Stopping at the top of the steps, on the wide porch, he introduced her and Suzanne to the men and women standing there. The men were dressed in dark suits and the women wore dark dresses and white aprons. The tallest man, with grey hair and an angular face was Aaron, the butler. The woman next to him, slender and tall, with a serious lift to her chin and her grey hair pulled back in a severe bun, was Mrs Mills. Next to her was a chubby-faced, smiling and grey-haired woman named Bertha, and the last man in the row was Loren. He was younger than the others, and broadly built, with hair that was either blond or red. Clara couldn't tell if the yellow hue from the moon and lamplight was altering the colour or not.

She bid them all hello, as did Suzanne, and told herself that she was relieved when Roger instructed Bertha to show them to their rooms. The short woman's wide smile was friendly and welcoming.

'Your luggage will be brought up to your rooms directly,' Roger said as he released the hold he had on her elbow.

Clara nodded her gratitude and as she followed the plump and smiling Bertha, silently questioned what these people must think about Roger bringing home two women, a child, and a dog. Sammy, never far from Abigail, was at her side as Clara walked across the threshold, and she couldn't help but glance over her shoulder, to see if any of the other servants were put out by the dog's entrance.

No one appeared to be, but then again, Roger had introduced Sammy to everyone along with the rest of them.

'This place is magnificent,' Suzanne whispered as they stepped into the interior of the home.

The grandeur of the foyer was breathtaking. Moulded arched doorways led off the foyer in several directions, including over the sweeping staircase that curved elegantly around a corner on the second floor and disappeared. The dark wood of the floors and walls gleamed in the lamplight and the smell of lemon oil filled the air.

'Would you like me to carry the little miss for you, ma'am?' Bertha asked.

'No, thank you,' Clara responded. 'I can manage.'

'Very well. Welcome to Clairmount. We are all excited to have you here. This way if you please,' Bertha said with a slight nod and a wave of her hand towards the staircase. 'Your rooms are on the second floor. It was a pleasure setting up a room for the little miss. It's been such a long time since there was a wee one in the house.'

'Thank you. We sincerely appreciate your hospitality,' Clara replied.

'Yes, we do,' Suzanne said, and complimented Bertha on the loveliness of the home.

The home was beyond lovely. It was extravagant, but Clara wasn't listening as the two other women chatted while Bertha led them up the wooden staircase and then down a long hallway with shimmering cream-coloured wallpaper and flocked gold scrolls. Her mind was on other things. So many things that she couldn't focus on any one thing. Even though their travelling was over for now, she still didn't know what tomorrow would bring or the next day. Or next week for that matter.

Her thoughts paused momentarily when Bertha stopped long enough to open a door. That room turned out to be Suzanne's. From the doorway, Clara could see it was large and lovely, but didn't dally longer than bidding her friend goodnight because Bertha explained, 'Your room is just down the hall, ma'am.'

Several doors later, Bertha opened another one. 'Here we are.'

The room had several lamps lit, each sitting on a table. There were four that she counted while entering the room. Tables. One had two chairs flanking it, one was beside a large four-poster bed that had lovely yellow chiffon material draped between the tops of the posts. A drawered dressing table with an upholstered bench and tall mirror sat along one wall, and held two lit lamps, and the fourth table was between two large wing-backed upholstered chairs facing a fireplace.

Bertha crossed the large room, which had a round rug of yellows and oranges that was as cheerful as the sun itself, and then opened another door. 'This is the little miss's room,' Bertha said.

Clara crossed the room and entered the next one, full of child-sized furniture, including a table and chair set, a crib, as well as a bed, and shelves full of toys. There was even a pallet of quilts folded up and laid beneath a window, which, after giving the room a once-over, Sammy claimed by walking in a circle atop the pile before lying down with a sigh that echoed in the room.

'Would you like me to put her in the crib?' Bertha asked.

Clara's hold on her daughter tightened. 'No.' Abigail hadn't slept alone since they'd moved into the root cellar. They, along with Suzanne, had shared the one mattress that they'd hauled out of the house and into the root cellar, and in truth, it had been less comfortable than the pallet that Sammy had claimed looked.

'There are several sleeping gowns and swaddling cloth here in the wardrobe,' Bertha said, opening a door on the cabinet with ornate scrollwork. 'Mildred, the upstairs maid, and I carried down a trunk full of clothes that had been the marquess's when he was a wee one.'

A little quiver rippled up Clara's spine. 'The marquess?'

'Yes. We washed and ironed everything, so they are as good as new. Any that had yellowed we threw out.' Bertha's wrinkled face took on a shine, so did her dark blue eyes. 'His Lordship was such an adorable baby. A real happy little boy.' She closed the cabinet door and sighed. 'Right up until his father died. Then he lost his smile.'

Clara was certain Bertha was referring to Roger, yet asked, 'What was his father's name?'

'Eldon. Eldon Roger Hardgroves, the third Marquess of Clairmount.' She sighed slightly. 'I'll never forget the night His Lordship was born. The old master had run through the house, shouting that he had a son. Roger Eldon Hardgroves, the fourth Marquess of Clairmount. He was so proud of that boy. So proud. We all were.'

Clara felt as if the room spun before her eyes. He was a marquess? All this time, he was a marquess and never told her?

Normality just got further away.

Roger had always considered Clairmount a lonely place. That's how he remembered it and the reason why he hadn't ever spent a lot of time here. Yet, tonight, he felt a sense of comfort with the familiar surroundings. A comfort he hadn't felt in years.

He knew a large part of that was because their travelling had come to an end. Clara and Abigail, as well as Sammy and Suzanne, would be able to rest well tonight, knowing they didn't have to climb back into the carriage tomorrow morning.

Instead, they'd be able to relax and get to know their

new surroundings, their home until Drew and Annabelle returned from Scotland.

He hoped that Clara would be comfortable here, and made a mental reminder to tell her about the library on the third floor tomorrow morning. She could sit up there and read to Abigail, and he'd tell her about the glass growing house. That used to be his favourite room.

Threading his fingers together, he slipped his hands beneath his head as he stared at the ceiling above his bed. Both mother and daughter could use several days of relaxing after all they'd been through. Suzanne, too, but having not lost a husband, she seemed to have weathered the storm that had been their lives the past several months better than Clara.

Abigail had weathered it better, too. Being so young, she knew no other life.

Clara had, though, and he sensed she was attempting to hold on to her old life. He couldn't blame her. Didn't blame her. Nor could he get her off his mind. Her delicate features, her trim, shapely body that could use a few more weeks of solid meals, for she was still a bit too thin.

She was resilient, yet for whatever reason, didn't want to accept it. Again, he could understand her reasonings, he just didn't know how to help her get past them. Which really wasn't like him. Normally, he tended to mind his own business, but this time was different. He'd spent hours in the saddle, thinking of little else except her and her situation, and during their evening stops, while she'd busied herself with menu planning for the next day, he'd gained more insight through conversations with Suzanne, concerning the life that Clara had known and left behind.

Because, in truth, there was another thought that plagued his mind when he thought of Clara. That of her husband, how he'd left her and went to war. He didn't blame the man for going to fight for his country. As odd as it was, he felt sympathy for him. Leaving Clara and Abigail had to have been difficult. Very difficult.

For them, too.

He knew the pain of watching his father leave, and then of never seeing him again. Though he'd been young, he remembered saying goodbye to his father that last time.

Unlike him, his father had loved the sea and chose to captain one of the many ships within his fleet as often as possible. He hadn't planned on going on another trip that year, had said he was staying home until spring, but then another captain had fallen ill, and his father had left. Roger remembered that morning, how he'd held on tight to his father's neck until his mother had pulled him away, told him that his father had to go to sea.

His father hadn't wanted to go, he was sure of that, but had gone because his mother told him to. Told him to leave his wife and child behind—the way Clara's husband had.

He would never blame a man for dying—no one could evade that for ever—but he did feel a sense of disappointment in Clara's husband for leaving her and Abigail on their own. Having grown up without a father, he didn't like the idea of Abigail having to do that. Nor did he like the idea of Clara searching for a man to take on that role. He'd watched his mother do that.

Roger heaved out a heavy sigh at the thoughts and memories floating about in his mind.

He'd be far better off not thinking about Clara or Abigail, or his father. Going back to minding his own business would be the smartest thing he could do right now, because then he'd be sound asleep rather the thinking about the woman sleeping down the hall.

Come morning, he'd send another message to Drew, telling him to come and get his guests as soon as possible.

He'd done favours for Drew before, but this one was taking its toll, that was for damn sure.

By morning, Roger wasn't overly sure that he should send a message after all. It wouldn't be right to ask them to cut their Scotland trip short, nor would it be fair to deprive Clara and the others a few weeks of relaxation before they had to travel again.

She was still sleeping. He knew because he heard Sammy whining at the nursery door as he walked past.

Upon opening the door to let the dog out, he heard Abigail's soft chattering. It had been years since he'd been in that room, the one that had been his when he'd been a child. The staff had told him last night that they'd prepared the room for Abigail, including hauling down the crib and other children's furniture that had been stored on the third floor after he'd outgrown it. Bertha had also assured him that she was prepared to take on the role of nanny.

He'd suggested that Clara would determine the role of a nanny. She was very protective when it came to Abigail, and he understood why.

Abigail was standing inside the wooden rails of the crib, and her chatter increased when she noticed him in the doorway. With a wide smile, she held her arms up.

Faces didn't come any cuter than her little cherub one. Though he probably should find Bertha to see to the child, he couldn't walk away from that face, and crossed the room, lifted her out of the crib, then walked to the door that was open to the adjacent room.

Lying on her side, with both hands tucked beneath one cheek, Clara was sound asleep. Roger may have stood there longer, simply watching her sleep, but he knew Abigail's chattering could waken her at any time.

Gesturing for Sammy to follow him, although he knew that wasn't necessary, Roger carried Abigail out of the room and quietly shut the door behind them.

Downstairs, he'd let Sammy outside, and instructed Bertha to swaddle Abigail with a clean cloth. Once their needs were seen to, both the child and dog joined him in the dining room for breakfast. That's where they still were when he heard shouts echoing down the hallway.

Hearing his name, Sammy barked and left his post next to Abigail's chair to run for the doorway.

Roger rose to his feet and crossed the room with concern rising inside him. 'Did you not inform Cla—Mrs Walton of the pull cord in her room?' he asked Bertha as she scrambled past the doorway.

Bertha skidded to a stop and gave a quick curtsy. 'Yes,

my lord, last night. She did not pull it. I will go see to her needs.'

'I'm sure she's looking for her daughter.' Roger waved a hand. 'Hurry. Tell her that Abigail is with me.' He had assumed that Clara would pull the cord upon waking, to summon the maid, and therefore know why Abigail and Sammy were not in their room.

From the sounds of her shouts, and the speed of footsteps, that clearly had not happened and Clara was upset.

Bertha's explanation was quickly cut short and Roger was making his way down the hall when Clara rounded the corner.

Her waist-length hair was in one long braid, and dishevelled from sleeping, and she wore only her night-gown—a loose-fitting gown of creamy white cotton that floated in the wake of her hurried footsteps—and damn if the sight of her didn't make his heart skip just as it had every morning since he'd met her.

However, the concern on her face is what sent him into action. 'Clara there's no need for concern,' he said, walking towards her. 'Abigail is fine.'

'Fine?' she huffed out and shoved past him. 'Fine would mean she was with me. Which she is not! The crib she slept in last night is empty! Empty! I knew I should have put her in bed with me! Who took her? Who?'

He pivoted on a heel and followed her towards the dining room, where Sammy was heading. 'I did. I apologise. You were sleeping. I assumed that you would pull the cord to alert the maid when you awoke, and they would let you know that Abigail was with me.'

'I don't need a cord! I need my daughter!'

He followed her into the dining room, where Abigail was sitting in the high chair that was pushed up to the table, still munching on her breakfast of eggs and toasted bread.

Abigail gave her mother a toothy grin and offered her a morsel of the bread she'd been about to put in her mouth.

Clara declined the offer with a kiss on Abigail's head and a whisper that Roger couldn't hear, but he could feel the tenderness between mother and daughter. He'd felt that since the day he'd met them at the dock. It could be that way between all mothers and their children and he'd just never noticed it before, or it could be something special between these two, because they were special.

'I am sorry, Clara,' he repeated, walking to the table. 'I did not mean to cause you concern. I heard Sammy whimpering at the door when I walked past it earlier, and noticed Abigail was awake.'

'At which point you decided to just take her, rather than wake me?'

She was mindful of keeping her tone even and low to not upset Abigail, and Roger followed suit in his response. 'You were sleeping. I assumed you were tired after our late-night arrival.'

'I was tired.' She shot him a glare. 'Mainly because I couldn't fall to sleep last night after learning that you'd been lying to us this entire time.'

'Lying to you about what?'

She huffed out a breath. 'Everything.'

He had no idea what she referred to. 'What do you consider everything?'

'We can start with the fact that you are a marquess.'

Her eyes were full of challenge, daring him to deny her statement. He wouldn't do that. There was no reason to. He'd known she'd discover it sooner or later. Actually, he'd thought she might have heard one of the inn owners say it. Several had addressed him with his title. 'Yes, I am. The fourth Marquess of Clairmount. I never lied to you about that.'

Planting a hand on her hip, she moved away from Abigail's chair, closer to him, before hissing, 'You never told us about it, either.'

'There was no need to tell you.'

'No need? No need indeed!' she said pointedly. 'We travelled halfway across the country with you.'

He held her gaze. 'Yes, you did.'

She shook her head, huffed out a breath. 'And we should have known your true identity.'

'You did know my true identity.'

'Not your title!'

He gave her a nod of acknowledgement, yet asked, 'What difference would that have made?'

She opened her mouth, but didn't speak.

'Would it have made the trip easier? Shorter?' he asked.

'No, of course not, but…'

'But what?' he pressed.

She tossed both hands in the air. 'But there was no need for you to hide your identity.'

He shook his head. 'I wasn't hiding my identity. If you remember, Captain Harris didn't have a chance to make a formal introduction before you began insisting that you were not about to travel anywhere with me.'

Her glare grew more direct. 'You could have mentioned it during our travels.'

He lifted a brow and repeated his question from before. 'Why? What difference would it have made?'

'Honesty,' she snapped. 'That's the difference! Because if you had, then I would have known you were being honest.'

'I was being honest,' he declared. 'If you had asked, I would have told you my title.'

'Why would I have asked?'

He shrugged. 'It appears to be of importance to you.'

'No, having you not tell me is the importance, because that makes me wonder what else you haven't told me.'

'What else is it that you want to know?'

Frustration flashed across her face. 'How am I supposed to know?'

Roger knew he shouldn't be basking in her frustration, because she had clearly been worried upon finding Abigail's crib empty, but he couldn't imagine a woman more beautiful than she looked right now. Her cheeks were flushed a rosy pink and her dark brown eyes sparked with life. He liked seeing that. During their travels she'd been sombre and task focused, other than when she'd gaze upon her daughter. She had endured more than many, including him, in a short amount of time, and he should have been mindful of that this morning.

'I am sorry about this morning, Clara,' he said in earnest. 'I did not mean to cause concern and it will not happen again. I am a marquess. I inherited the title upon the death of my father. I do not wear it like a feather in my hat.' He could point out that some do and expect everyone to notice it, but he wasn't one to needlessly put down others. 'Nor do I put a lot of credence in it. It simply is what it is. Some say I'm a lot like my father in that way. Perhaps I am, and perhaps I'm not. I don't remember much about who he was as a man, other than that he was my father, so I can't say for sure either way. As far as other things that I didn't mention, I suppose I should tell you that I own the ship that brought you to England. As with my title, it seemed an unnecessary detail to share when we first met, as our first conversation was focused on getting you and your companions in my coach so we could begin our journey.'

Her jaw dropped slightly. "Your ship?"

'It's one of several that I own, part of the shipping conglomerate that I inherited from my father, along with my title, and Clairmount. I also oversee another large shipping company that I will one day inherit, upon the death of my grandfather, my mother's father. Because of that, I have ships that sail in and out of the United States regularly. It is for this reason that Drew and Annabelle asked me to find you and Suzanne.'

Those amazing brown eyes of hers searched his face as if trying to decipher if he was telling the truth or not.

She must have determined he was, because she gave a slight nod. 'Thank you for that information.'

Roger wasn't sure why he found her so fascinating, but he did, and so he chose to tell her the rest of the truth. 'You once asked if Annabelle liked me when we first met, and part of the reason she didn't was due to my title. She was quite adamant about how Americans had once fought a war against the crown, and that titles of nobility held no place in her country. Your country.'

Clara frowned slightly as she nodded.

'I assumed that you, like Annabelle, would be put out by a title. Therefore, I saw no reason to infuriate you any more than you already had been at that time. Also, if you had been in full health during the journey you would have realised that the staff at nearly every inn we'd stopped at addressed me as "Your Lordship", or used my title.'

Her frown increased. 'I did hear them say "Your Lordship", but I assumed that was because of your mannerisms and dress and…' With a sigh, she let her voice fade away.

He gave a nod and then continued. 'I should also mention that Annabelle is now the Duchess of Mansfield.' The rest of Annabelle's story was hers to tell, not his.

Clara's eyes widened. 'The Duchess of Mansfield?'

'Yes.'

'You mean her husband…?'

'Yes, Drew is the Duke of Mansfield.'

She stared at him for a stilled moment, and then, shook her head. Blinked several times, then twisted so he couldn't see her face.

He went with his instincts and gently grasped her shoulders with both hands to twist her back around. 'I'm sorry. I didn't mean to overwhelm you with information.'

Tears slipped out of her eyes and down her cheeks.

'I truly hadn't meant to upset you,' he whispered and pulled her closer, into an embrace.

She sobbed quietly as she buried her face in his shirt front.

He held her tighter and kissed the top of her head. 'I'm sorry. So sorry.'

Stiffening, she lifted her head, pushed herself out of his embrace. 'I just want things to be normal again. I just—' She spun around and hurried back to Abigail. Pulling the chair away from the table, she picked up her daughter, mumbled, 'Excuse us,' and hurried out the door.

As if questioning if he knew what he'd just done, Sammy looked at Roger, then at the door, and then with a large doggie sigh, he clambered to his feet and followed in Clara's wake.

Roger watched them leave and seriously questioned his own intelligence.

Chapter Five

Clara paced the floor of Suzanne's room, which was as elegant as her own. This room had a bright blue rug on the floor and blue and white draperies, as well as bed coverings, and hosted an ornate roll-top desk near a large window, which Suzanne was already making good use of, while perched on a chair covered in light blue fabric. 'Can you believe it?' Clara asked. 'He's a marquess, and Annabelle is a duchess, married to a duke.'

'Yes, I can believe it,' Suzanne answered.

Clara paused long enough to stare at her friend and blink. She couldn't understand why Suzanne, the person whom she knew almost as well as she knew herself, wasn't the least bit stricken by the news.

'It's not all that unbelievable,' Suzanne said. 'England is full of people with titles. I don't see why you are so shocked. Only a man of means would have been able to search for us on Annabelle's behalf, and afford to trek us here, to his home, and allow us to stay here, and provide us with clothing—'

'I know all that, but don't you think he should have told us?'

'Why? What difference would it have made?'

Frustration boiled inside her, and she spun around to pace across the rug so quickly, she nearly stepped on Sammy's tail. He was distracted, watching intently as Abigail played with a set of square blocks, stacking them atop each other.

'It would have made a difference,' Clara said, attempting to keep her voice calm.

'How so?'

Clara drew in a deep breath, hoping it would help her think, but she could still feel Roger's arms around her. Still feel how he'd kissed the top of her head. At that moment, she'd wanted to wrap her arms around him and hold on. Just hold on.

That made no sense.

All it did was frustrate her even more. Spinning back around to face her friend, Clara held up one finger. 'I know one great difference it would have made. I wouldn't have found out from Bertha last night! I couldn't fall to sleep afterwards, thinking about it, and when I did, I awoke to discover he'd kidnapped my child right from under my nose.'

Suzanne set her pen in the holder and rose from her chair. 'He did not kidnap your child. He took her downstairs and fed her breakfast.'

'Without my knowledge.'

Suzanne stepped close enough to grasp Clara's upper arms. 'Because you were sleeping!'

That bothered her too. Knowing he'd seen her sleeping. There was something very intimate about that. 'He could have woken me.'

Suzanne let out an exasperated-sounding sigh. 'And then we could be standing here talking about how he'd entered your chamber without your permission. Because that's what this is about. What all of this is about.'

Confused, Clara frowned. 'No, it's not.'

'Yes, it is. Roger hasn't been able to do anything right in your eyes since we stepped foot in England.'

Clara opened her mouth, but closed it again when she couldn't summon a reply.

'Your daughter lights up when she sees him, even your dog adores him, but you can't find a single thing to like about him. Not one.' Suzanne shook her head. 'The entire household thought something awful had happened at how you were running through the halls in your nightgown, screaming for Sammy.'

Clara's face burned at the memory of that. What had she been thinking? She'd been so shocked to find the crib empty, the room empty, that she'd panicked. Panicked like she never had before. All she'd known was that Sammy would be wherever Abigail was. That she could count on.

It was the only thing she could count on. 'I just want our lives to be normal again,' she said. That won't happen if Annabelle is a duchess. That's not normal. Neither is living in a marquess's home. Nor being hugged by him. Even it it felt so amazing. So real.'

'Clara,' Suzanne said softly, 'you have been my dearest friend since I moved to Hampton to live with Aunt Adelle, and I cherish our friendship. I was there the day they brought the news to you of Mark's death, saw how it stole the life from you for a moment. I was scared, afraid that you might never be whole again, but you snapped back. Within minutes you were comforting his mother, his father, making coffee and serving everyone the pie you pulled out of the oven as if knowing we were coming over that day.'

Her breath was caught somewhere deep in her throat, yet Clara managed to say, 'Because there hadn't been anything else I could have done.'

'Yes, there was. You could have sat down and cried, or screamed and yelled, told us all to leave so you could be alone, or reacted a dozen other ways. But none of them would have been you. You always reminded me of a cat, landing on your feet, and even if you'd hurt one foot, you acted as if you hadn't and kept going. I was amazed by your stamina, and without you, I don't know where I'd be right now.'

Clara's eyes stung. 'Without you, Abigail and I may not have survived.'

Suzanne shook her head so hard the pencil that she had stuffed in the twisted bun of her long blond hair came loose and she had to slide it back in place. Clara grinned at the automatic action of her friend. Suzanne had been stuffing her pencil in her hair since they'd been in school. She'd clearly never outgrow the habit.

'We survived because of you,' Suzanne said. 'If it had been just me, I'd have given in long ago, but you were so determined that we stay put. It was that determination that convinced me to do what I could to help.' Suzanne closed her eyes for a moment, and they were glistening when she lifted her lids. 'Clara, there was nothing more we could have done. Nothing. We would have starved if we'd stayed any longer. We both know that. We both know that leaving with Captain Harris saved us.' A tiny sob sounded before she continued, 'We will never have the life we had before again. Before the war. I'm sorry, Clara, but that life is gone.'

Clara's heart, which she'd thought was bruised and broken beyond repair, evidently hadn't been because it cracked right down the middle. 'I don't want it to be.'

'I know you don't.' Suzanne wrapped her arms around her. 'But it is.'

Misery arose inside Clara, making her throat burn and leaving her tongue-tied. She didn't want to believe what Suzanne was saying could possibly be true, but at the same time, she knew it was, and knew she'd been afraid to admit that since leaving the farm.

'It's just been so hard,' she finally whispered. 'Leaving the farm that Mark bought for us. I promised him that I'd be there when he returned.'

'He's not coming back,' Suzanne whispered. 'We both know that, and we both know that Mark loved you. He would never have expected you to go on living there, not like we had been, not for any reason.'

Clara did know that. Mark hadn't been a martyr and wouldn't want her to be one, either. Yet, there was still a strong inclination inside her that said she had to return home. 'I know he's not coming back, but I will return to the farm, build it into what we had dreamed about, talked about doing together. I have to do that.' A knot formed in her stomach. 'I'm afraid, Suzanne.

Afraid that if I get too comfortable here, that I'll forget about Mark, forget about the farm, and I can't do that.'

'You won't. I know you won't. You'll get back home, and I'll go with you, I will help you.'

'No, I'm not asking that of you. You—'

'I know you're not asking. I'm offering. Once the war has ended, we'll return together and grow enough vegetables and fruits to feed half of Virginia.'

Suzanne knew that had been Clara's dream, to have a garden so big that it would take all day to hoe. Since she'd been a small girl, she'd loved making things grow and multiply. Everything from grains to fruits and vegetables, and plants and flowers. So had Mark; that was one of the many things they'd had in common.

'However, until then,' Suzanne said, 'until the war is over, let's just accept this—' She waved a hand, gesturing around the circumference of the room. 'All of this for the adventure that it is.' Glancing down at Abigail and Sammy, Suzanne said, 'An adventure of a lifetime.'

Clara glanced at her daughter, who was still playing with the blocks. Abigail was too young to comprehend, but that didn't stop a winsome grin from forming on Clara's face. It had to be every little girl's dream to live in a palace, and here, for the next few weeks at least, her daughter could live that dream. 'It is an adventure of a lifetime, isn't it?' she asked Suzanne.

'Yes, it is, and I'm recording every moment in my journals.' Suzanne sat down in her light blue chair. 'Just think, Abigail's granddaughters could one day read about her adventure in England.'

Clara sat down on the bed. 'I hadn't meant to sound ungrateful for all Roger has done for us. I was just shocked to learn he's a marquess.'

Suzanne sat down beside her. 'That doesn't change who he is at all. He's a really nice man.' She patted Clara's leg. 'Just because he's a man, doesn't mean he can't be a friend. I think of him as a friend.'

Clara nodded, but couldn't quite grasp the idea. Perhaps she needed to think about that, and to accept things as they were for the time being. Watching Abigail play, she asked, 'Do you think Annabelle's home is this nice?'

'Probably,' Suzanne replied. 'Have you seen the library yet?'

'No. All I've seen is this room, mine and Abigail's rooms, and...' Her face grew hot thinking about her interaction with Roger while she'd been wearing only her nightgown. 'The dining room.'

After she'd made her fast exit, Bertha had brought a breakfast tray up to her room. She'd eaten, dressed in her yellow gown and put a clean dress on Abigail before coming to speak to Suzanne.

'Come, let me show it to you. I was up there earlier this morning.' Suzanne rose from her chair. 'It's on the third floor. Mildred told me about it last night.'

'Who is Mildred?' Clara picked up Abigail.

'The upstairs maid.' Suzanne grinned. 'Can you even believe that? We went from living in a root cellar to an English estate with an upstairs maid. It's like the greatest adventure imaginable.'

From where he sat behind the big desk going over ledgers, the muted voices sounded joyful, like the far-off sound of birds chirping on a bright and sunny morning. Roger glanced up at Alice Mills, known as Mrs Mills to all the household staff. Until this moment, he'd never wondered if there was a Mr Mills. Not that he knew of. Then again, his mother had hired Mrs Mills to run the household years ago. He'd also never seen the woman crack a grin in all those years.

With her pointed chin protruding upwards, it was merely her eyes that glanced downward, towards him as she stated, 'Bertha is giving the guests a tour of the house.'

'Is she,' he said, closing the leather-bound book that had accounted for every dime spent as always. Though he'd read through each line, his mind had been on Clara, and still was. She'd wanted her life to be normal again. He couldn't make that happen, but he could encourage her to make her life as normal as possible while being here. 'Will Bertha include the growing house in her tour?'

'No, my lord. That hasn't been used for years. Not since before I became employed here.'

He pushed the chair away from the desk and stood, crossed the room to take a peek down the hallway.

The trio of women looked like a small regiment the way they walked side by side down the hallway. Short, and aging, Bertha was flanked on one side by Suzanne and the other side by Clara, wearing her yellow dress and carrying Abigail, with the ever-present Sammy following closely at her heels.

Roger leaned against the doorframe and watched as they walked closer. He might want to avoid her for a bit longer, considering her quick exit out of the dining room, but he'd much rather find out whether or not she'd forgiven him for not mentioning his title. Being forgiven by anyone had never been a concern of his in the past, in part because he hadn't made it a habit to lie or act in a way that would beg forgiveness. The other part was if someone was upset with him, he figured that was their problem not his.

A quick flash of a thought, one that left as fast as it came, suggested that he should consider the idea of wanting to know if Clara had forgiven him as a warning.

He frowned slightly, wondering if he should have held on to that thought a little longer, just to give it a bit more credence, but the thought slipped away as the woman approached.

'Hello, my lord,' Bertha greeting with a slight curtsy.

They stopped and Roger stepped into the hallway. 'Hello, ladies.' He attempted to keep his gaze off of Clara due to how she was studying him with what appeared to be deep consideration. He also attempted to tell himself that it was her problem to not forgive him, but as usual, when it came to her, neither of his self-directed instructions were doing much good and his gaze found hers.

She quickly dipped her head, gazed down at the floor as a hint of colour filled her cheeks.

Abigail, however, didn't have anything to forgive, and she held her arms out to him. He smiled at the child's ease of showing what she wanted, when she wanted it, and reached out to take her from Clara.

'We aren't done touring the house,' Clara said, not releasing her daughter.

Abigail gave her mother a brief glance before stretching towards him again.

He slid his hand under her tiny arms to lift her from Clara. 'I am done with the ledgers and am going out to the stables. I'm sure Abigail and Sammy will enjoy that more than touring the house.' He held Clara's gaze. 'That is if you don't mind.'

She released her hold on Abigail. 'I don't mind.'

'All right then, that's where we'll be when you're done.' He gave Bertha a quick nod. 'You'll show her how to get there.'

'Yes, my lord,' Bertha said. 'Of course. We won't be long.'

'Take your time,' he said as Abigail leaned her head on his shoulder. 'We'll be fine.' With a nod to the ladies, he turned towards the doorway of his office and informed Mrs Mills, 'Our business is completed for today. Thank you.'

She gave a stiff curtsy. 'Yes, my lord.'

Chatting to Abigail about the horses, he carried her down the hallway and out the front door. At the sight of green grass, Abigail giggled and wiggled to be let down, and Sammy shot down the stone steps like someone had lit his tail afire.

Roger laughed and hurried down the steps before putting Abigail down on the ground. 'You two are like a couple of spring fawns the way you love to frolic in the grass.'

Sammy barked and Abigail set into her toddling run, arms out at her side to help her balance.

Watching them, Roger imagined them holed up in a root cellar for days, weeks, months, on end. That made him think of his own childhood, compare how he'd been given every material thing a child could want, as well as clothes aplenty, and how he'd never known the pang of hunger.

At Abigail's age, he'd still known the love of a father, and of a mother for that matter. It wasn't until years later that he longed for those things. He would have given up all the gifts, all the clothes, even a meal here and there, to feel loved. To know that if he'd held his arms out to someone, they would have picked him up, held him close.

He shook his head to make the thought go away, be absorbed back into his mind, where things lived that he couldn't seem to shake away completely.

His childhood was one of those things.

The main thing actually.

It wasn't as if he believed that his mother hated him, they just didn't see things eye to eye after his father had died, and that had continued on, into adulthood.

A delightful squeal from Abigail pulled his attention back. Espying what had her so excited, he warned the dog, 'Sammy, no.'

The dog shot back a look filled with disappointment, but his tail never stopped waging.

'That is a cat,' Roger told the dog while scooping Abigail up into his arms. 'You are a dog, and bigger, but you do not want to encounter that cat.' Solid black, except for a white patch beneath his chin, Ports was not only a large and old cat, he was ornery.

Ports chose that moment to plant all four legs on the top of the rock fence wall he'd been sitting on, and arching his back, gave out a growl followed by a long hiss.

Abigail wrapped her arms around Roger's neck and hid her face from the cat while Sammy leaped behind him and peeked around one thigh, no doubt wondering what the hell kind of critter was on that fence.

'That will be your only warning, boy,' Roger told the dog. Then, he levelled a glare on Ports. 'You stay away from this little girl or your nine lives will be up.'

The cat gave another hiss, then jumped down and with his tail standing straight up and jerking, he sashayed off towards the barn where he belonged.

Sammy let out a muffled bark, as if saying good riddance.

Roger reached down and patted the dog's big square head. Like Clara and Abigail, Sammy had put on weight. His belly was now round rather than sucked in and not a rib could be seen.

'That, my friend, is Ports. The barn cat. He's good at his job of keeping the rodents away, but I can guarantee that he'll like you as much as he likes humans. Which is nil.'

Whether it was from seeing the cat, or hearing the warnings, Sammy was weary and walked close to Roger's side as they made their way to the stable built of stone and as old as the house itself. Jacob was inside the stable, talking with Loren, who had been Clairmount's groom and groundskeeper for several years.

The three of them discussed the horses, how Jacob planned on leaving for Southampton tomorrow morning, and a few other subjects while Abigail sat atop a white mare that was as old as she was gentle. Still, Roger stood next to her, with one hand on the mare's back, ready to grasp the little girl if she lost her balance.

That didn't seem likely; she was engrossed with the horse, giggling and patting its neck.

Sammy's bark alerted them to someone approaching moments before Clara walked through the wide opening of the double set of wooden doors.

As if it would just never get used to the sight of her, Roger's heart made that fluttering, double beat action that momentarily stopped his lungs from breathing, before he found the wherewithal to invite her forward.

He also noted how easily a smile formed as she recognised Jacob and greeted him politely.

Jacob and Loren bid them farewell, and went about their business, while Roger introduced Clara to Flower, the horse.

'Flower?' She ran a hand down the length of the horse's nose. 'That's an interesting name for an all-white horse.'

Roger couldn't contain the laugh that came straight out of nowhere, or the memory that caused the laugh. 'I was little, three or four, and had been out here, in the stable, with my father. Flower here was being born and the groom needed help. Afterwards, when we went inside, my mother said that we both stunk like the stables. My father looked at me and said, 'I think we smell as good as flowers.'

Clara's laugh was as light and soft as a musical note. 'So you named the new horse Flower.'

'That I did. It was a fitting name, too. She's as gentle as a flower.'

Glancing downward, a blush covered her cheeks. 'I um, I'm sorry about this morning. There was no call for me to act so…' She huffed out a sigh. 'So unreasonable.'

'Apology accepted, but only if you accept mine as well. I do apologise for taking Abigail from her room, and for everything else.'

She shook her head, even as she said, 'Apology accepted. I should never have been worried. I know that she's safe with you.'

'I'm glad that you know that.' He reached out, pushed a wayward twist of hair that had fallen from the knot at the nape of her neck and was hiding one of her eyes. 'You've done a good job with her, Clara. Raising her on your own as you have.'

'Thank you, but she's still young and has a lot of raising yet to come.'

'I suspect she does, but I'm confident that you'll continue doing a good job.'

She blinked several times, and when she looked at him again, there was moisture pooling in her eyes. 'I wasn't doing that good of a job. We were living in a hole in the ground, scrounging for food. There's nothing to be proud of about that.'

'Yes, there is. None of that was your fault. Your country is at war. You were left to your devices.' That still caught inside him, left a burning ball of frustration. He just couldn't seem to get over how she'd been left

all on her own like that. There was no one to blame—
he just didn't like knowing that it had happened to her.
She deserved to be taken care of, protected. 'You made
the best of the circumstances. Had you done anything
other than what you had, you may not have survived,
and that would have been an awful thing.'

She leaned the side of her face against Flower's and
sighed. 'I didn't know what to do. I had some money
at first, and had I known, I could have used that, taken
us someplace safe, but I kept thinking things would
get better, that the war couldn't continue much longer.'

He wrapped his fingers around her hand, squeezed it.
'There was no way for you to know how long it would
last. To this day, no one knows when it will end.'

She nodded and looked at her daughter, who was still
enjoying her seat on Flower's back.

'You can't blame yourself, Clara,' he said evenly. 'It's
in the past, and now it's time to move forward.'

She nodded, but the sadness still shimmering in her
unshed tears belied her nod.

He gave her hand another squeeze. 'If not for yourself, move forward for Abigail. Let her experience an
unhampered world while she can.'

Clara lifted her face away from Flower while re-
moving her hand from his hold and laid it on Abigail's
leg. 'Let her live in a palace while she can,' she said
softly, reverently.

'A palace? Is that where she wants to live?'

With a smile, she said, 'This place is as close to one
as I've ever seen.'

He chuckled. 'Clairmount is nothing more than a

manor house. But fear not, I'll see that she visits a palace.' He lifted Abigail off the horse. 'Buckingham Palace.'

'The queen lives in Buckingham Palace,' Clara said, touching the tip of Abigail's nose.

'Yes, she does,' he said. 'That is also where Drew and Annabelle were married.'

Clara's eyes widened. 'They were?'

He nodded. 'As sure as I'm standing here, they were' Tickling Abigail's tummy, he settled her on his hip. 'Come, I want to show you something.'

A flash of apprehension flashed in Clara's eyes. 'What?'

'You'll see.' Once they'd left the stable and walked around the long, neatly manicured hedge, he put Abigail down so she and Sammy could run across the low-cut grass that encompassed the back yard.

'The outside of your home is as lovely as the inside,' she said, taking in the hedges and flower beds.

'Thank you, but I can't take any credit for that. Mrs Mills does an excellent job of overseeing all the aspects of the house, inside and out. Has for years.'

'She does appear to be very competent, as do the others I've met.'

'You've met them all?'

The expression on her face as she glanced up at him was adorable. 'I have no idea if I met them all or not, nor can I remember all their names. Bertha rattled them off so fast my head was spinning.'

He chuckled. 'That is Bertha. She can get in more words per minute than anyone else I know.' They paused their steps because Abigail and Sammy had stopped to investigate a butterfly fluttering about. 'Do me a favour,' he said. 'When you do learn all of their names, teach them to me.'

With a perplexed look, she asked, 'You don't know all of their names?'

'No, I don't.'

'But many of them have been here for years.' She shrugged one shoulder. 'At least that's what Bertha said.'

'I'm sure they have, but I've seldom spent any length of time here since I was a small boy.'

'Why? Where did you live?'

The butterfly flew away, and they all continued their walk along the back side of the house. 'Shortly after my father died, I was sent off to school, up near London. That's where I met Drew. Then my mother remarried and I started going with Drew, to Mansfield for holidays and breaks.' During those years, he'd discovered how badly a child could want to be loved. Want to be needed. 'The longer breaks, I would go live with my grandfather in Southampton so I could learn all about the shipping companies that I would one day manage. My grandfather—my mother's father—took over my father's company upon his death while also managing his own, until I was old enough to take over.'

'Your grandfather lives in Southampton?'

He wasn't surprised that she picked up on that. 'Yes, but staying at his house would not have been ideal. My grandfather often has guests and my townhouse there is too small.' His mother was often at his grandfather's house, unless she was in London, at the home of her latest husband—her third one. The second died a few years ago. 'You'll all be more comfortable here at Clairmount.'

Silent for several long moments, when she spoke it was a question on a separate topic. 'How did your father die?'

'The ship he was captaining went down in a storm.'

'Do you captain ships?'

'I do when it's necessary, but unlike my father and grandfather, I'm not a sea dog. I respect the sea. I appreciate the profits she's provided my family for years, but I also resent her for all she's stolen from people. The lives and dreams.' He hadn't meant to say any of that, it just came out without thought. However, it was all very true.

Luckily, they were nearly at their destination so he could change the subject. 'What I want to show you is around the corner of the house. My father had it built.'

Chapter Six

Clara was still processing how nonchalant Roger had sounded while talking about his childhood, thinking that there had to be a lot more that he wasn't saying—because the non-caring attitude he'd portrayed didn't fit him—when they rounded the corner of the massive house. Then she stopped and pressed a hand to her breastbone. Attached to the outside wall of the house was a huge glass structure that ran nearly the entire length of the home. She hadn't seen this during the tour from Bertha.

'You can get to it from inside, past the kitchen and laundry,' Roger said. 'There's also a door from outside.'

She had heard of glass growing houses, where people could grow plants and flowers year-round, but had never seen one. Excited to see what was growing inside, she frowned as they walked closer because it didn't appear as if anything was growing on the other side of the glass.

'It hasn't been used for years,' Roger said, while picking up Abigail and opening the door that was framed with wood, but hosted a large glass panel. 'Not since my father died. He used to bring plants and seeds home from around the world and attempt to grow them here.'

Her heart pounded as she stepped inside. It was warm outside, but the added warmth of the sun shimmering through the glass and the glorious scent of dirt, or the earth itself, was wonderful. Long and narrow, with glass making up three walls and the ceiling high overhead, the space was filled with tables piled with pots, gardening tools and other bric-a-brac, and along the centre was an aisle of wooden, raised beds filled with dirt. Grey, dried out dirt, but it still made her hands itch with the want of digging in, prepping the dirt, and planting seeds.

'What type of plants did he bring home and grow?' she asked, noticing extremely large pots.

'All types and sizes. He had a banana tree that he brought home from the Caribbean, but it never produced fruit.'

'Banana tree?'

'Yes, bananas are a tubular fruit, very sweet and quite delicious, but they don't ship well, so a visit to the Caribbean or other tropical location is the only way to sample one.'

'You've sampled one?'

'Yes, while sailing with my grandfather years ago.' His grin made his eyes twinkle. 'I tried to bring some home, but they rotted long before the trip was over.' Grinning, he added, 'But they were delicious while they lasted.'

His delight was evident. 'Has that happened to other things you tried to ship home?'

He laughed. 'Dozens and dozens of other things.'

She wanted to know more, so much more, but had a hard time deciding what to ask and finally settled with, 'Why did your father try to grow bananas? Did he like them that much?'

He set Abigail down to explore at will. 'I'm not sure how much my father liked them, but they are a favourite of my mother's.'

'She's eaten them, too?'

'Yes. She sailed with my father several times.'

The dullness in his voice caused more questions to fill her mind. It was as if he lost all his cheer when he spoke of his mother, and that reminded her of how Bertha had said that he'd lost his smile after his father had died. It wasn't any of her business, but that didn't stop her curiosity, even as she attempted to quell it by asking, 'How large was the banana tree?'

A faint smile sat on his lips along with a thoughtful gaze as he looked around the room. 'I remember it being tall, but it couldn't have been. This ceiling is only about ten feet tall.' He stood and walked to the far corner. 'I remember it being over here. It must have been in one of these large pots.'

There were several large earthen pots, the largest ones she'd ever seen. 'I wish I could have seen it. A banana tree. I've never heard of one.'

'Well, like I said, it never produced fruit.' He walked back to centre of the room, looked around. 'This place needs a good cleaning.'

The floor was made of stone and needed a good sweeping and scrubbing, as did the tables, and the glass panels could use a good washing with vinegar water to make them sparkle. 'Why don't you use it?'

'I'm not here enough, and the gardener has enough to keep him busy with the gardens, orchards, and grape-vines.'

A deep sense of sadness at such an amazing space not being used washed over her. 'This is legacy, Roger. One your father left you. He must have enjoyed being out here. I can only imagine that he'd like for it to still be used.'

'He loved being out here.' He scooped up a handful of dirt from the bed in the centre of the room and let the dried-out soil fall between his fingers. 'Suzanne mentioned that you liked to grow things. That you had a large garden before the war struck. During your time here, you're welcome to use this area.'

For a moment, her imagination—with visions of her spending hours in the glass house, cultivating the dirt and planting, and aiding the growth of tiny seedlings—nearly went wild, then she pulled herself back into reality. 'We won't be here that long.'

'No, you won't, but it could give you something to do while you are here.' He walked along a table near the wall, looking at the various pots and other miscel-laneous items. 'I will request it be cleaned out. If you want to use it, you can. If not, at least it'll be clean if someone else does.'

There was so much she didn't know about him, in-cluding who that someone else might be. 'Your mother?'

His laugh sounded fake, and also bitter. 'I doubt that she's stepped foot in this room since my father died.'

Grief. She could understand that. 'It holds too many memories for her,' she said.

He brushed his hands together, ridding his palm of any lingering soil. 'Hardly. My mother remarried soon after my father died. And again, after her second husband died. She's on husband number three now.'

Clara clearly heard the distaste in his tone. 'That angers you?'

'Angers me?' He shook his head. 'Hardly. She can get married as many times as she wants. I simply refuse to follow in her footsteps. Or to be cajoled into it.' He lifted Abigail off the floor and playfully tossed her in the air until she was giggling. 'I think it's about time for the midday meal.'

He was very good at redirecting Abigail's attention, but Clara's curiosity couldn't be distracted that easily. His mother's marriages clearly disturbed him, but surely he planned on marrying someday. He was a marquess, had a legacy, businesses, to pass down to heirs. Didn't he want that?

She and Mark had talked about that, about passing down their farm to their children someday, and she would. She would make sure the farm was passed down to Abigail. Somehow.

Roger opened a wooden door, held it for her to exit the glass room. She recognised the hallway, and twisted, held her hands out towards Abigail. 'I'll take her upstairs to clean up before eating.'

'Off you go,' he said to Abigail while handing her over. 'I'll see you in the dining room.'

Abigail's tiny brows formed a deep frown as she looked at him, almost as if questioning how he dared hand her over when she clearly hadn't been ready to be handed off to anyone. Not even her own mother.

Clara wasn't upset by that. How could she be? Since meeting him, he'd given Abigail everything she needed. Not only food and clothes, safe travels and a comfortable place to sleep, but also his undivided attention.

Once again, Clara questioned if she was allowing her daughter to grow too attached to him, and she wondered what she should do about it.

A heavy sigh built in her chest. She managed to keep it inside until they'd parted near the stairway, where she carried Abigail upwards, while he continued down the hallway.

Once the sigh was out, another one instantly started to build at the way Abigail twisted in order to keep her eyes on Roger for as long as possible.

She had married a man she'd loved. Set a future in place for him and her, and the children they would have, and life had been exactly as she'd dreamed.

Then the war had come, and she'd vowed to be at the farm when Mark returned. When he'd died, she'd accepted the loss. Accepted that she'd lost her husband, lost the love and friendship they'd shared. Accepted that she'd be alone the rest of her life.

She'd been fully prepared to live that life. Had been living that life, then, out of nowhere, the sailors had arrived, hauled them to England, and she'd met Roger.

Roger Hardgroves. The fourth Marquess of Clairmount.

A man who must have more money than he knew what to do with, considering how he'd already provided for them and how this…this palace, was simply one of his homes.

He was more than that, though, and that's the part that was impacting her the most.

In his calm, unhurried way, he'd made her realise that while she'd been focused on her life, on what she'd accepted and would live without the rest of her life, she hadn't taken into consideration what that meant for her daughter.

Abigail had needs, too. Clara loved her with all her heart and always would, and she knew her daughter loved her in return. However, the way Abigail had so quickly taken to Roger, said that had been something she'd been lacking.

Clara knew what it was like to have a father's love. She knew that better than others because it had been all she'd had, and she'd wanted her children to have both a mother and a father.

That wasn't possible now.

She'd accepted the life she would have, one that didn't include Mark. She couldn't change that. The part of her that had loved Mark had died with him. She'd given him a part of herself, the part of her that had been created to share with a husband, with the love of her life.

Now that part of her was gone, just like him.

The meal may have been the most sombre one that he'd had with the trio of women since he'd met them.

He hadn't expected that. Clara had seemed excited when he'd shown her the growing house. Roger had caught Suzanne's attention and glanced towards Clara, silently asking if she knew why Clara was so subdued, but Suzanne had merely shrugged.

He wondered if Clara's silence had something to do with what he'd said about his mother's marriages. Perhaps she was more like other women than he'd thought. Was finding a second husband on her mind? A knot formed in his stomach. She was sure to find one. A willing man to be her husband and a father to her daughter.

Abigail was her normal happy self, but she was also clearly sleepy. Her little eyelids had grown heavier as she'd eaten, and now that her plate was nearly empty, her little head was nodding.

Clara noticed and, leaving her own plate nearly untouched, she set her napkin on the table. 'If you will excuse me. It's time for a nap.'

Roger stood and pulled back the long-legged chair that allowed Abigail to sit with them at the table so Clara could easily lift out the sleepy child.

After mother and child had left the room, he broke the thick silence by saying to Suzanne, 'I hope you are finding the accommodations satisfactory.'

'Very, thank you. You have a lovely home and everyone has been very welcoming.' She set down her fork and knife. 'Clara agrees. She just, well, she hasn't been herself since we left America. She understands that we had to leave, but I think she feels as if she abandoned Mark, her husband, by leaving.'

'It was confirmed that he'd died, wasn't it?' Roger

felt a twinge inside his chest. 'I mean, he's not, perhaps a prisoner of war, is he?'

Suzanne shook her head. 'He's dead. His brother was with him when he died and came home long enough to break the news to his parents. I was there when they broke it to Clara.'

Hearing the news of a death was one of those things that a person never forgets. 'That had to be very hard on her.'

'It was, but she rebounded quickly, did what she had to do, not only for herself and Abigail, but also for the neighbours and anyone else she could think of. She had a huge garden and shared it with everyone, right up until the soldiers came that first time. They took the horses and cow, the pigs and chickens, and burned down the barn.'

Interested, he asked, 'Where were you while that happened?'

'We hid in the root cellar. Sammy had alerted us to their approach. They returned and raided the house, but they didn't burn it down. Over the following months, others stopped by, scrounging through what was left. Some stayed for days, but they never found the root cellar.'

He'd known they'd been through hell and back, but until this moment hadn't imagined all of it. Still couldn't. 'You were very brave women.'

'No, we weren't brave, we were scared out of our wits, and the truth is, those sailors, when they arrived, saved our lives. I'm sure of that.' Suzanne laid her napkin on the table and gave him a nod. 'You are the reason we are alive today. If you hadn't ordered Captain Harris to find us before returning to England, we...' She shook her head. 'Clara would have died defending her home, protecting her daughter.'

With a nod, he said, 'And you would have defended her.'

'Yes. I would have.'

That wasn't surprising. It was clear how close the women were. 'Did you live with Clara before the war?'

'No, I lived in my aunt's house in town, but she died a few years ago. I'd ridden out to Clara's farm with her in-laws when they went out to tell her about Mark and stayed at the farm with her. If I'd gone back to town that night, I probably would have died along with her father and in-laws. My house, along with theirs and many others were burnt to the ground. About the only people who survived on that side of town were those who took to the water.'

Tragedy came in many shapes and forms, and these women had had their fair share. 'If you need anything, or know of anything that Clara or Abigail need, please don't hesitate to ask. I have the means and the ways to provide it, and I want to provide it.'

She nodded, but then shook her head. 'We already owe you for what you've done and have no idea how we'll ever repay you. I know that's weighing heavily on Clara.'

The money he'd spent on their behalf was of very little significance. 'I don't expect, nor do I want repayment.'

A pretty woman in her own right, her faded blue eyes took on almost a haunting glimmer. 'I was sent to live with my aunt in Virginia after my mother died. There were no other options except to accept the charity of the people who paid my transport to Virginia and the charity of my aunt for taking care of me upon arrival, but Clara has never accepted any kind of charity, and I know her well. Very well. Therefore, it would behoove you to believe me when I say she won't accept it this time, either. It's not an easy thing to accept, not even for a child.'

The honesty of her tone struck a chord in him, gave him something to think about that he'd never had to consider. He'd been born into a wealthy family, had servants waiting on him since the day he was born, and though he'd never had to accept charity himself, he thought he understood how some people might feel about it. 'That's why Clara was so adamant about taking care of the meals during our travels,' he said, aloud, though he wasn't sure he'd meant to.

'Yes, it was, and I'm sure right now, she's trying to think of a way she can earn her keep while being here.' She glanced around the room, then back at him. 'With the number of servants you have, she may have a hard time coming up with something, and that's leaving her out of sorts.'

He let that settle for a moment, then said, 'If I can come up with a way, would you help me convince her?'

Suzanne let out a soft laugh. 'Convincing Clara of anything isn't easy—you've already experienced that—but yes, I will help in whatever way I can.'

Convincing Clara wasn't going to be easy, but he was up to the task. 'All right then.' He pushed away from the table. 'I'm going to find Bertha, send her up to sit with Abigail, and if you could think of a way to have Clara show you the glass room in about half an hour, that would be good.'

Suzanne agreed, and while she went upstairs, he found Bertha, who was more than willing to take charge of Abigail. Afterwards, he found Mrs Mills. He'd already asked her to send someone to clean the glass room, and now told her not to send anyone, that he was going to do that himself.

Though her stern expression barely changed, he could sense her surprise and confusion, but gave no further explanation. Instead, he caused her more confusion by asking where he'd find a broom and other items he might need.

He'd never used a broom before, but if it would help Clara find the *normal* she was looking for, he'd learn to use it, because he understood that she would never find the old normal that she'd had. He had to help her find a new normal. One she could embrace.

Almost right to the minute, half an hour later, Clara and Suzanne walked into the glass room.

'What on earth?' Clara asked, gasping and pressing a hand to her chest.

He'd done his best to create more of a mess, and her face told him he'd done an excellent job of it. 'There wasn't anyone available to get this room clean and organised, so I thought I'd do it myself.'

She opened her mouth, closed it, then drew in a breath so deep and long it made her trim, yet supple, breasts rise and fall. 'Why do you want it cleaned?'

'Because you were right.' He leaned on the broom

handle. 'My father loved this room. It is a legacy. One I should have taken note of before now. Once it's cleaned, I'm going to hire someone to grow things in it. It will be nice to see it full of plants and flowers again.' He wasn't convinced of that, but he had seen how her eyes had lit up upon walking into the room, and Suzanne had confirmed how much Clara enjoyed growing things.

Grasping the broom again with both hands, he gave the floor a hefty sweep that caused another whirlwind of dust to rise in the air.

'Have you ever used a broom before?' she asked, coughing and batting at the dust.

He made a point of swiping at the dust motes filling the air with one hand. 'I've swabbed many a ship's deck.'

'Well, that's not quite the same,' she said.

'Maybe you should do the sweeping,' Suzanne said, under her breath, but loud enough that he heard.

'That is a very good idea,' Clara said, approaching him, hands out to take the broom. 'You could move the large pots out of from under the tables, if you don't mind.'

'I don't mind at all.' He handed over the broom and included a wink with his smile. 'I'll take all the help I can get.'

He chuckled at the blush that flooded her cheeks, and at how she didn't need any more encouragement in order to take charge.

She took to that role like she'd been born into it, and within minutes, Roger realised what he'd assumed was going to be a little bit of sweeping and rearrang-

ing, was actually going to be as much work as unloading a cargo ship.

Once the floor was swept, pots of every size and
shape were carried outside, emptied, and left to be
scrubbed clean before they'd be carried back inside.
Tables and counters were cleared, scrubbed clean, and
every item was cleaned before it was replaced back on
a table or counter.

Roger deduced that Sammy must have decided Abigail was safe under Bertha's watchful eyes, because
he'd ambled into the room, and then outside, where he
lay, near the door, watching the work as if it was of
great interest. Or perhaps boring, because he was soon
snoozing.

Mrs Mills had snuck a peek at the activities happening and had returned with aprons for both Clara and
Suzanne, to protect their dresses, and when Abigail
arose from her nap, Bertha carried the child into the
glass house. She didn't stay long, instead insisting that
she take her charge outside and would return when it
was time for tea.

The more they cleaned, the more things Roger came
across that brought more memories of his father. Those
that had been tucked away inside him for years and
years.

That was especially true when he pulled the heavy
canvas covering off the large cabinet up against the
back wall. He could almost see his father sitting at the
desk, head bent and pen in hand.

'Oh, my goodness,' Clara said softly. 'What a gorgeous piece of furniture.'

Made of solid oak, with tall, carved doors on the top and deep drawers on the bottom, the cabinet doubled as a desk. Roger pulled out the sliding table that was hidden between the upper cupboard and the lower drawers. 'It was my father's desk.'

'I've never seen anything like it,' she said.

Curious, Roger pushed the desktop back into the cabinet and opened one of the lower drawers. He grinned at seeing the stacks of envelopes. Memories of carefully filling those envelopes washed over him.

Clara knelt down next to a deep drawer. 'These envelopes are all labelled and dated.' Digging deeper, reading the writings on each envelope, she added, 'It's seeds! All kinds of seeds.'

He knelt down, took out a handful of envelopes. 'These are close to twenty years old, or older. He let me count the seeds and put them in the envelopes for him.'

'You did?' Her eyes were shimmering. 'This is a true treasure.'

'Treasure?' He shook his head and dropped the envelopes back into the drawer. 'They are too old to grow.'

'No, they aren't,' she insisted. 'With a little soaking in sugar water, I bet they'd still grow.'

'Are you willing to find out?'

Frowning, she glanced up at him.

'I'll hire you and Suzanne to finish getting this place in order and then plant some of these seeds, see if they will grow.'

'You don't have to hire us. We'll gladly do that.' She was sorting through the envelopes again. 'I just don't recognise a lot of these names, and wish I did.'

He stood and opened one of the overhead doors. There he found exactly what he'd expected. 'You'll find information about every envelope in these ledgers.' He lifted one out and flipped it open. As with the envelopes, he instantly recognised the left-handed slant of his father's handwriting.

She lifted out another ledger and let out an excited gasp. 'This is amazing.' Flipping through the pages, she said, 'Everything is here. Names, dates, descriptions, drawings, where the seeds came from, their growing cycle. Oh, my! This is…this is truly amazing.'

Her face was aglow, and watching as she flipped through the pages, Roger felt a significant spike of desire. He knew the feeling well. When it came to her, he'd been able to squelch it. For several reasons. She'd been ill, she was a widow with a child—which was on the top of the pole of the type of women he stayed away from—she was Annabelle's friend. The list went on. He had thought of numerous reasons during the long hours riding Smokey, and each and every one of them had been good, sensible.

Yet, right now, not a one was strong enough to douse the flame that had been lit, nor to quell the quickening of his pulse.

He couldn't pull his gaze off her, not even when she looked up. Their eyes locked and the flame inside him flared as they stood there, staring at each other. The draw between them wasn't one-sided. That, too, was something he knew well, and recognised.

She looked away first, and her hands shook as she

closed the book, put it back on the shelf. 'I—I should find Abigail.'

As quick as a bird, she turned and flew across the room, out the door.

Roger closed the book in his hands, put it back on the shelf, and stood there, staring at the room for an extended length of time before he put one foot in front of the other, walked to the door. Turning about, he stared at the room again.

There had been reasons, good reasons why he hadn't spent a lot of time at Clairmount. The main one was the one he hadn't considered until this moment.

At one time, this place, this entire house, had been a happy place. A home.

That had changed with the death of his father, and that was why he'd stayed away. He didn't want a home or anything that went along with it. Because when you have that happiness, that love and connection, and then lose it, the grief is crippling. He'd lived through that once and wouldn't do it again.

With that thought settling, he entered the hallway, and he wondered if he should join a travelling acting troupe. He was a damn good actor. Had been for years, and continuing that legacy, he acted as if all was exactly as he wanted the rest of the day. During tea, he'd commented on how wonderful it was to see the glass house coming to life again. Afterwards, however, he explained that he had some things to see to, and that the women should asked Aaron to assist them with any heavy lifting.

There was nothing he needed to see to, other than

keeping his distance from Clara. He didn't want to be attracted to her. Didn't want to become any more attracted to her than he already was.

He saddled a horse and visited John Richards, the overseer of the tenant farmers on Clairmount land. He met with John a couple times a year, so a visit wasn't out of the ordinary.

He returned in time for dinner and maintained his role of being a host to his guests. He also suggested that if Clara wanted other seeds, Aaron would take her to see John, who could provide whatever she needed.

Then, the following morning, before anyone else rose, he asked Aaron to let the guests know that he'd been called to London, saddled Smokey, and rode away while the sun was barely peeking over the horizon.

Chapter Seven

Clara told herself she was relieved that Roger was gone. More than relieved, she was grateful. It was as if her prayers had been answered. Something had happened between them when she'd found the seeds yesterday. Something that should never have happened.

She was still shaken by that moment, when her entire being had imagined what it would be like to be kissed by him. She hadn't been able to sleep last night, and when she had fallen to sleep, she'd dreamed about kissing him.

No, that hadn't been a dream. It had been a nightmare.

The worst nightmare imaginable.

She'd kissed Roger in her dream, but worse than that, Mark had caught her and Roger kissing.

It had been awful, and left her so traumatised she was still sick to her stomach, but was doing her best to make sure no one noticed. Especially Suzanne. She still looked at all of this as an adventure, and that they should enjoy it. There was nothing to enjoy about being unfaithful to your husband.

Suzanne wouldn't understand how devastating that was.

Clara did, and as soon as breakfast was over, she collected Abigail and headed for the glass growing room, hoping the work would get her thoughts back in line.

Never, ever, had she so much as had a fleeting thought about kissing anyone except for Mark. She'd loved him.

She still loved him.

Would always love him.

She'd known him all her life. Had only known Roger a very short time. Not even two complete weeks.

Annabelle couldn't get back from Scotland soon enough.

'You forgot an apron,' Suzanne said, standing in the doorway that led to the hallway of the house.

'I guess I did.' Clara met Suzanne in the centre of the room and took the starched, white apron. 'Thank you. There is no need for you to help today. I can manage.'

Suzanne slipped the loop of her apron over her head. 'I figure I should earn my keep, too. I asked Aaron to carry out a couple buckets of hot water to wash the pots outside.'

Clara's mind was a befuddled mess. A complete, befuddled mess, but Suzanne was right. They did need to earn their keep, but that wasn't why she'd agreed to restore the glass growing room. The small amount of work it would take, wouldn't begin to repay Roger for all that he'd done for them. She'd agreed because Roger wanted it restored in memory of his father. She'd seen that in his eyes when he'd told her about the banana tree. He hadn't admitted it then. He hadn't even admitted it when he'd said he wanted it restored, but when he'd uncovered that desk, that look was back in his eyes again.

That's what she'd been looking at, when the thought about kissing him had struck.

A thought that had startled her senseless.

Abigail, who had been enjoying toddling around the table legs with Sammy, had walked over to the door, and with a little squeal, she shot out the door to the yard that Suzanne had left open.

Clara hurried after her, so did Sammy.

Already standing near Suzanne, Abigail was chatting. Saying one word, over and over again.

Clara listened more intently, then told Suzanne. 'I think she's saying *dog.*'

'I think she saying *Doger,*' Suzanne replied.

'Doger?'

Abigail squealed and clapped, while looking around expectantly.

'Yes,' Suzanne said. *'Doger.'*

The word got another excited reaction from Abigail, who repeated the word again.

'I wonder what she's attempting to say,' Clara said. Besides *bye-bye*, she hadn't said other words, other than *mama*, which she'd been saying for some time.

'She's saying Roger,' Suzanne said. 'And wondering where he's at.'

Clara's heart nearly stalled in her chest, both at Suzanne's statement and how Abigail repeated *Doger* several times.

That couldn't be. Just couldn't be. 'No,' Clara denied. 'She's saying *dog*, or *doggie*.' Kneeling down, she patted Sammy's head. 'He's right here, Abigail. Here's your doggie.'

'Goodnight and God bless,' Suzanne muttered. 'When have you ever called Sammy *doggie*, or even *dog*? Never, that's when. I doubt that Sammy knows he's a dog, let alone Abigail. She's saying *Roger*, with a *d* instead of an *r*.'

'Doger! Doger!' Abigail repeated, and again several more times, getting upset.

'She's looking for him,' Suzanne repeated.

Clara wasn't convinced, leastwise, she wasn't going to admit it, that's for sure, until she had no choice, which was moments later when Aaron carried two buckets of water around the corner of the house.

'Doger! Doger!' Abigail squealed and took off her in toddling run, until she got close enough to realise it wasn't Roger, then she spun about so fast, she tripped, tumbled headfirst onto the ground.

Clara quickly gathered her off the ground and patted her back as Abigail buried her face in her shoulder, half mumbling and half sobbing, 'Doger. Doger.'

It was enough to break Clara's heart all over again.

'I'm so sorry, ma'am,' the tall, grey-haired Aaron said with sincerity. 'I didn't mean to frighten the little miss.'

'You didn't,' Clara said, kissing the top of Abigail's head.

'Oh, the poor wee thing,' he said, setting the water buckets on the ground. 'She was so happy, running towards me, but when she realised it was my ugly mug, she nearly jumped out of her skin.' He gave Abigail's back a tender pat. 'I will go find her a sweet biscuit Maybe that will help.'

'Oh, that's not necessary,' Clara said. 'I'm sure she'll be fine in a moment.'

Not taking no for an answer, Aaron gave Abigail's back another soft pat. 'Don't fret, now, little miss, I'll be back in a wink.'

As he hurried off, Clara knelt and twisted Abigail around to face the worried dog. 'Look, here's Sammy.'

Abigail released her hold on Clara's neck and wrapped her arms around the dog's neck. 'Ammy.'

Clara's heart sank at the clarification that Abigail hadn't been saying *dog* or *doggie*.

'Goodnight and God bless,' she whispered, stealing her friend's words, because they were better than the ones floating through her mind. Words she'd never speak in front of her daughter. She never cursed. Never had cause to. Until this moment. If Abigail hadn't been near, she might have cussed like a drunken sailor straight off the boat over how foolish she'd been at letting her daughter get so attached to Roger.

Clara would direct a few choice words in Roger's way, too. For being so…so…everything. For being the first man that Abigail got to know. For being so kind and caring to all of them. For kissing her in that horrible dream last night.

Hurried footsteps brought her mind back around. Besides Aaron, carrying one of the light and airy cookies they'd had yesterday with tea, Bertha was hurrying towards them, too, her arms pumping in time with her footsteps.

Upon arrival, they both knelt, Aaron holding out the cookie and Bertha with both hands pressed against her bosom.

'Here you are, little one,' Aaron said softly to Abigail.

'Hear she took a tumble, I did,' Bertha said. 'Came to have a look-see myself.'

'She's fine,' Clara said.

They both were convinced of that when Abigail gave them a toothy grin and took the cookie.

After much fussing, including checking for skinned knees, Aaron made his way back inside the house, but Bertha insisted upon staying and keeping an eye on Abigail, and Sammy, so Clara and Suzanne could complete their work.

'His Lordship has to be so happy about this,' Bertha said, gesturing to the glass growing room. 'This had been his father's pride and joy, but after his death the marchioness tried, but she wasn't able to find anyone who could keep the plants alive and so they died. She locked the doors then, said to leave it alone.'

'Oh.' Worried, Clara asked, 'Will she be upset to have it cleaned?'

'Heavens no, Lady Elaine will be delighted. Especially knowing it was His Lordship who ordered it. She's wanted him to have more interest in Clairmount for years, but, well, it's not my place to say more, but it sure was a waste, having the place empty all the time.'

'All the time?'

Bertha nodded. 'I can count on one hand the number of times the marquess or the marchioness have been here over the years. It's so sad the way they avoid each other.'

Clara had been curious, very curious about Roger's mother, but hadn't dared ask him. Yet, if Bertha made comments, she would listen, out of politeness if nothing else. 'Avoid each other you say?'

Bertha shook her head sadly. 'Yes, ma'am. The two of them walk on eggshells when they are around each other. It's enough to break a heart, that it is. The marchioness hasn't had an easy time of it, with two husbands dying on her. I do hope this one doesn't up and kick the bucket, too.' Lowering her voice, Bertha continued, 'If you ask me, she married again the second time only to give His Lordship a father, but the marquess, even as a young lad, wasn't having any of that. He had his grandfather, still does, and that was all he needed, in his mind. The rest of us know that William Cross is little more than a sea dog. No manners whatsoever. Course, I've only met him the one time, when he came here and hauled the marquess off to the sea. Lady Elaine was at her wits end over that, especially since it had only been months since the lad's father had died at sea. When they returned, she sent His Lordship off to school, that she did. Right quick.'

'How old was he?'

'Let me think…' Tapping a finger against her chin, Betha tilted her head from side to side. 'He must have been nine.' Nodding, she confirmed, 'Yes, nine, because by the time he was ten, he no longer came home, not even for holiday. He would go home with the Duke of Mansfield and—' Bertha clamped her mouth shut. 'Forgive me. I should not have rambled on so. Should not have said anything. Mrs Mills will have my head if she knows I did. Excuse me. I'll take the little miss back outside.'

And with that, Bertha and any more information that Clara might have learned, was gone, with Abigail in her stout arms and Sammy on her heels.

His London townhouse had been the one place that Roger had spent the most time and he was usually quite comfortable and satisfied here, but after three days, he was as restless as an alley cat at midnight.

There had been a missive waiting for him here from Drew, stating they had received his message about finding Clara and Suzanne and that he would send another note before leaving Scotland.

Garrison, the only household staff Roger retained at his London townhouse, much like Jacob was the only one he retained for his place in Southampton, had informed him that the message had only arrived shortly before Roger had, otherwise it would have been sent on to Clairmount.

It made sense that Drew would have sent it here. In the message Roger had sent, he'd stated that he would deliver the women to Clairmount and travel on to London himself.

That had been his original plan, and he was glad he'd followed it.

He was also wondering how Clara and Abigail were getting along. He missed seeing both of them.

Missed them a great deal.

Which confirmed that coming to London had been the right choice.

Ideal except for the even more than usual hustle and bustle. Everyone was preparing for the International Exhibition. Opening day was only a few weeks away, on May first. Buildings to host the world's fair in South Kensington had been under construction for years, and exhibitions from around the world would be on display for several months after the opening day. He'd visited the site numerous times, watching the construction, especially the two large glass domes, and was interested in seeing the new maritime engines that were to be introduced to the public during the opening days. Rumours had it that there was also supposed to be a machine called a refrigerator that could produce ice. Either the engines or the refrigerators, or both, could greatly benefit the shipping industry.

Yet, even that, thinking of those new inventions and of advancing his companies, didn't keep his mind off Clara. It appeared as if he was a glutton for punishment when it came to her.

Roger tossed another invite on his desk and threaded his fingers behind his head as he leaned back and swung his feet up to rest his heels on the desktop.

The buzz in London had confirmed that Queen Victoria would not be attendance. She was still in mourning after the death of Prince Albert, and so her cousin, the Duke of Cambridge, would preside over the events from a throne built beneath one of the glass domes.

The duke was also hosting a ball the week before

the start of the exhibition and half of London was on pins and needles, waiting to see if they'd receive an invitation or not.

Roger wasn't. He was guaranteed one. So was Drew. Prince Albert had practically been a second father to Drew over the years, and Albert's death last December had affected them both. It was like the end of an era.

The end of another era had come about when Drew had married. The two of them had vowed bachelorship together, when they'd been young, but Drew had changed his mind after meeting Annabelle. After meeting Annabelle himself and seeing the two of them together, Roger had seen that coming, and he'd been happy for both of them, still was. He just wouldn't follow in Drew's footsteps.

Nothing would change his mind about getting married. He couldn't let his mother win. He'd been angry with her for telling his father to leave, but afterwards, after his father's death, he'd been crushed by the way she'd sent him off with his grandfather, then off to school. All he'd wanted had been to be home with her, but that hadn't been what she'd wanted. She'd wanted to forget he existed, get on with her life. Remarry.

Disgusted at himself for letting his thoughts go down memory lane, he dropped his feet to the floor.

There was always a good game of gambling at one of the many gentlemen's clubs on Pall Mall Street. That was exactly what he needed. Something to put him back into the life he'd chosen for himself. The one where he didn't have to think about anything or anyone, other than himself. And the wonderful life he had being a bachelor with money to spend on the games, drink, and if he chose, a willing female companion.

Little more than a couple of streets from his house, he recognised a man and woman pushing a baby carriage. He'd heard that Viscount Harmon and his wife had had a baby last winter. A boy. He'd also heard that the viscount was not the father. His wife had had an affair with a commoner, with the precise goal of getting pregnant. The two of them had been married for over five years and this was their first child.

Roger caught his thoughts with a bit of disgust. He was a gossipmonger. Had been for years. If there was information to be had about nearly anyone, he had ways of finding it. But he never repeated it, other than to Drew if the information was important.

Him seeking information had started years ago, when he'd caught wind of how gossips were saying that one of his friends' widowed mother had been on the lookout for a new husband. He couldn't recall if there had been a scandal about it, but it had made him start keeping an ear out in case anyone mentioned his own mother.

'Hardgroves,' Carl Harmon said, as they approached. 'Haven't seen you for a while, old chap.'

A thick and stocky man, and shorter than most, Carl Harmon was a kind man. His carrot-coloured hair had provided him with a few choice nicknames over the years, which he'd taken in his stride.

'Good day,' Roger greeted, with a nod towards Mrs Harmon, who was a remarkably common-looking woman. It was odd that he'd never realised that before today.

'I dare say, you haven't seen my son, have you?' Carl asked.

'No, I can't say that I have,' Roger admitted.

Carl's chest puffed out a bit more as he stepped closer to the buggy and pulled back a blanket covering the sleeping baby. 'He's a handsome devil. If I do say so myself. Which I do often enough.'

With Carl so excited he could barely contain himself, Roger attempted to come up with a compliment, but all he could think was that the poor kid was as bald as a billiard ball. The carriage, however, was an elegant one. 'He sure has a nice carriage. Looks like he's content sleeping in it,' Roger said. His mind went to Abigail. She was too big for such a carriage now. So full of adventurous spirit, she'd climb right out of the rolling bed, but he sure would have liked for her to have had one like this one.

'Just a short walk puts him right to sleep,' Carl said, smiling at his wife, who nodded in agreement.

'It certainly is a fine day for a walk,' Roger said, once again void of any other comment, because he felt like an intruder. The look Carl and his wife shared held more than an agreement about the baby falling to sleep. Rumours were often false and he was glad that the one he'd heard didn't appear to be affecting Carl and his wife. They looked as if they were on top of the world, as they should be over their child.

Roger congratulated them on their son, bade the couple a good day and continued on his walk, but any interest he may have had in the gambling hall on Pall Mall was gone.

He'd never wanted a child. Never wanted to get married. Not long ago, he'd told Drew to have two sons. One to inherit all of Drew's holdings, and the other to inherit a couple of shipping companies. That right there had solved the only reason he would ever get married—someone to pass down his shipping holdings to, but not in the way his mother wanted.

She'd got what she'd wanted years ago.

The street was busy, and he didn't notice the coach until it stopped next to him.

'Hello, Roger,' the woman said out the window.

Roger sucked in a deep breath, then nodded. 'Hello, Mother.'

Chapter Eight

Clara had made up her mind about one thing, Clairmount in spring was utterly gorgeous. In the past week, flowers in the numerous flower beds had popped into bloom and their fragrances filled the air. From her inspections of the plants, different ones would continue to bloom all summer long.

Donald Goodale, the gardener and groundskeeper, was a wealth of knowledge when it came to the plants she didn't recognise. Married to Mildred, the upstairs maid, Donald had been working at Clairmount for ten years. Prior to that, he'd been a tenant farmer on Clairmount land, but turned his farm over to his son and daughter-in-law. He told her he still helped them when needed and claimed that the marquess was the fairest landowner in the area.

Clara easily believed that. Roger was a fair and honest man, and though she tried her hardest not to, she missed him.

She told herself that was only because she was excited for him to see the glass greenhouse. The cleaning had been completed, the soil had been replaced in the bed and the pots, and most excitingly of all, there were already a few tiny seedlings popping up through the dirt.

Mrs Mills had provided her with an empty ledger to record what, where, and when she'd planted each seed. She still had high hopes for those that hadn't yet sprouted, even after she'd soaked them in sugar water and nicked the harder seed shells with a sharp knife.

Over the past week, she'd scoured through the journals that Roger's father had created about the seeds and thoughtfully selected varieties that she was sure would sprout and grow enough to be established by the time Annabelle returned from Scotland.

Donald had agreed that he'd take care of the plants after she left, and she appreciated that because it meant that she had a plan in place. At least one for the plants. A plan for her and Abigail was still unknown.

The lilting giggle of her daughter floated in through the open door of the glass house that led to the yard, and despite all the emotions that Clara couldn't get in control, when it came to her daughter, she couldn't help but smile, knowing that her daughter was happy. And healthy and well.

Although Abigail was still looking for Roger every day and her chattering often included the word 'Doger'.

Bertha and Abigail, along with Sammy, appeared in the doorway moments later, and the frown on Bertha's normally cheery face, caused instant concern.

'Did something happen?' Clara asked, while inspecting Abigail as she took her from Bertha's arms.

'No, ma'am,' Bertha said. 'Other than Aaron is looking for Mrs Mills. A message has arrived for her, but he can't seem to locate her. Have you seen her?'

'Not since earlier this morning,' Clara replied. Although stern faced, Mrs Mills had been nothing except kind and accommodating since they'd arrived, and was always close at hand.

Frowning, Bertha shook her head. 'It appears that no one has seen her for a couple of hours, and that's certainly not like her. Mrs Wells said they had discussed the menu for the week, and she made a list of things she would need from market, but Mrs Mills never came back for the list.' Bertha wrung her hands together. 'Everyone is quite worried.'

'Let's remain calm,' Clara cautioned, noticing how Bertha was wringing her hands. Clara questioned if there was a horse and carriage missing, as well as suggesting that the house was very large and perhaps an area had been overlooked. She and Bertha made their way inside, to the kitchen, where they found Aaron and the cook, Mrs Wells. Both looked as worried as Bertha.

Once again, Clara encouraged everyone to stay calm and quickly determined that an organised search was needed. Soon, everyone was gathered together in the kitchen, and she assigned search areas to each person.

Clara, with Abigail and Sammy, said she'd search several rooms on the ground level, but as she left the kitchen and moved down the first hallway with Suzanne, who was heading to search another section of the ground level, Sammy sat down near a door and wouldn't leave. Questioning his actions, because he usually avoided being separated from Abigail, Clara opened the door. A set of stairs led downward to a darkened area, and Sammy's bark had Clara looking at Suzanne.

'I'll find a lamp,' Suzanne said, while turning back towards the kitchen.

Sammy was already going down the steps and Clara followed, calling Mrs Mills's name as she walked. Sammy disappeared into the darkness before she reached the bottom of the steps, but Suzanne, along with Aaron, holding a lamp, appeared at the top and hurried downward.

'I opened the door earlier, while searching, but there was no light, so I didn't come all the way down here,' Aaron said. 'Alice wouldn't be down here without a lamp.'

'Sammy thinks something is down here,' Clara said, hoping the dog wasn't taking them on a chase after some kind of rodent or something.

'Alice!' Aaron shouted. 'Are you down here?'

There was a thump sound, and Sammy barked.

'This way,' Aaron said. 'Mrs Wells already checked for supplies, so I don't know why Alice would, but the food storage room is right over here.'

Sammy barked again and sat down near a door.

Aaron pushed open the door. 'Alice!'

Mrs Mills was lying on the floor, with a section of shelving pinning her legs. 'Hold still,' Clara instructed while she stood Abigail next to Sammy and rushed over to Mrs Mills.

'Thank goodness you found me,' Mrs Mills said, with tears in her eyes.

'Are you hurt?' Clara asked.

'I don't think so, but I can't move my legs.'

Clara grasped Mrs Mills beneath the arms. 'I'm going to pull you out while Arron and Suzanne lift the shelf off your legs.'

'I was so foolish,' Mrs Mills said. 'I climbed up the shelf so I could reach the empty baskets for the market trip and the whole thing tipped over. There's food everywhere.'

For the first time in ages, Clara wasn't worried about the food. 'Don't worry about that.'

'But look at this mess I created.'

'Messes are easily cleaned up,' Clara said while tightening her hold on Mrs Mills. 'Ready?'

'Yes.'

Aaron and Suzanne lifted the shelf high enough for Clara to help Mrs Mills scoot out from beneath it, but the other woman's moan had her asking, 'Where does it hurt the worst?'

'My leg. My right one.'

Clara quickly examined the leg, and though she couldn't feel anything broken, bruises were already forming. 'Where is the closest doctor?' she asked Aaron.

'In the village,' he replied. 'About an hour away.'

'Suzanne, please go find Loren, tell him we need his help getting Mrs Mills to her bed, and then ask Donald to summon the doctor.'

The next several hours were a bit chaotic. Loren and Aaron got Mrs Mills carried up the steps and into her room, while Clara asked Mrs Wells to brew a pot of tea and add lemon to it, hoping that might ease some of Mrs Mills's pain while they waited for the doctor's arrival.

The somewhat pudgy doctor, who didn't have a single hair on his shiny, round head, was breathless when he arrived, no doubt because he'd entered through the front of the house and the servants' quarters were in the back. 'My lady,' he greeted with a slight bow. 'Forgive me, I was not aware the marquess had married.'

It was a moment before Clara understood that he was thinking she and Roger were married. She was about to correct him, but, concerned the doctor might not see to Mrs Mills if someone in Roger's family hadn't requested him, she withheld commenting on his statement, and opened the door to Mrs Mills's room. 'Mrs Mills had a mishap. Her legs were pinned under a shelf that had toppled over. The right one appears to be more injured than the left.'

He set his bag on the chair near the foot of Mrs Mills's bed. 'Thank you, my lady, you can leave now, rest assured—'

'No,' Clara interrupted. 'I'll stay, you might need help.'

'Yes, my lady,' he said while he opened his bag.

Luckily, Alice's leg wasn't broken, but it was badly bruised and the doctor said she should stay off it for at least a week, which agitated the woman greatly because the message that had arrived earlier was from Roger's mother, the marchioness, who was planning on visiting and would arrive by the end of the week.

'I can't stay in bed,' Alice insisted. 'There is too much to do with Lady Elaine coming.'

'Don't worry, it will get done,' Clara said. 'You just tell us what needs to be done and we'll do it.'

'That wouldn't be proper. You are guests.'

'Guests,' Clara said, searching for a way for the other woman to accept the assistance, 'who are totally capable of helping and want to help.'

'That's kind of you, but it just wouldn't be proper.'

'Let's worry about what needs to be done and not what's proper.' Clara was nervous about Roger's mother's visit. She might not appreciate having strangers in her home, especially Americans who didn't fully understand all the rules of society here. However, Clara did understand how to take care of a home. She'd been doing that her entire life. 'The food storage room has been cleaned and Loren has reattached the shelf to the wall, so it will never fall again. Suzanne will go to market with one of the kitchen helpers, and Martha is already airing out the marchioness's room for her arrival.'

The ride to Clairmount gave Roger plenty of time to think. As if he'd needed more. Time or thinking. That's all he'd done since leaving. He'd planned on staying away longer, but running into his mother last week had changed that plan. She'd heard that he had guests staying at Clairmount.

Hence the reason he was back home. She'd be arriving three days from now.

The only thing he had to be glad about was that she wouldn't be hosting a party at the estate.

That, and the fact that he'd been able to quickly escape talking to her on the street that day, and had used every moment since preparing for this, his return. The freight wagon would arrive tomorrow.

Clara's inevitable arguments about how they couldn't accept the clothing and other items that would show up tomorrow echoed in his mind as he rode. Clothing was not a luxury, yet she was sure to say that so many would be far too extravagant.

He might have bought a few more than any of them needed. He'd simply told the seamstress that two women and a little girl needed to be outfitted and paid the price she requested to have everything ready posthaste.

The sun was setting, painting the sky with a variety of hues of red when he turned onto the road leading to Clairmount, and he felt a sense of homecoming that he'd never had before. He was excited to see Clara, and to see Abigail, because, he rationalised, he was anxious to know if they'd settled into a more normal life than they'd known the past year.

His rationalisation wasn't all that believable, not even for him, a man who loved being a bachelor, loved living alone, because he knew the truth. He missed them. Missed Clara and Abigail. He even missed Sammy.

He saw the dust before the carriage, and even as the vehicle approached, he questioned who it might be for they'd obviously been at Clairmount.

Roger stopped Smokey in the middle of the road, and his heart did a somersault upon recognising Dr Murphy.

'Is something amiss at Clairmount?' Roger shouted before the doctor's single horse came to a halt.

'Not to worry, my lord. The Marchioness, Lady Clara, summoned me the other day to see to an injury of Mrs

Mills. Rest assured it was a mild injury. She is healing quickly and should be up and about again in no time.'

Roger was relieved, yet questioned the doctor on what had happened before the two parted. It was then that something the doctor had said clicked in Roger's mind.

The Marchioness, Lady Clara.

Roger heeled Smokey into a faster gait.

Loren met him in the driveway. After a brief greeting, in which he was informed that all was well and that Clara would be able to tell him more about Mrs Mills and her injury, Roger walked up the steps of the house. The odd sense of nervousness inside him was foreign. It was contradictory to be nervous and filled with a sense of homecoming at the same time.

Then again, everything about his life had been contradictory the past couple of weeks. Including Clara. He had thought she might not be like other widows, looking for her next husband, yet, here she was, claiming to be his marchioness, his wife.

He did not need a wife, nor want one. Never had.

A bark on the other side of the door made him smile. Maybe a dog is what he needed. He might have to look into getting himself one after Drew returned and his guests had left.

The door opened. 'Good evening, my lord,' Aaron greeted, holding the door wide. 'Welcome home.'

Sammy was also there to greet him, with his tail wagging and big brown eyes looking hopeful for a pet.

'Thank you, Aaron.' Roger removed his riding gloves and coat, handed them to the butler and then bent down to give Sammy a good rubbing behind both ears. 'It's good to be home.'

Glancing towards the doorway to the drawing room, a unique sense filled him as his gaze met Clara's.

She blinked slowly, glanced the other way, and his gaze roamed over her. A sharp, hot, flame of desire shot through him. She had on her green dress, the one with the sash around the waist that highlighted the perfection of her womanly figure. She was a remarkably beautiful woman.

Her hair was pulled back, and she was smoothing one side with a hand.

He braced himself against the ache of desire, walked closer. 'Hello, Clara.'

'Hello.' She drew in a breath that caused her breast to rise and fall. 'We—I didn't know you were coming home today.' A blush covered her cheeks, even as she lifted her chin. 'Supper will be served shortly.'

'Good. I'm hungry. It's been a long ride.'

'Doger!' Abigail said excitedly as she toddled out of the room and ran on short legs towards him.

Roger scooped Abigail up into his arms. 'You learned how to say *doggie* while I was gone.'

'She's not saying *doggie*,' Clara said with her cheeks turning rosy. 'She's saying *Roger*.'

He looked from her to Abigail, then chuckled. 'Well, I'll be damned.'

Clara cleared her throat.

'Oops, sorry,' he apologised for the curse word, yet was amazed by the warmth that filled him as Abigail hugged his neck.

'Doger,' she said in her cute little voice.

That may have been the moment his life changed for ever. Then again, it may already have changed and he just knew it for certain at that moment.

Not sure how to deal with that epiphany, he glanced around. There was a large vase of flowers on the side table in the hall, a table he didn't remember being there, but other than that, the house looked the same. It was always neat and clean, yet it felt different. Flowers couldn't make a place feel different.

People did that.

Certain people.

Once again, his gaze locked on Clara's and a few of the thoughts flashing through his mind should probably make him blush, but he wasn't embarrassed. He'd thought about bedding her before. More than once.

She, however, would be mortified to know that's what he was thinking.

'There are seedlings,' she said.

'Excuse me?' he asked, trying to clear his thoughts.

'Seedlings. In the glass house. Several of the seeds sprouted. They weren't dead, just dormant and needed a little coaxing to come back to life. Would you care to see them?'

'I would.'

She hesitated slightly, as if afraid to step closer to him, then took a step forward.

He pivoted on a heel to walk alongside her. She walked evenly as they moved forward, yet Roger sensed a nervousness in her, as if she'd like to bolt away from him. It took all he had to not reach over, take a hold of her hand and tell her that she had nothing to be nervous about, nothing to fear.

Or did she? Was she afraid of him learning she'd told the doctor they were married? What purpose would that serve? She'd told him more than once her goal was to return to America. To the farm she'd owned with her husband. Being married to him wouldn't increase the chance or the speed of that happening, because if they were truly married, her place would be here, beside him, in England.

Had he misunderstood what Dr Murphy had said? Had the man meant his mother had summoned him? But his mother wasn't due for days yet, and she was now married to a viscount, and no longer used her marchioness title. The servants here still referred to her as such, he'd heard that on occasion, but he was certain Murphy had said Lady Clara.

As they moved down the hallway, he noticed more vases filled with colourful flowers, and he noticed that each room they passed had the drapes pulled open, filling the rooms with the glow from the setting sun.

The doors and drapes were normally closed, the rooms unused. The entire house had been more unused than not for the past several years. When he was here, it was usually only for a few days, or a week at most to check in on the tenant farmers. Or on the rare occasion that he'd been requested to visit by his mother.

He couldn't put off the inevitable, so he simply said, 'My mother will be making a visit to Clairmount soon.'

'We know,' Clara said. 'She'll arrive on Friday. A message arrived a few days ago.'

'Is that why you are so nervous?'

She glanced at him, shook her head, and then huffed out a breath. 'It does make me slightly nervous. It is her home and—'

'One of her homes,' he interrupted. 'It's also my home. You have no reason to be nervous. My mother is a very kind person.' That was true. No one had ever said a bad word about his mother. He was the only one who'd had issues with some of her actions. Mainly those that had included finding him another father. He'd never wanted that.

Clara gave a nod. 'The staff has assured me of that.' A grimace filled her face. 'Oh, dear, I nearly forgot to tell you about Mrs Mills. She had a slight accident. She will be fine, but the doctor suggested that she not use her leg for at least a week. Perhaps more, depending on how the bruising heals.'

He withheld the fact that he'd met the doctor along the road. 'What happened?' he asked.

'She was attempting to collect an empty basket off the shelf in the storage room for Anita to make a trip to market, and the entire shelf tipped over. She became trapped beneath it.'

That sounded worse than the doctor had made it out to be. 'Goodness! How severe are her injuries?'

He listened intently as Clara related the tale of Mrs Mills's absence and how she was discovered in the food storage room. Needing to check on his employee himself, he asked Clara to wait a moment and opened the door to the kitchen as they passed. Aaron was there as expected and he asked the man to let Mrs Mills know that he would like to call upon her in her room.

'We can look at the seedlings later,' Clara said.

'No, the light will be gone in a few minutes, and I'm sure Mrs Mills would like a few moments before I enter her room.'

Clara's smile included a knowing expression. 'I'm sure she will, but she can't leave her bed.'

'That's why I asked Aaron to let her know in advance. I would never enter her room without her permission.' That was true, but he questioned if he'd explained that because his subconscious wanted her to know that would include her bedroom. Yet, if invited, he would be there in a heartbeat.

The way she looked up at him, with a gaze that was soft and tender, made him want something that went beyond desire, yet was simple. He wanted her to look at him like that for ever.

She blinked and looked away, as if she too realised there was more in her gaze than she'd wanted.

'Well, um, I chose seeds that, from your father's journals, were fast growing,' she said, moving down the hallway. 'Some haven't sprouted yet, but I'm still hopeful.'

Abigail squirmed in his arms. He set her down and followed as she ran after her mother. Full understanding struck when they entered the growing room and the little girl ran to a corner that had clearly been set up for her to play in as her mother worked. There were several pots and old spoons, cups, and other items for her to play with in the dirt.

Here, like the rest of the house, he felt a change. Not because it was neat and organised, or even with the way the setting sun gave the entire room a warm glow. There was a life in the room that had never been there before, one that he couldn't attribute solely to the tiny green seedlings.

He inspected the plants that Clara was so proud of, and commented on their growth, all the while paying more attention to how the glow on her face was more enchanting than that of the room. He'd never wanted to kiss a woman more than he wanted to kiss her in that moment. That want had been there since he'd walked in the house, and he wondered how long he was going to be able to live with it. He doubted it would kill him, but it was torturous.

'You've done an amazing job, Clara,' he said, doing his best to sound normal. 'It's clear how much you enjoy gardening.'

'I've always loved watching things grow.' She glanced at Abigail in the corner and at Sammy lying near the door. 'Growth is an amazing process, in everything.'

He nodded, although he'd never paid that much attention to things growing, but she was right. It was an amazing process. He'd seen her grow over the past couple of weeks—in strength and confidence.

'Mr Goodale has agreed to take care of the plants after Annabelle returns and we go to live with her,' she said.

Her going to live with Drew and Annabelle had been his goal, and there was no reason for him to not be looking forward to that happening. No reason whatsoever.

Except for the fact that his life had changed. 'Will Donald have time?' Roger asked. 'I know he still helps his son with their farm.'

'He assured me it wouldn't be a problem,' she said. 'But if it will be for you, I can make other arrangements.'

Roger wondered what those other arrangements might entail, but chose to not question it aloud. 'It won't be a problem for me. If Donald has agreed, then he'll do it.' The room was growing darker now that the sun had slipped beneath the horizon. 'Shall we go check on Mrs Mills?'

Chapter Nine

Clara knew full well that it wasn't her place to stand beside Roger while he visited with Mrs Mills, but he'd asked her to join him, claiming it would make the housekeeper feel more comfortable, and Clara knew that was true.

She also knew that it wasn't her place to be overseeing his household staff, but there again, she'd been asked, and had wanted to help in any way she could. Mrs Mills had insisted that everyone else had their own duties to see to, and overseeing that those duties were completed was impossible for her to do while in bed.

Clara had been overseeing households her entire life, for her father and then her own. Granted, both homes had been much smaller and there hadn't been servants at either place, but she'd been responsible for everything. Things were more complicated here, complex due to the staff and the rules of society that she'd never encountered before, such as strict guidance as to the division between family and staff. Guests were to be treated along the lines of family, which she attempted to abide by as much as possible, but some things were just too rigid. If there were things that needed to be done, and she was capable of doing those things, then she did them. Including cleaning. She'd been cleaning her entire life and knew how to use a broom and mop, and numerous other household tasks.

Mrs Mills repeated how her accident had come about to Roger and claimed that everything was ready for his mother's visit, all because of Clara. Mrs Mills also insisted that if not for Clara and Sammy, she might still be lying in the storage room. Which was clearly untrue—someone would have found her—but Clara didn't rebut the woman's claims. Roger's smile said he knew the truth.

As he had been while she'd been ill at the inn, he was very caring about Mrs Mills's injury, and assured her that her health and healing was the utmost of everyone's concern.

Clara's nerves leaped beneath her skin as he questioned the doctor's orders. She hadn't told anyone how the doctor continued to assume that she was Roger's wife, and had hoped that no one else had noticed. Hopefully, no one would ever know and she wouldn't have to explain why she hadn't corrected the man. She wasn't overly certain why she hadn't.

Upon exiting Mrs Mills's chamber, Roger said, 'Thank you, but I do apologise for you having to take on so much.'

'Mrs Mills makes it sound like I've been doing much more than what I have. With so much help, it's barely been any work.'

'It's clear that Mrs Mills appreciates it, and so do I,' he said.

Clara's heart thudded due to the way he looked at her. Or maybe, just because he was here. She had missed him. That concerned her, and though she told herself it was only because of all he'd done for her, she couldn't help but wonder if it was more than that.

She would have to think about that, and about what to do about it, but at the moment, a kitchen maid appeared in the hallway and requested a moment of her attention.

'Excuse me,' Clara said, and stepped away from away from Roger. 'What is it, Anita?' she asked. At one time she'd wondered if she'd ever remember the names of so many different servants, but now she not only knew their names, she knew them. And liked them, including Anita, who was the cook's young niece and had only been working here for a few months.

'Forgive my interruption, ma'am,' Anita said. 'Mrs Wells is wondering if you'd like supper delayed a bit longer, giving the marquess time to freshen up after his ride home.'

Clara felt the heat of chagrin for having not thought of that herself upon his arrival. Then again, she hadn't been able to think about much when he'd stepped in the house. All she'd done was stood there, ogling him. A part of her had wanted to rush forward and greet him much like Abigail had. Her daughter hadn't stopped looking for him, each and every day, as if she was sure that she'd find him sooner or later.

She didn't want to admit it, but Clara had known that he'd come home sooner or later, too, and there had been an excitement and a comfort knowing that he would be home. That she would see him again. 'Yes,' Clara said to Anita, 'please ask Mrs Wells to wait half of an hour before serving the meal, and do thank her for me. I know how difficult it is to keep things warm.'

With another curtsy, the young girl said, 'I will, ma'am. Thank you.'

'Is something amiss?' Roger asked as Anita hurried towards the kitchen.

'No. There's enough time for you to freshen up before the meal is served.' Clara held her arms out to Abigail. 'And enough time for me to clean up this little one.'

Abigail shook her head and leaned closer to Roger.

He chuckled and kissed the top of Abigail's head before handing her over. 'Off you go, baby girl.'

Abigail wasn't impressed and her frown showed it, as did the way she said, 'Doger?' As if questioning how he dared hand her off.

He laughed again and tickled Abigail under the chin until she grinned. 'That's better.'

Then, he winked at Clara and moved towards the stairway.

It was a moment before she could move due to the commotion his wink caused inside her. Goodnight and God bless, but that man did things to her that were not right.

Simply not right.

'Doger,' Abigail said.

'Yes, Roger is home,' Clara replied with a sigh and headed down the hallway.

She ended up taking Abigail up to their rooms to

wash her face and hands because that way Clara could also check her appearance in the mirror. Just to make sure no pins had come loose in her hair. She wasn't checking to see if she looked pretty or not. There was no one here that she wanted to look pretty for, it was just that...

The air in her lungs was so heavy it hurt as she heaved out a sigh.

Mark was the only person she'd ever wanted to think that she was pretty. The only man she would ever want to think that, and she was mad that he'd died.

She shouldn't be, because it hadn't been his fault, but she was, because if he hadn't died, she wouldn't be here. She'd be home, with her husband and their daughter, living the life she was supposed to be living.

A life she was used to, one she knew.

Instead, she'd become used to living here, in a palace with servants, and this life was nothing like her life used to be. It was also a life that she would never fit into. It was too foreign. Living like nobility wasn't for her. She was meant to be a farmer's wife. An American's farmer's wife.

'Doger.'

Clara let out another sigh, picked up her daughter and left their rooms, all the while trying to convince herself that she couldn't wait to return to America. To her farm.

Roger and Suzanne were already in the dining room, and during the meal, Roger told them about London and the balls that were happening right now as well as the upcoming exhibition.

Suzanne was totally enthralled, and had a plethora of

questions, which Roger kindly answered, and although Clara didn't want to admit how interesting the things that he talked about sounded, in truth, she was quite captivated by it all.

He had a way of making things sound bigger than life, yet simple at the same time. He also had a way of making everyone laugh, especially when he told them about the ball that Drew had hosted shortly after Annabelle had arrived. It had been a masquerade ball, and some of the costumes he described were outlandish, especially when he said that one woman had worn a giant teacup on her head.

'Now, I know you're jesting,' Clara declared as they made their way into the drawing room after eating.

'No, I'm not. You can ask Annabelle when she arrives.' A sheen of teasing made his eyes twinkle.

'I will,' she said.

'I will be there,' he said.

She lifted a brow. 'So you can convince her to go along with your story?'

He laughed. 'No, so I can see your face when you learn I'm telling the truth.'

She shook her head, but couldn't stop from giggling.

'She'll also tell you that I was the genius who came up with the idea to have the masquerade ball.'

Clara laughed louder. 'A genius?'

He pretended to be hurt, made a show of giving her a frown. 'You don't think so?'

'That you are a genius?' she asked, playing along with him.

'Yes.'

She laughed. 'I am not going to answer that.'

He blew on his knuckles and rubbed them on his lapel. 'Well, I am.' Giving her a feigned look of shock, he asked, 'It's not that hard to believe, is it?'

'Yes,' she said, enjoying the bout of playfulness. She hadn't laughed like this for a long time.

'Why? Have you ever met a genius before?'

'Not that I know of.'

'There you go—now you have.'

She laughed harder as they all sat in the drawing room. Continuing the game, she said to Suzanne, 'Be sure to note that in your writings.'

Suzanne laughed. 'I most certainly will. And I'll mention the teacup hat.'

'In that case,' Roger said, resting one foot on his opposite knee, 'let me tell you about some other costumes.'

He told them about costumes and ball gowns, and decorations, and outrageous-sounding foods, not only from Annabelle's ball, but many others, and had Clara pressing a hand against her stomach at times because she laughed so hard. He described things in such a way that she could see them in her mind, and it made her wish that she'd seen them in person.

The people and the ballrooms, the decorations and food, as well as the woman who had worn a wig that had been so tall that she'd bumped into a lit sconce and knocked it off the wall, and how her husband had dumped the punch bowl over her head to make sure she didn't catch fire.

By the time Clara crawled into bed, she was exhausted

from laughing, but also happy. She couldn't remember the last time she'd fallen asleep with a smile on her face.

That night, she dreamed about going to a ball.

However, as with her last dream, it had turned into a nightmare.

She had been at a ball, dancing with Roger. Everything had been as beautiful and glamorous as he'd described and she'd been in awe, enjoying herself, until the music had ended and then she'd felt everyone looking at her, pointing and laughing.

That's when she'd noticed that she'd been wearing her old threadbare dress that she'd been wearing when she'd arrived in England. In her dream it had been in even worse shape, with ugly patches and a ragged, torn hem, and her toes had been grubby, dirty, and sticking out of her shoes.

People had laughed louder and she'd tried to run, but had been surrounded by people in fancy dress, and couldn't find an escape route no matter how hard she tired.

That's when she'd awoken, and hadn't been able to fall back to sleep.

As she lay there, staring at the ceiling, she couldn't recall a time when a dream had been so vivid. She hadn't needed confirmation that she didn't belong in England, in this world of nobility, wealth and luxury, but, nonetheless, her dream provided that.

Everything else proved that, too. Even though she loved spending time in the growing room, loved the plants, the soil, the warmth and brightness of the sun shining through the glass, she didn't fit there, either.

It was an adventure, like Suzanne claimed, but she didn't have time for adventures. She had to create a plan that would get her and Abigail back to America. A plan that included making the money she would need in order to return to Virginia and rebuild the farm.

Though she would never have wished for Alice to be injured, taking over the running of the household could provide information that she could put to use. Not until after Alice healed and Annabelle returned, but after that, she could find a job as a housekeeper in order to earn the money she needed.

By the following morning, Clara was convinced that her dream last night not only confirmed a plan was needed, but it also created an urgency in her to put it in place as soon as possible. She couldn't keep dreaming about Roger. That could tarnish Mark's memory, the love they'd shared, and she could never let that happen.

'Excuse me, ma'am,' Aaron said from the doorway of the growing room that led to the house. 'The pedlar is here. Mrs Mills said that you would see to him.'

'Oh, yes, of course.' Clara glanced out the window to check on Abigail and Bertha as she removed the gloves that had been provided for her use and set them on the table. 'Thank you, Aaron.'

He gave a slight bow. 'I will accompany you and carry the purchases.'

She considered telling him that wasn't necessary. The only thing on her list to purchase was tea and she was sure she could carry that by herself, but had already learned that it was part of his duties. Mrs Mills had said that the pedlar had the freshest tea and she wanted plenty on hand for when Roger's mother arrived.

Earlier this morning, while going over the day's tasks with Mrs Mills, Clara had put a small amount of money from the household cash box into the small handkerchief pocket sewn in the waist seam of her dress for purchasing the tea from the pedlar. He included Clairmount on his rounds once a month, and Mrs Mills was happy that he was due to come just prior to Roger's mother's visit.

Clara smoothed the skirt of her dress, making sure the money was still there and gave Aaron a nod of thanks while walking through the door he held open for her. She was still working out the differences between the American dollar and the British pound, so having Aaron nearby could be a benefit if she questioned anything.

Short, with curly grey hair and one eye that didn't open, the pedlar was standing near the back of his large enclosed wagon, complete with painted glass windows and a shingled peaked roof. The entire wagon was painted bright red with gold writing listing the various goods he sold across the side of the enclosure. Two tired-looking dappled grey horses were hitched to the wagon, and she glanced over her shoulder to where Aaron followed. Slowing her steps, so he was within hearing distance, she said, 'Please be sure he waters his horses before he leaves.'

'Yes, ma'am,' Aaron agreed.

'Good day, my lady,' the pedlar greeted with a deep

bow. 'I'm honoured to make your acquaintance. Emil McDonald at your service, right this way.'

As she had with the doctor, Clara considered correcting how he had addressed her, but again, wondered if he would forbid selling to her if he didn't think she had the authority to purchase on behalf of the household. Aaron could vouch for her, but not correcting the man's assumptions seemed easier.

He opened the door and waved a hand for her to climb the solid wooden steps into the back.

She didn't need to climb the steps. The interior was lit up by the two large windows on the sides and from where she stood, she was slightly in awe over the amount of goods neatly stacked on shelves and in crates on the floor. Withholding the desire to take a closer look, just out of curiosity, for it had been so long since she'd done any shopping, any browsing, Clara said, 'We are merely in need of tea this morning, Mr McDonald. The usual amount, please.'

The smile on his face said that he'd noticed her accent, and that it definitely wasn't English. Clara lifted her chin and waited for his response with a smile on her face.

'I have it right here.' He climbed the steps and picked up a small wooden box. 'But first, please allow me to show you the new yard goods. Beautiful, heavy material, perfect for draperies. It's that time of year and I'm sure you are anxious to make changes to the home.'

The hopeful look on his face was endearing, and truthfully, if it was her house and she had the funds, she would look at the material, because, though they were still in fair condition, windows in several rooms could use new drapes. Light coloured ones that would enhance the beauty of the room, of the house.

'No, thank you, just the tea for today, please,' she said.

'Oh, my lady, if you please,' Mr McDonald said, having already set down the box of tea and picked up a bolt of cloth. 'Look at this. It's the finest you'll find. Direct from the Orient.'

The material he held up for her to view was a lovely cream colour, and she couldn't stop herself from stepping closer to feel the weight of the fabric and examine the gold thread that was woven into the material in delicate flower shapes. It was thick, perfect for draperies, and stunning. It would go perfectly in the drawing room. That was her favourite room, and this material on the windows would look so nice with the olive-green furniture and white stone fireplace. If there was enough, she'd make a tablecloth for the round table near the set of windows in the one corner.

But that was all wishful thinking. This wasn't her home, and despite the desire to have the place looking as lovely as possible, it wasn't her place to make costly changes. She drew her hand away from the material and stepped back. 'That is lovely, but we just need the tea today. How much will it be?'

He gave her an amount, and though she was still learning the currency, it seemed awfully steep for a box of tea. She understood that he needed to make a living, but wasn't about to be cheated, either. Pedlars back home had a reputation of manipulating prices depending upon the purchaser, and it appeared that happened here, too. 'Would that be for two boxes?' she asked.

He lifted a brow. 'No, just the one.'

'I see. Well, perhaps we are not in need of tea today.' She waited a moment, letting her words settle, before continuing. 'Unless of course, you could see fit to provide me that box of tea for a fair price. I may not be British, but I do know when someone is attempting to take advantage of me.'

'Oh, no, my lady, that is not at all what I was attempting to do.'

'Of course it wasn't.' She gave him a nod. 'Thank you for stopping today, Mr McDonald.'

He quickly set aside the material and picked up the tea. 'I could sell this box of tea to you today for half price.'

Clara settled a look upon him that said she still wasn't going to be bluffed. 'You mean for the fair price?'

His smile was quick, and his nod said they fully understood each other. He wouldn't attempt to swindle her and she wouldn't be swindled. 'Yes, my lady.'

'Very well, then. I will take the one box.' She pulled out the money, counted out the sum and handed it to him. Taking the box of tea in exchange, she said, 'I would like you to pull your wagon over near the stables, where Aaron will see that your horses are watered before you continue on your way.'

'Thank you, my lady. That is very kind. Good day, to you.'

She nodded. 'Good day to you, Mr McDonald.' She turned, nodded to Aaron and then walked into the house, feeling a sense of pride for having made the purchase for the correct price.

Every housekeeper should be prudent with household funds, and that was something she'd become very skilled at years ago. Waste not, want not.

Roger straightened his stance from where he'd been leaning against the bottom half of the stable door. The top half was open, and he'd watched the exchange between the pedlar and Clara. He hadn't been able to hear what either of them had said, but from the body language and the outcome, he knew Clara had made her purchase for a fair price. However, even though he hadn't seen her face, he could tell that she'd been drawn to the material the pedlar had shown her.

He waited until the man had pulled his wagon to the stable, where Aaron had already requested that Loren provide buckets of water for the horses, before pushing open the bottom half of the door and walking over to the wagon. 'Good day.'

'Good day, my lord,' the pedlar replied. 'The lady of the house requested water for my horses.'

For whatever reason, or perhaps no reason at all, Roger chose not to correct the man about Clara's position. 'I'm aware of that. Please allow them to drink their fill.'

'Thank you, they've already had a long journey today.'

Many pedlars included Clairmount on their routes and he couldn't say if he'd ever conversed with a single one of them. 'Tell me, the material you showed the lady, was that for a dress?'

'No, my lord, that was drapery material, but I have other fabrics, fine dress goods, if you're interested.'

Draperies? He had no idea how one knew when new draperies were needed, but asked the man, 'Would you mind waiting here for a short while?'

'No, my lord, not at all.'

He found Clara leaving the kitchen. 'Excuse me, could I ask your opinion on something?'

She hurried to the doorway where he stood. 'Certainly. What is it?'

He took a hold of her elbow to steer her along the hallway. 'I would normally ask Mrs Mills, but with her incapacitated, I'd like your opinion on the condition of the draperies.'

'Draperies?' She stopped walking. 'Did Mr McDonald tell you about his material? You have to be careful with him, he's a—'

'A pedlar,' Roger intervened., 'He peddles goods, sometimes for a higher price, sometimes for a lower price.'

She grinned. 'That is correct.'

'He's watering his horses, as you instructed, and his visit reminded me that someone had mentioned the draperies might need to be replaced soon. It could have been Mrs Mills, or it could have been my mother. I know nothing about draperies, but if he has suitable material, it might be a good time to purchase some, before my mother arrives.' It was a little white lie, but the truth was, he liked the changes she'd made to the home so far, and he wanted her to have the freedom to make more, if that is what she wanted.

She bit her lip, and he couldn't tell if it was because of excitement, or scepticism.

'If you say that they don't need to be replaced, then I won't worry about it,' he said.

'They are still serviceable,' Clara said, once again walking beside him. 'But they are starting to fade from the sun. I've pulled them all open and tied them back. In fact, most people probably wouldn't notice, but...' She shook her head.

'But you did?'

'Yes, and a lighter colour would brighten the rooms considerably.' A blush rose into her cheeks. 'But it's not my place to suggest that they be replaced.'

'Oh, but it is. You are filling in for Mrs Mills, and if, in your opinion, new ones would make the house more welcoming, it would be my opinion that they be replaced.' He steered her into the drawing room. Again, draperies did not fall into his expertise, but noticing the number of windows, he added, 'I'm sure there is someone in this house who knows how to sew. I wouldn't ask that of you.'

She crossed the room and held up the bottom of one dark green drape. 'It's merely a matter of cutting the right size, hemming the edges, and pleating the top while sewing the rod pocket. Simple stitches that would not take long at all.'

'Did you happen to notice if the pedlar had any suitable material?'

'He had a lovely cream material with gold stitching that would look striking in this room.'

This time he was certain it was excitement in her tone and on her face. 'What about other rooms?'

'I didn't examine other fabrics, but I could look for you. However, it might be an expensive overture to do all the rooms.'

Money wasn't his concern. He didn't want her to wear herself out. 'What if we just did a few rooms, and next time he comes, I could purchase material for other rooms. I'm sure my mother would be impressed.' That much was the solid truth. He'd never shown an interest in Clairmount and the fact that he had would impress his mother. Not that he was looking to impress his mother. He'd never want that. His goal for years had been to never do anything that she wanted him to do.

'Well,' Clara said, 'I could recommend a few rooms that could use them the most.' She went on to explain what colours would look best in each of the rooms, demonstrating that it had been something already on her mind.

'Would you mind overseeing the project?' he asked. 'Picking out the material and instructing the maids on their sewing?'

Her frown grew as she looked at him for a few silent moments. 'Are you sure Mr McDonald didn't mention something about draperies?'

Roger had told white lies before, but he didn't want her to distrust him, therefore he admitted, 'He mentioned that he had drapery material, as well as many other fine goods.'

Her gaze became more thoughtful. 'Are you nervous about your mother's visit? Is that why you came home?'

'No, I'm not nervous, and yes, that is part of the reason I came home.' He took a step closer to her. 'Because I don't want you to be nervous about it, nor did I want you to face her alone.'

'I'm hardly alone, but thank you for your thoughtfulness. It's hard not to be nervous,' she said quietly. 'It's her home.' Bowing her head, she continued, 'She may not appreciate it being used by guests when she's not here.'

He lifted her chin with the tip of one finger. 'She won't mind in the least. Believe me, and believe me when I say that she'd be impressed with new draperies.'

She shook her head slightly and sighed. 'You will need to be careful of Mr McDonald, he might try to charge you twice what the material is worth.'

'Oh?'

Straightening her spine, she said, 'He tried to charge me twice what the tea was worth.'

'How did that work out for him?'

She shrugged. 'It didn't. I would have let him drive away before I'd have paid such an extravagant price.'

'Well, then, besides picking out the material, I believe I will let you negotiate the price.'

She acted unsure, and he wasn't completely sure what compelled him to act—other than he'd been thinking about it since meeting her—but he leaned over and gave her a quick kiss on the cheek. 'Thank you.'

She opened her mouth, stared at him.

He didn't move, but braced himself for her to spin

about and run away. He had no idea what he'd do then. Follow her, apologise, or simply let her go.

Marching past him, she said, 'We need to catch Mr McDonald before he leaves.'

Chapter Ten

Sometimes his good ideas turned out to be not so good, and later that afternoon, Roger was wondering if both of his latest good ideas were backfiring on him at the same time.

'No,' Clara repeated, hands on her hips and lips pursed.

Her stance and expression reminded him a great deal of the first day they'd met. So did her stubbornness.

'I can't accept all this.' Shaking her head, she corrected, 'We can't accept all of this. Two dresses each was one thing, but this—dozens of them, for both Suzanne and I, and dozens more for Abigail—is too much. Simply too much. She'll outgrow them before she can wear that many, and...'

Roger half listened as she went on about extravagant spending and luxuries, mainly because he was listening to how she said things more than what she said. Her accent, especially when irritated, was beyond captivating.

So was she.

She was also a very efficient woman. After choosing four bolts of cloth and negotiating a price that was agreeable to both her and the pedlar, she'd set up a mini factory in the house. Between measuring, cutting, and sewing, there was not an idle set of hands in the house. Even Mrs Mills was included, stating that a person didn't need two legs in order to sew.

He had escaped the managed chaos by taking Abigail and Sammy outside, where they eventually ended up in the paddock, with him walking alongside Flower while Abigail sat on the horse and Loren led them around the paddock with a lead rope. No one who knew him well would have believed it if they'd seen it. He was sure of that.

That was also where he was when the freight wagon arrived, and how he'd ended up in Clara's room, where he'd instructed everything be delivered, figuring that she and Suzanne could pick and choose between the dresses.

However, the way she was reacting, one would think she'd rather run around naked.

That was an image that took hold in his mind.

'What are you grinning about?' she asked, sternly.

He wiped a hand across his mouth, but his smile was stuck in place. 'I'm smiling because I had the intuition that you would react much the way you are over the items that the freight wagon delivered.' That was the ultimate truth. Stepping closer, he grasped her upper arms. 'I do not believe that clothing is a luxury.'

'It is when there are this many items.'

'You are going to need more than two dresses for the rest of your stay in England, and once Annabelle returns, there may not be time for you to go shopping be-fore moving to Mansfield.' He was thinking off the top of his head, and wasn't liking the thought, but it was one that she might agree with. 'I was simply trying to make sure that you'd have everything you need.'

'That's just it. I don't need all of this,' she said. 'Nei-ther does Abigail.' She pointed to the stack of toys he'd also purchased. He didn't know what had been bought, merely instructed the store owner to pack up things a little girl would like.

'This tea set is made of real china,' Clara said, ges-turing to the basket holding a child's tea set. 'If she drops a piece, it will break.'

'Then I'll buy her a new set,' he reasoned.

She shook her head and blinked her eyes several times. The moisture on her thick lashes struck him harder than her vocal arguments.

He rubbed her upper arms. 'Abigail needs toys to play with, all children do.'

'I know that.' She gave him one of those high-chinned looks of dignity. 'I also know that I can't have her get-ting used to things that I can't afford to provide for her once we leave here.'

She had a point. One he hadn't thought of and one he didn't want to think about. Yet, it was true. If she did return to America, like she was so set upon doing, she may have a difficult time providing for herself and Abigail. He couldn't tell her that returning to America was a foolish idea, because that was her home, and it was only natural that she would want to return. It just wasn't what he wanted.

He questioned that acknowledgement silently. It wasn't fair for him to think about what he wanted. That's what his mother did to him. Always had, and it had made him want the exact opposite of whatever it was that she wanted.

Clara's tiny, muffled sob, struck like an arrow to his heart and he pulled her closer, up against his chest.

'I can't keep doing this,' she sobbed softly.

'Shh…' he whispered, rubbing her back as she slumped against him. 'There, now, everything will be all right. I promise.' It was one hell of a promise, but it was one that he'd accept and fulfil.

'No, it won't,' she whispered between sobs. 'We don't belong here.'

He felt just the opposite. Inside him, something was screaming that she completely belonged in his arms.

She cried harder and he rocked back and forth, while holding her tight. He had more than enough money to make sure that no matter where they were, they would be taken care of financially. 'I'm sorry. I didn't mean to upset you. Whatever you want, I'll help you get it.' He rested his chin on the top of her head. 'Everything is going to be fine.'

Clara knew nothing was ever going to be fine, but her ability to speak was taken away by the sobs rumbling in her throat. It felt as if a dam had broken inside her. All the tears of sadness, fear, and anger that she'd been holding inside chose this very moment to let loose, and she couldn't stop them. Couldn't control them.

Being held by him made them flow faster. It had

been so long since someone had held her, had told her that everything was going to be fine, that all she could do was hold on as the sobs racked through her and the tears flowed.

She'd cried when Mark had died, and when her father had died, but only in private. She hadn't wanted to scare Abigail, nor had she wanted others to think she was weak and wouldn't be able to manage on her own.

Suzanne had seen her cry, but only a small amount, because Suzanne had lost everything, too, and she'd had to be strong for her friend. They'd been strong for each other. Right now, for whatever reason, she felt weak in his arms. Not a bad weak, just an exhausted one. She'd been exhausted for so long, but had still held it all in. She didn't have that ability right now. It felt as if everything that had piled up inside was pressing to be released.

As if understanding her thoughts, he whispered, 'There now, let it out, Clara, let it all out. You'll feel better if you do.' His hold tightened even more. 'Just cry until you can't cry anymore.'

Unable to stop, she had no choice but to cry. Cry for Mark, her father, the town of Hampton, friends who had lost everything, the fear of the soldiers finding them, the scarcity of food and wood for warmth, and so many other things from the past year, including leaving. She cried for herself, for all the pain and fear, and for Abigail, for all her daughter had lost and would never know. She also cried for Roger, for his kindness, generosity, and understanding.

When the tears finally dried, she was surprised to

discover she was sitting on the bed, still cradled in Roger's arms. Her swollen eyes burned and she blew her nose in the handkerchief that had found its way into her hand. An unladylike thing to do, but she'd just sobbed her heart out in his arms, so there was no more embarrassment to be had.

He leaned back slightly and lifted her chin with one finger. 'Feel better?'

She nodded, then shook her head. 'I'm sorry.'

He ran a finger along the edge of her face. 'After my father died, my grandfather told me to get on my horse—Flower at the time—and ride. Ride and cry. Cry until there were no tears left. He said that if I didn't, it would get trapped inside me and fester.'

'Did you listen to him?' she asked.

'Yes, I did.' His smile was endearing. 'When my grandfather gives an order, he expects it to be followed.'

A thought made her smile, and she voiced it. 'Much like you.'

He shrugged.

A sigh pressed heavily, and she released it. 'My father made Mark promise that he would never make me cry when we got married, so when he left for war, I didn't cry, because I didn't want him to have broken his promise.' She'd never told anyone that. Not even Suzanne or Annabelle.

He brushed hair away from her face. 'Did you cry when he died?'

'A little, but his parents had lost him, too, and I didn't want to make them feel worse, and then…' She shook her head. 'There were so many other things to cry about, that it just seemed useless. Like a waste of time. There was so much to do. So many others had lost everything. I still had the garden and food to share.'

'You've had a lot of things bottled up inside you for a long time,' he said.

She did feel lighter, in a way she couldn't explain. 'I suppose so.'

'I wonder if there is something else you suppose?'

Confused, she asked, 'What?'

'You had food to share with others, and you did that. I have money to share. Money to buy you and Abigail, and Suzanne clothing and other things you need.' He held her chin to make sure she didn't look away. 'Don't you suppose that's the same as you sharing your food? Don't you suppose that others thought that you were being extravagant when you gave them so much, yet you were simply providing them with what you thought they needed?'

There was a correlation to what he was suggesting, but it wasn't the same. She didn't regret sharing what she'd had with others, yet she also clarified, 'But we ran out of food, out of money.'

'I won't run out of money. I have more than enough to buy whatever you need, whatever Abigail needs, and I want to share it with you, just like you wanted to share your food with others.'

She leaned back enough to put space between them, because being in his embrace was becoming too comforting, too natural. 'That's not the same,' she justified, 'and it's improper.'

'Improper? By whose standards? Those who have

never been in need, or perhaps by those who set standards that they themselves don't follow?'

She was still processing an answer when he gestured to the trunks and crates full of clothing and whatever else he'd seen fit to purchase. She'd only looked inside the first couple of crates and packages before she'd begun arguing with him. Arguing in front of Suzanne and Abigail, and the two men who had been hauling all of the items up to her room. Suzanne had taken Abigail and left the room, and Roger had instructed the men to leave everything else in the hallway, which meant there was more.

'The freight drivers have left by now,' Roger said, running both hands over his thighs. 'I suspect we could store this in the box room until we can decide what to do with it all.'

She closed her eyes. To not accept his gifts was rude. Very rude. He was simply being his natural, caring self. He could give gifts to anyone he wanted. He clearly had the finances, the wherewithal to do so. Why was she refusing them? To what avail? Was it because she had nothing to give him back in return? Planting seeds and keeping house didn't compare to the amount he'd spent.

That just showed how different they were. How different his life was from hers. She'd been brought up to work for whatever you wanted, to never expect, or accept a handout. While he'd been born into a life of benefits and luxuries, and was clearly on the other end of the spectrum, was used to providing handouts to those who needed them.

She had also been raised to make the best of every

situation. 'I'm sorry, Roger. Once again, I've behaved badly. I know you were just being nice, and I—'

'Why don't you want me to be nice to you?'

'It's not that—' She stopped herself, because that was at the root of it all. 'It's the other way around,' she said. 'I don't want to like you.'

'Why?'

There were plenty of reasons, including how she kept dreaming about him. About kissing him, and dancing with him, and none of that could ever happen. 'Because I shouldn't. I loved my husband.'

'I'm sure you did, and I'm sure he didn't mean to die. Didn't mean to leave you and Abigail with no one to care for you, but I'm also sure that he wouldn't mind if someone helped you. Provided the things you need.'

'I'm sure he wouldn't, either,' Clara admitted. 'He'd be grateful to you, and I should be, too. I am. I just—'

'Don't want to like me.'

'I do like you, and that's the problem,' she said.

'How is it a problem?'

'Because I need to make sure that Abigail knows who her father was. Knows he loved her from the moment she was born, before then, even. That he'd bought a farm for her to live on. He'd planted apple trees for her to pick apples from as she grew up.' Her throat swelled. 'That's all gone now. I'm all she has, and I have to keep his memory alive. He was a wonderful man. I'd known him my entire life. We grew up together. His parents owned the feed store next door to my father's livery station. We planned on getting married for years, but waited until he'd saved up enough money to put down on the farm that he bought for us.' She pinched her lips together to hold in a sob. 'Abigail was born in December, his brigade left town in April, and he died in August.'

Roger took a hold of her hand. Squeezed it. Clara wanted that to make her feel worse, to make her feel uncomfortable, but it didn't. She felt the warmth of his touch deep inside. In hidden, protected places.

She couldn't look at him because she was not only afraid of betraying Mark, but of betraying herself, too. 'I have to make sure that Abigail knows he loved her.'

'Clara,' Roger said softly. 'Abigail is going to know that her father loved her. She's going to know about the apple trees and the farm, and that he died defending his country. Died a hero, because you will make sure of that. Just like you've made sure that she has everything she's needed. Nothing will change that, because that is who you are. Her mother.'

Clara kept her gaze on her knees, but they'd grown blurry due to the tears welling in her eyes again. 'I haven't done a very good job so far,' she said, nearly choking on the words.

His hold on her hand increased. 'I beg to differ. Abigail is a happy, healthy little girl.'

'Because of you. You sent Captain Harris to find us.'

'It is true that Captain Harris is in my employ, and followed my orders. Orders I gave because of my friendship with Annabelle and Drew. However, you agreed to come with him, and to come here, with me, because you knew that was what was best for your daughter. If not for her, you wouldn't be here. I'm certain of that.'

Clara couldn't deny that, and nodded. 'I would do anything for my daughter.'

'I know that, but what you don't understand is that I'm not asking you to do anything. Not even to like me. All I want is to provide the things you both need. Because that's what right.'

She looked at him, and even with tears still blurring her vision, could see the compassion in his eyes. 'You have to expect something in return.'

'No, I don't.'

'Everyone expects something for—'

He pressed a finger to her lips, stopping her from saying more. 'Expectations can lead to disappointments.'

She knew that, and nodded, but because she felt as if she was losing ground with the battle going on inside her, as soon as he removed his finger, Clara said, 'I will make sure she always remembers you, too, once we return to America. That she always knows how good you were to us while we were here.'

Chapter Eleven

After his father had died, Roger had decided that he'd never want to be anything to anyone. However, at this moment, he knew he didn't want to simply be a memory, either.

At the same time, he wasn't sure what he did want. Or maybe he was afraid of what he wanted, because it wasn't what she wanted.

He gave Clara a nod, acknowledging he'd heard her pledge, then asked, 'We don't need to store this stuff in the box room, then?'

'No. Thank you for your generosity. I do appreciate it. Appreciate all of the things you purchased. They are things that we need.'

'You're welcome.' He stood, and feeling out of sorts, walked towards the door. 'I'll let you see to the unpacking.'

'Thank you for being so understanding, Roger.'

He gave another nod, even though he didn't understand what she thought he understood. She didn't want to like him because she didn't want to forget her husband. The two things weren't connected.

He fully understood why she would want to hold on to memories of her husband to share with Abigail. He had been older than Abigail by several years when his father had died, but in all reality, most of what he knew about his father came from things people had told him.

He had a few memories, a few vivid visions, and though they were mere snippets in time, they were enough for him to know he had a father. A father who had loved him.

Opening the door, he stepped into the hallway, but his mind shifted when he turned around to pull the door shut and saw her still sitting on the bed. What would Clara have thought he expected from her? Abigail was her daughter, and Clara could tell her about her father. He would never attempt to stop that. Not even if—

The conclusion that formed struck like a lightning bolt. 'Did you tell Dr Murphy that we were married?'

The blush that flushed her face was beet red. Bloody hell! Is that what she was after? A marriage proposal? His mother! Clara had already known she was on her way when he arrived. Had his mother somehow already convinced Clara they should marry? He stepped back into the room and pulled the door closed behind him.

A wave of outrage at the lengths his mother would go to washed over him. 'Did you?'

'No,' she said, shaking her head. 'He assumed as much when he was summoned here. I didn't correct him because I was worried that he wouldn't treat Mrs Mills if someone in the family hadn't summoned him. Your rules of society are confusing and complex.'

Nodding, Roger gave himself a moment to think.

He had no reason to not believe her, but there was also no reason for the doctor to have assumed such a thing. Other than this was the first time in his life he had brought anyone home. People certainly could make assumptions from that. 'What about the pedlar?' he asked.

'I didn't tell him that, either, but again, I didn't correct the way he addressed me or his assumptions that I was the lady of the house.'

'Why?'

'I don't know,' she said, with still flushed cheeks. 'It was just simpler to not say anything, and that was wrong. I'm sorry, I should have corrected him, and the doctor.'

He believed she hadn't purposefully led people to believe they were married, but someone had, and he knew who. His mother wouldn't stop until she had what she wanted, and he wouldn't stop until she didn't get it.

Clara stood. 'I am sorry, I assure you it wasn't on purpose.'

'I believe you,' he said. 'I'm sure my mother was behind it.'

'Your mother? How?'

He leaned back against the door as a clearer picture formed in his mind. 'I should have seen this coming.'

'Seen what?' she asked, frowning deeply.

Frustration grew. 'She's attempting to make you a marchioness.'

'Make me...' Looking more confused, she asked, 'Why?'

'My mother would like nothing more than to see me married and hasn't kept that a secret, therefore, all the servants here know that's her goal. I'm sure the moment

I sent word that I was bringing guests here, a message was sent to her.'

'It is her home,' she reasoned.

'True, and because I've never shown an interest in taking it over completely, she continues to oversee the staff. Staff who would have spoken to the doctor, to the pedlar, prior to them meeting you. Staff who would do anything she asked.'

Clara was staring at him like he'd lost his mind.

He knew he hadn't. 'Doesn't it seem strange to you that a shelf that has never been unstable before would suddenly fall over?'

'I suppose so,' she said, quietly, thoughtfully. 'But it could have just been an accident.'

'I don't think so. Nor do I think it was the pedlar's idea to mention new material for draperies to you. Someone wanted you to take over Mrs Mills's duties so I would see how capable you are at running a house. Of becoming a marchioness.'

'Why would they want that?'

'Because getting married, having an heir to inherit titles and holdings, is of the utmost importance to those of noble backgrounds. It's priority number one to my mother, and to my grandfather. Both have expressed concerns over my vow of bachelorhood.'

'I don't want to be a marchioness. I'm returning to America,' she said, nearly breathless.

'Yes, I know.' She'd told him about returning to America several times. Roger rubbed his chin. There had to be a way to use this to put an end to his mother's goal. Put an end to it for ever. 'I should have seen this coming, known they would have taken advantage of your situation, and now that I know their scheme...' He walked across the room to look out the window, hoping to come up with a plan.

'Now that you know their scheme, what?' Clara asked after several moments.

'I'm not sure yet,' he replied, 'but I may need your help.'

'My help?' she asked, with a quiver in her voice. 'Doing what?'

He turned around, faced her. An odd pang struck at the idea, but still he said, 'By simply telling people exactly what you've told me. That you will be returning to America as soon as the war is over. And that I will be assisting in your return.'

'You will?'

'Yes, I will.'

'What if the war doesn't end for months?' she asked, 'After we've gone to live with Annabelle?'

'Whenever it ends, whenever you are ready to return, I will provide transport for you on one of my ships.'

'How will that help you?' she asked.

He wasn't upset with her. None of this was her fault. It was his mother's, for turning even this, his want of helping Clara into something he couldn't have. That angered him, and he walked to the door. 'Because it will show my mother that her little scheme didn't work. That her meddling will never work.'

Once in the hallway, he let out a muttered curse. Clara was still in love with her husband, would always love her husband, and it angered him that his mother's meddling had tried to manipulate her into something she didn't want.

* * *

Hours later, Clara was still thinking about her conversation with Roger. She could understand his desire to not be tricked and felt a keen sense of loyalty to him over that. So keen that telling people he'd take her back to America after the war ended felt disloyal. He'd helped her so much, and she'd done so little in return, yet still expected him to do more by providing transportation back to America. That wasn't like her.

She needed to return, but couldn't expect him to help her get there. She wouldn't expect it, yet had said that she would say that, hadn't she?

It was all so confusing. All she could think to do was to fulfil her promise of having the house in perfect shape by the time his mother arrived.

That wasn't very difficult. It was already a beautiful home, and with so much help, the drapes for the drawing room were completed and hung up by that evening. A new table cloth covered the round table near the window, and just as she'd imaged, the room looked utterly stunning.

The front parlour, which Mrs Mills explained was Roger's mother's favourite room, would get new curtains next. A lovely rose-coloured material to match the room's furniture, with gold cording to tie them back. Then the study, which had been his father's favourite room. She'd chosen a tan brocade for that room to match the brown leather furniture, and the final room would be the second parlour, which was called the tea room because it is where guests were normally served tea, again according to Mrs Mills. The material for that room was a light yellow with tiny specks of white.

All the draperies would be sewn and hanging by the time his mother arrived, she'd make sure of that. None of her seedlings were large enough to display in pots, but she found some lovely ferns growing near a wooded area beyond the manicured yard and asked Donald to dig them up. She planned on planting them in some of the decorative earthen pots and setting them on stands in the rooms near the windows. Each of those rooms would need to have a few pieces of furniture rearranged to give them a fresh look.

'Are you sure you don't want this one?' Suzanne asked. 'It's extraordinary.'

Clara glanced at the dress. For the last hour, the two of them had been going through the trunks and crates, dividing out the gowns, dresses, shoes and slippers, underthings, and nightgowns and accessories.

'That is beautiful,' Clara admitted. 'The blue is nearly the same shade as your eyes and will look stunning on you.' It was most certainly a ball gown, not simply a dress, and Clara was certain she would never have need for that. She was choosing the dresses she would keep by a simple standard: dresses that she thought a housekeeper would wear. The staff at Clairmount all wore matching dresses, uniforms one might say, and that might be true wherever she found a job. Even though Roger had said that he'd provide her with transportation home, she was going to find a job and pay him for both her and Abigail's passage.

'This will be the last one for me,' Suzanne said, laying the dress with a pile of others.

'But there are still several left,' Clara said.

'I have over a dozen,' Suzanne said. 'The rest are for you.'

Clara glanced at the gowns draped on the bed, over chairs and trunks, and already hanging in the standing wardrobe. 'I'll never need all of these. I'll certainly never be able to haul them all back to Virginia.'

'I think that's something we can figure out when the time comes,' Suzanne said. 'I'll help you hang all these up, and then you can help me carry mine to my room.'

Clara helped, and later, while lying in bed, she couldn't help but think about why Roger's mother wanted him to get married so badly. As a mother, she hoped that Abigail would someday fall in love and get married, because she wanted her daughter to know how wonderful it was to share her life with someone she loved. Even though Mark had died, the time they had shared had been wonderful and had created Abigail.

Is that what his mother wanted, too?

Why didn't Roger want that?

Grief. He'd told her that was the reason, and she'd agreed, but there is grief in loneliness, too.

There had to be more to his reasons, and though it was none of her business, she wanted to know what had put him off marriage. At one time she'd looked forward to spending the rest of her life married, now she was destined to spend it alone.

Not completely. She had Abigail, but Roger didn't have anyone, and that didn't feel fair.

He would make a wonderful father. Abigail adored him. Other children would, too. His children.

She could imagine a little boy, with green eyes, black hair and a quick, charming smile, exactly like his father's. He would be kind and generous, and loving. Very loving. She dreamed about that little boy, that night. A sweet dream that she couldn't quite remember in the morning, but knew it hadn't turned into a nightmare because she'd slept soundly and woke up even more determined to get the house in order for Roger's mother's visit.

The days that followed were busy, but many hands make light work. All of the draperies were sewn and hung and several rooms hosted potted ferns and vases filled with fresh cut flowers from the flower gardens. She also prided herself on how well the rooms looked where she'd requested the furniture be moved about. Roger had helped with some of the heavier pieces, and during those times, she realised that a friendship had formed between them. A fun one, where they laughed and teased each other.

'My mother is going to love this room more than ever,' he said, walking into the parlour.

That was another thing Clara had noticed the last few days. He actually seemed excited about his mother's visit. How can that be if he distrusted her so much?

'You've done an amazing job, with all of the rooms. All of the house,' he said.

'I've hardly touched all of the house,' she replied. 'Nor can I take credit for all the work. Everyone helped, including you, but I am happy with how all the rooms look. Especially this one. It's so welcoming.'

'It is.'

She glanced at the single vase of flowers. 'I am afraid that I'm cutting flowers faster than the garden can produce. I hope your mother won't be disappointed by that.' Although she was nervous about meeting his mother, she was also very curious.

She was also torn by the relationship between him and his mother in another sense. He'd said his mother was kind, and that she had nothing to fear in meeting her. Then why was there contention between the two of them? It couldn't totally be because his mother wanted him to marry. Bertha had said the contention between them had been there for years. Ever since his father had died.

'Do you ride?' he asked.

She chuckled slightly at his abrupt change of subject and instantly noticed how good that felt. How good a question that sparked a memory about her father felt. Up until now, she'd refused to recall happy memories. 'My father owned a livery stable, and I was his only child. I learned to ride at a very early age in order to help exercise the horses. Lucky for me, though, Annabelle loved tending to their other needs.' After Clara and Mark had married, Annabelle had continued to help with the horses at the livery, which had been so thoughtful. Clara had worried a great deal about her father when she'd moved out to the farm Mark had purchased. That had been the most difficult part of her marriage, leaving her father alone.

'Would you care to take a ride with me?' Roger asked. 'I'd like to show you something.'

The last time he'd said that, he'd shown her the growing room, therefore, she didn't question her quick response, 'Yes, I would.' Only then did another thought form. 'But…' She left the rest hanging in the air as she walked towards the doorway.

He lifted a brow. 'But?'

'I can't ride in a side saddle.' She stopped next to him in the doorway. 'I never learned and I don't want to.'

His frown was a bit mocking. 'Is that proper?'

She understood his frown, because he was teasingly mocking her. That had happened during the past few days more and more often, as their friendship had formed and become stronger. Teasingly in return, she slapped his arm. 'I don't care if it's proper or not. I'm not hanging both legs over the same side of the horse. That's an accident waiting to happen.'

'Very well. I don't have a Western saddle, though, only English ones.'

'As long as there are two stirrups, one on each side of the horse, I can ride in it.'

'All right, then.' He gave her a quick up-and-down glance. 'Do you need to change?'

She was wearing one of her new dresses, a lovely lilac coloured one, with a V shape of white lace down the front and around the sleeves and hem. However, it was also very practical and serviceable, and lightweight enough to tuck around her legs and out of the way once she was in the saddle. 'No, this one is fine, but I will collect a bonnet and let Bertha know where I'm going. Abigail is sleeping.'

He bowed slightly. 'I will meet you out front in fifteen minutes.'

Excitement filled her as she hurried up to her room. She hadn't ridden a horse since before Abigail was born. Once she and Mark had married, they always travelled in a wagon, especially after she'd become pregnant, and then the horses were stolen and she never left the farm. She had to pause for a moment and acknowledge how those memories didn't pull her down into a dark and gloomy place. They were just memories. Some of them, like riding, she could smile about, remember fondly.

She had always enjoyed riding and was looking forward to whatever he wanted to show her, and being excited right now, felt good.

In fact, she'd felt different ever since she'd bawled her eyes out in his arms and told him about Mark. About needing Abigail to know her father had loved her. Roger had been right about keeping things locked inside her. Things had been festering. Things that she couldn't do anything about. All she could do was accept that her life was different than before. She could never go back to that life, but she could remember it with joyfulness rather than sorrow. That was how she wanted to remember things, and that was how she would tell Abigail about things when she was old enough—with joyfulness, not sorrow.

Clara was waiting on the front steps when Roger rode up on Smokey, leading a brown horse with three white feet named Buck. Due to Abigail's love of the stable—her grandfather would have been so proud of that—Clara knew all of the horse's names, and also knew that Buck didn't buck.

The English saddle didn't have the deep swells of the Western ones she'd grown up using, but it served its purpose.

They rode across the back yard, past the barn where the animals, other than the horses, resided, and was another one of Abigail's favourite places—her daughter's love of animals was never-ending—and into the woods. Clara hadn't ventured this far before, and was surprised when after a short distance, the trees gave way to rolling hills.

Hills that were covered with wildflowers. Everything from bluebells in the open areas, to cowslips in the more shaded, wet lowlands. There were also primroses, purple orchids and foxgloves, as well as several varieties that she'd never seen so didn't know the names of, but would soon learn. There were so many flowers, in so many different directions that she pulled on the reins, stopped Buck so she could simply stare.

After a moment, she turned to Roger, who was grinning.

He also held up an empty feed sack. 'I brought a couple of bags so you can collect as many as your heart desires.'

She laughed and once again scanned the colourful displays in all directions. 'Let me just say this in advance.'

'What?'

'I won't blame you if you get bored and return without me,' she shouted while urging Buck into a gallop.

Roger quickly caught up to her, and they galloped, side by side, through fields and valleys, and up the side of a hill, all the way to the peak, where she could smell the sea.

The happiness inside her was light, wonderful, and she lifted her face to the sunlight, breathed deeply.

'How close are we to the ocean?' she asked. The smell reminded her of home, of the farm, where the distinct scent of the sea would fill the air on certain days. It was such a good memory, one that made her smile grow.

'The English Channel is about two miles from here. We can ride over there if you want to see it.'

She pondered that for a moment. 'Are there fields of flowers along the way?'

'No, just crops that belong to the tenant farmers.'

That, too, she pondered before saying, 'Donald claims you are the fairest landowner for miles around. That others stand in line, waiting and hoping that a piece of your property becomes available.'

He looked directly at her, as if pondering something himself. She couldn't say what, but as usual, was curious.

'I wouldn't know about standing in line,' he said, glancing away. 'But I do believe that the farmers are the ones who put in the work and that they should be the ones to reap the rewards.'

She knew how hard farmers had to work to make ends meet, to have a crop that paid more than what had been invested, and could image how much more difficult that was for those who didn't own the land and had to pay for its use along with the rest of the costs. Don-

ald had claimed that all of the tenant farmers on Clairmount property were far better off than those on any
other property, and told her how Roger even provided
seed and other support to his farmers, as well as negotiating for them to get the best prices for their crops.

She would like to meet some of the farmers, and to
see the English Channel, but not today. 'Perhaps we can
ride to the Channel another day,' she said. 'Because by
the time we are done picking flowers, you are going to
be exhausted.'

'Oh, I am, am I?'

'Yes.' She climbed off Buck's back. 'We are going to
start with the pink flowers right over here. They remind
me of little pincushions.'

'Pincushions?' he asked while dismounting Smokey.

'Yes, you know, you put your pins in them while
sewing.'

'No, I don't know. I've never done a lot sewing.'

She giggled and continued walking towards the flowers. 'Have you done a lot of flower picking?'

He took Buck's reins from her and tied both horses to
a shrub. 'No, I can't say that I have.'

'Well, I do hope you've brought along a knife,' she
said. 'We need to cut the stems at an angle so they will
last longer.'

'I do have a knife, and a bag. Two bags, actually.
His and hers.'

It had been so long since happiness had bubbled inside her, she almost didn't recognise the feeling, and
when she did, she couldn't stop herself from laughing.
Nor from enjoying picking wildflowers.

At times they would walk from one field to the next, at other times they would ride, carefully laying their bags of bounty across their laps. She couldn't imagine a man who would help pick wildflowers, but there was one, and he was right here beside her.

They were in a field of daisies when Roger said, 'We'll have to bring Abigail with us next time. She'd enjoy all the flowers.'

Kneeling side by side, because she was holding the stems while he carefully sliced them, she met his gaze. 'You have been so good to her, right from the beginning.'

His grin softened and his eyes glowed. 'She's an adorable little girl. Just like her mum.'

Clara's heart stalled, then began to race as their gazes stayed locked. The desire to kiss him went beyond all she'd ever known, to the point it made her feel light-headed. She'd been married, had a child, and knew all there was to know about men and women and the birds and bees, yet right now, she felt out of sorts. Didn't know what to do. She couldn't act on any of the things that she was feeling, but at the same time, she couldn't look away.

Chapter Twelve

Roger had never been to war, never been on a battle-field, but there was one hell of a conflict going on inside him over whether he should or should not kiss Clara. They'd formed a special kind of friendship the past few days, and she seemed happy, content. He didn't want to ruin that, but a man knows when a woman wants to be kissed, and Clara wanted that. He could see it in her eyes, feel it in the air between them, and he wanted it just as badly.

Yet, if that happened, things would change—that was a given—and where would they be then?

Here again, if anyone who knew him, saw him right now, hesitating to kiss a beautiful woman, perhaps the most beautiful woman in the world, they'd think he was half-rats—so drunk he couldn't walk. He wasn't. He was stone sober.

So stone-cold sober that he remembered that his mother was trying to trick him into seeing the positive side of marriage. He should have figured that out back in London, when she'd appeared on the street corner.

He hadn't questioned it, because she'd always found him when he was in London—and practically everywhere else.

However, he hadn't expected her to go to these measures. They hadn't seen eye to eye, but she'd never taken steps to trick him. She had this time, and had involved the staff, which he still wasn't totally sure what he should do about. He couldn't have staff that he didn't trust, yet at the same time, no one had done anything mean or hurtful to Clara, or him.

Still, he didn't like being manipulated in any way and wouldn't tolerate it.

However, because of all that, he had promised that he'd take Clara back to America. Whenever she wanted to go. A promise is a promise. Therefore, he had to return her just as he'd found her.

Un-kissed.

Un-kissed by him, that is.

For if he did kiss her, his mother would be getting what she wanted, and that he wouldn't allow to happen.

Flustered at himself for thinking the entire thing through and coming up with a completely plausible answer for not kissing Clara, he shifted his mindset. He couldn't let the moment go completely. Not with the way her eyes were sparkling. Rather than kissing her, he leaned a bit closer. 'I wonder.'

She gasped, blinked, asked, 'You wonder what?'

'If Abigail's mum, is…' He waited a moment before gently poking her in the side. 'Is as ticklish as her daughter.'

Clara squealed and leaped back. 'No.' She pointed

her handful of daisies at him like a knight wielding a sword. 'No tickling.'

'So you *are* as ticklish as Abigail,' he said, advancing on her.

She twirled her daisies at him. 'No, I'm not.'

He slowly continued his approach. 'You're not?'

'No! I'm not!' She pivoted and ran, straight to her horse. Fast and agile, she was in the saddle lickety-split.

'We aren't done picking flowers,' he shouted while running to Smokey.

'Yes, we are,' she shouted over her shoulder while urging Buck into a gallop. 'I no longer trust you.'

He swung onto Smokey's back. 'No longer trust me?' Hell, if that was the case, he should have kissed her.

Her giggle floated in her wake. 'I trust you, but we have plenty of flowers.' Twisting, watching as Smokey gained ground on Buck, she asked, 'You did remember your bag of flowers, didn't you?'

'Aw, tarnation!'

She laughed.

He spun Smokey around to go back and get his bag off the ground. Another action that no one would ever believe was him.

With the bag on his lap, he easily caught up with her, because she'd stopped her horse and waited for him. 'We can pick more flowers. I promise I won't tickle you.'

She shook her head. 'Thank you, but I do believe that we have enough. Our bags are quite full and I don't want them to get squished.'

A moan bubbled in his throat. Lord, but she put an ache in him like no tomorrow, and every word she said, every look she gave him, twisted that ache a bit tighter. At this rate, he'd be howling in pain before they made it home.

With a slight frown, she asked, 'You don't have any idea what time your mother will arrive today?'

She'd asked him that before, and his answer would be the same as it had been, but he'd answer, because he needed something to get his mind on a different track. 'No. It all depends on what time her carriage left London yesterday and where they spent the night last night. She could arrive anytime between now and midnight tonight.'

'I do hope that I have time to have a vase of flowers put in her room before she arrives.'

'You'll have plenty of time,' he replied.

'How do you know?'

'Because my mother will make the rounds of greeting all the servants, making small talk and introducing those who haven't met him to Stuart.'

'Her husband, your stepfather.'

'Her husband,' he agreed, or corrected, depending upon how one wanted to look at it. No matter how many times his mother chose to remarry, he would never claim to have any father outside of his own. That had been another one of her goals, and he'd never let her win then, either. 'Stuart Voss.'

'Do you not care for him?'

Roger shrugged. 'I don't know him. Have only met him twice, I think.'

'You think? You don't know for sure?'

He shook his head. 'I know I saw him once in London, but it might have been twice.'

'Saw him? Have you never spoken to him?'

Her concern made him a bit uneasy. Perhaps he could have been a bit more welcoming to Stuart. 'I said hello to him in London that one time for sure.'

She looked at him, shook her head, looked away. Then looked at him again, with a frown. 'How long have they been married?'

He wasn't sure. 'Two years, I think. It could be three.'

They rode in silence for a distance before she asked, 'What about her second husband. Did you know him?'

'Duane Carter. I met him several times over the years.'

'Did you like him?'

'I can't answer that. I didn't know him well enough to say if I did like him or didn't.'

'Didn't you ever live with them?'

'No. There was no need. After my father died, I went to boarding school and was either at Drew's house, or my grandfather's house, or once in a while, here at Clairmount, until I was old enough to live on my own. Then I moved into the townhouse in London.'

'Is that where you live when you are not at your house in Southampton, or here?' she said.

He wasn't sure if he lived anywhere, he just had places where he stayed, yet he replied, 'Yes.'

There was sadness in her eyes when she stopped Buck to stare at him, rather intently. 'Haven't you ever wanted just one place that you could truly call home?'

He opened his mouth, but then stopped what he'd

been about to say, because it had been a lie. Instead, when he spoke, it was the truth. 'Yes, Clara, I have. But I guess I just haven't found it yet.'

'I hope you do, Roger. Someday.' She nodded, blinked. 'Everyone needs a home. A real home.'

The seriousness between them felt heavy, constrained, and he didn't want that, not after the fun they'd had. Determined to lighten the mood, he said, 'Someday, Clara, I hope that you admit that you're ticklish.'

She laughed. 'I am not ticklish.'

'I believe you are,' he said, urging Smokey to start moving again.

'I believe you will never find out,' she replied as Buck caught up to Smokey.

'Is that a challenge?'

Merriment filled her face, even as she shook her head. 'No, it's a simple statement. Much like the sky is blue. Or the stars are bright.'

'But the sky isn't always blue, and stars aren't always bright.'

She let out an exaggerated sigh. 'You have an argument for everything, don't you?'

It was his turn to laugh. 'Me? I dare say, you are the one inclined to argue.'

'It takes two. One can't argue with themself.'

'Have you tried?' he asked.

Even her giggle had that accent that he found so enchanting. 'Have you?'

'I do it all the time,' he replied. That was true. He was still arguing with himself about not kissing her when he'd had the chance, and regretting it.

* * *

The happiness inside Clara remained after they returned to the house. For the first time in a very long time, the smile on her face wasn't fake. She didn't have to purposefully plant it on her lips. It simply was there. Her footsteps felt lighter, too.

She could try to convince herself that it was because of the gorgeous flowers, but she would be lying to herself. Though the flowers were indeed lovely, some of the most unique ones she'd ever seen, deep down, she knew that it was more than that. For the past several days, she felt as if the puzzle pieces inside her were slowly sliding back into place, making her whole again. It was difficult to describe and even harder to explain, even to herself, but it was as if she was becoming herself again. Not necessarily the person she used to be, because there had been lasting changes to her life that would affect her for ever, but a new version of that old self that was ready to live again. Embrace life and all it had to offer.

'Oh, but, ma'am, we don't need flowers in the kitchen,' Mrs Wells said, hands folded together as she gazed at the vase of flowers.

'Yes, you do,' Clara replied, positioning the vase on the work table, where it would be out of the way, yet still provide joy to the room. 'Flowers should be enjoyed by everyone.' After adding greenery from the hedges to the flowers, she'd been able to fill enough vases that nearly every room had a bouquet in them, including the staff quarters.

Clara swiped her hands together. 'Now, is there anything you need help with?'

'No, ma'am.' Mrs Wells then went over the list of things that would be served for tea as well as supper.

Special attention was being given to both meals in case Roger's mother arrived in time for either, or both. Clara had never heard of afternoon tea until arriving at Mansfield and then discovered that many of the upper-class homes served four meals throughout the day, with tea being in the late afternoon, when back home it would have been supper time. Here, however, supper was served much later, often due to social obligations.

Those obligations didn't occur here, at the country estate, but the staff kept the schedule as such, nonetheless. Clara had learned that it was that way at most country estates. There were many things that were different from how she'd done them back home, and she absorbed every bit of information for when she'd seek employment after Annabelle returned.

She was also putting it all to good use right now, while taking over for Mrs Mills. It still seemed strange that Mrs Mills, and Aaron, could be in on what Roger was convinced was a scheme, for they had been nothing but kind and generous to her. However, last night she had noticed a rag with ink on it lying on the table in Mrs Mills's room, and wondered if the woman wasn't using that to make her leg look bruised.

'That sounds perfect,' she replied to Mrs Wells. 'I have some things to see to in the growing room, but don't hesitate to find me if I can help with anything.'

'Yes, ma'am, thank you. And thank you for the flowers. I've never had a vase in the kitchen before.'

'You are very welcome, and as long as I'm here, I'll make sure you have a vase in here.' Another wonderful memory formed. 'My father told me that my mother loved flowers, so if there were flowers blooming outside, I had a vase in my kitchen at home. Both at my father's house, and then my farmhouse. I didn't have any memories of my mother, and that made each one he'd told me about more special.'

'That is a special memory,' Mrs Wells said.

'It is,' Clara replied, glad that she could embrace that memory again. That was something she hadn't allowed herself to do since Mark had died. She wasn't sure why. Perhaps she'd just thought her life had to be miserable. In all aspects.

She left the kitchen and made her way into the growing room, hoping to record the changes to her seedlings in the journal. With all the sewing and other tasks the past few days, she hadn't used a ruler to measure the growth of each plant, but knew by looking at them that they had grown.

Through the wall of glass, she saw Abigail and Bertha walking towards the far side of the house. They must have been at the barn again, because Ports, the big tomcat that Abigail had befriended was tailing along with them. Ports and Sammy hadn't become friends yet, but they tolerated each other, mainly by keeping their distance from one another.

Clara found her ruler and turned to measure her plants, smiling at herself because Abigail couldn't get enough of being outside and looking at the animals. That was fine with her. It was a miracle that they weren't all as blind as bats after living in the dark root cellar for months on end.

She had been concerned that Bertha was neglecting other duties while seeing to Abigail, but Mrs Mills had said that Bertha had no other duties. Her job at Clairmount had been a nanny to Roger, and she'd never been assigned to anything else, nor let go on the chance that she might be needed at some point.

She had asked Roger about that, and he'd laughed, said that Bertha had seemed old to him when he'd been little, and now that she was older than then, he saw no reason for her to seek employment elsewhere.

'I thought I would find you here.'

Clara's heart leaped as quickly as a smile formed on her face. She twisted towards the door where Roger stood, one hand braced against the frame, and the sight of him left her as breathless as ever.

His shirtsleeves were rolled up past his elbows and his stance made the material of his white shirt stretch over his muscles. He was so very handsome. So masculine. His shoulders were broad and firm. She knew that not only from crying on his shoulder, but from that first day, when he'd helped her into his carriage.

His arms were hard with muscles, too, and his chest. She knew that, but there was so much she didn't know about him, and wanted to. Wanted to know everything there was to know about him. 'What do you do?' she asked.

'What do I do?' Frowning, he added, 'Or what was I doing, because I was just helping Loren in the stables.'

She nodded, then shrugged. 'No, I mean… I meant, I know you own a shipping company, but what do you do? If we weren't here, if your mother wasn't due to arrive soon, where would you be?'

He pushed off the wall and stepped into the room. 'Well, let's see. I could be in Southampton, unloading or loading cargo. Yes, I have men who do that, but I like to see exactly what we are shipping and receiving. I spend a lot of time in London, too. I have warehouses there. It's where we distribute a lot of goods from the shipping companies and the produce that the tenant farmers grow. I like to know that they are given the fairest prices possible, so I spend more time there during harvest times.'

Taking that in, she asked, 'The freight wagon that arrived here, the men that delivered all of the things you bought, they are in your employ?'

'Yes, they are. Why?'

'I was just wondering.'

He'd stopped next to her, close enough that it was causing her heart to beat faster.

He touched the side of her face. 'The truth of it is, Clara, that if I never worked a day in my life, I'd still have more money than I'll ever need. The shipping companies, the warehouses, even the tenant farming, are all overseen by excellent people. People I pay well and treat fairly, and in exchange, they fulfil their duties without my assistance.' His hand slipped off her face as he glanced around the growing room. 'My father was a ship captain, first and foremost. He spent a lot time sailing, therefore, all of his other holdings—the tenant farms, the shipping company, other ship captains, the warehouses—were all run by good men. Fair and honest men, who stayed on after my father died. Many are still working for me, and those who have left taught me what to look for in their replacements.'

She was watching his face as he spoke, and felt there was something else. Something he wasn't saying, therefore, she remained quiet, waited for him to add it.

He grinned. 'If you ask people who know me, they'll say that I do as little as possible.'

She shook her head. 'You are always busy. Always doing something. Just now you were helping Loren.'

He nodded, but then shrugged. 'In all honesty, Clara, I'm not needed anywhere. Never have been.'

If felt as if a chunk of her heart let loose, for him. The solemnity on his face, in his tone, said he truly believed that wasn't needed by anyone. That couldn't possibly be true.

He shook his head. Grinned. 'Except by Drew. We needed each other for years.' He winked one eye. 'So, if you weren't here, I'd be in Southampton, assigning yet another ship's captain to search out word of your whereabouts.'

That she knew was true, and a soft, sweet sensation swirled deep inside her, knowing that he wouldn't have stopped looking until he found her. 'There were other captains besides Captain Harris?' she asked.

'Several others. You seemed to have disappeared. It was dangerous, but I knew Tristan was savvy enough to break through the blockade without losing his ship, my ship, so I told him to not return without knowing your specific whereabouts.'

'Lose your ship?'

He grimaced, whispered, 'Your country is at war. There is a Union blockade that is illegal to cross. My ship and everything aboard it could have been confiscated.'

Remorse, along with a splattering of shame over how she'd acted, washed over Clara. 'I hadn't thought about that, but it's true. You could have lost your ship.'

'It was worth it.'

Because Drew had asked him, needed him, to find her and Abigail and Suzanne. The regret in Clara grew. It all made so much sense now. Why he'd searched for them, insisted that Captain Harris not return without them. Because he felt needed. Rather than being grateful for all he'd done, all he'd risked, she'd thwarted his every move, his every act of kindness.

She took a hold of his hand, squeezed it. 'Thank you for not giving up. We needed you. Needed you to find us. To provide us with transportation and food, and clothing and a place to stay. We still need you.'

Looking at her, with a deep, penetrating gaze, he slowly shook his head.

'Yes, we do, and we thank you for all you've done for us so far.' Her words were barely a whisper because she was worried about what he might think about her action, but it was the only way she could think to display her gratitude.

Stretching on her toes, she pressed her lips against

his cheek. The warmth of his skin against her lips and the scent of him—a mixture of fresh air, masculinity, and the soap he must have used to wash up after helping Loren with chores—went straight to her head. It was so wonderful that she didn't want to move, even though she knew she had to.

Slowly she lowered her heels to the floor, and when her neck couldn't stretch any further, she had no choice but to let her lips slip off his cheek.

She was afraid to look up, to meet his gaze.

He cupped her chin, lifted it, and held it in place as his eyes searched her face.

Clara couldn't blink, move, even speak. His gaze was making her as breathless as if he'd kissed her square on the lips, rather than her kissing him on the cheeks.

Then he did just that.

Kissed her.

His lips were warm, firm, and purposeful. So was his kiss. It consumed her mind and body, leaving her incapable of doing anything except melt completely into his embrace.

The desire that rippled through her was like nothing she'd ever experienced when he nibbled her lips, then parted them with his tongue. The kiss deepened into one so thorough that she was dizzy, her knees wobbly and gasping for air when his mouth released hers.

Clara's first instinct was to run, to dash out the door or down the hallway into the house, but then she remembered *she'd* been the one to kiss him first. Lifting her chin, which was still about as wobbly as her knees, she met his gaze eye for eye.

He grinned, winked at her.

She'd been blushing since she'd met him, but right now her entire face was on fire. Goodnight and God bless, but his tongue hadn't just been in her mouth, hers had been in his! And her arms were still around his neck, her body still pressed up against his.

He chuckled and kissed the tip of her nose. 'Is now a good time to tell you that my mother has arrived?'

'Hog spit!' Clara hissed, only because she needed a moment to gather both her wits and her equilibrium. They were both returning, quite quickly, and she released his neck, pressed both hands against his shoulders. 'Why didn't you tell me that when you first walked in here?'

'I would have, but you started asking questions,' he said.

That was true, she had, but still! She pressed harder and wiggled against how his arms were still wrapped around her waist. 'You should be out front saying hello.'

He released her waist, but took a hold of her hands. Both of them. In firm, warm grasps. 'Not without you.' He leaned closer, so their noses almost touched. 'If you don't mind.'

Mind? She wouldn't mind if he kissed her again, which told her that her wits had not returned. There wasn't time to go chasing them down, either. 'I don't mind,' she said.

'Good, because we are in this together, remember? I said I'd need your help.'

She huffed out a breath. 'Yes, I remember.'

As if she could forget that.
Forgetting anything about him would be impossible.
Utterly impossible.

Chapter Thirteen

A kiss had never affected Roger the way that one had. He might still be reeling from it long after he was cold and in his grave. Clara was a passion-filled woman, one who had been holding it in, and being the recipient of it being released was something he'd never forget.

If not for knowing they'd have soon been interrupted, they'd still be kissing. He was sure of that.

He was also sure that he'd never been excited about seeing his mother, but he was today.

As a kid, he'd dreaded seeing her because it reminded him that she was all he had left of his family. In his young mind, he'd thought that if he didn't see her, he could go on pretending that his father was simply at sea, would be home someday. As he'd grown older and accepted the truth that his father was never returning, he found it easier to stay away than to try and rebuild anything between him and his mother. She hadn't needed him and he hadn't needed her. He hadn't needed anyone, but Drew.

That hadn't been something he'd planned on telling Clara, but it had flowed out of his mouth. The reward had been worth it, but that hadn't been why he'd told her. She instilled honesty in him. Not that he was ever dishonest with anyone, he just often chose to skid around certain topics. That wasn't possible with her. Furthermore, he felt safe telling her things, and that was unusual. Rare.

She was a rarity, too, like a jewel. Unique and one of a kind.

Still holding one of her hands, he turned, to lead her out of the room, but a snarling meow and a rumbling bark filled the glass space. Racing so fast he was little more than a dark blur, Ports shot through the open door that led outside and ran straight to the one that led into the hallway, with Sammy right on his tail.

Roger caught Clara's eyes, her look of shock, and then, simultaneously, they took off, side by side, joining the meowing and barking chase echoing down the hallway.

Roger knew there was no use shouting for the cat or the dog. One was too engrossed in the escape, the other in the chase, which was fair, because that was what cats and dogs often did.

Clara, on the other hand, was shouting Sammy's name, and he most likely couldn't hear her over the meows, snarls, growls, and barks.

The race continued around corners and down hallways, straight towards the entranceway. Probably because Ports knew that was the way out.

'I'll open the front door,' Roger said, while they were

both still running. 'Let Ports out and shut it again before Sammy gets out.'

'How? They are both ahead of us!'

'I know, but I'm thinking they'll stop there.'

'And get in a cat and dog fight!' she shouted in return.

'I'll break it up!'

'You'll get bit, or scratched, or—'

A scream echoed down the hallway, from the entrance way, and they both surged into a faster run, rounded the corner just in time to see Ports leap onto the side table and Sammy attempt to skid to a stop, but the slick floor had him sliding beneath the table. Sammy hit the wall with a thud, and rolled into the table legs.

Between the cat and the dog, the table shook and Roger noticed the vase of flowers that was teetering, about to fall. All he could think about was the amount of time Clara had taken to pick the flowers and arrange them in the vases. He'd never know why, but suddenly, saving the vase seemed like the most important thing. He dived forward, arms out, and caught the vase as it slid off the table, then he rolled onto his back, and skidded to a stop.

That—lying on his back, clutching a vase of flowers from which not a single drop of water had spilled—was how he greeted their guests, who were standing in the open doorway, staring at him. 'Hello, Mother. Stuart.'

Clara slid to a stop beside him and dropped to her knees. 'Are you all right?'

'Yes. Perfectly fine.' He grinned, nodded at the flowers. 'As are the flowers.'

Her face was as red as some of the flowers, yet she held her composure, took the vase, and set it on the table. She then snapped her fingers at Sammy and pointed down the hallway. Head down, the dog crawled out from beneath the table and, with his tail between his legs, walked in the direction she'd pointed.

She repeated the action at Ports, but pointed towards the open door. He leaped off the table and with his tail straight up and jerking, he walked between the guests and out the door.

Grinning, Roger bounded to his feet.

'Doger! Doger!' Abigail said, running towards him from the hallway, with a breathless Bertha running behind.

He scooped Abigail into his arms.

'Ammy! Orts!'

'I saw Sammy and Ports,' he told her. 'Everyone did.'

His mother let out a laugh, before she said, 'Oh, my word, this is the cutest little girl I have ever seen.'

Roger gave a nod of agreement. 'Allow me to introduce you to Miss Abigail Walton, and her mother, Clara Walton.' Nodding at Clara, he continued. 'Clara, this is my mother…' He paused because he wasn't sure what title he should use, for she had several. 'Lady Elaine,' he finally said. 'And her husband, Viscount Stuart Voss.'

There was an exchange of curtsies, bows, and hellos.

To completely break the ice that might otherwise fill the air, Roger went with the obvious. 'I'm sure you recognised Ports,' he said to his mother. 'And that was Sammy, who was sent down the hall to think about his bad behaviour.' He jostled Abigail. 'The two of them are in competition to be someone's favourite animal.'

Abigail giggled, as if fully understanding and enjoying what had been said. He knew she simply liked being jostled while he carried her.

'Well, I don't blame them,' his mother said. 'Would Abigail let me hold her?'

Hearing her name said by a stranger, Abigail bashfully buried her face into his shoulder. 'Perhaps later, once she gets used to you,' he said.

'You were always a shy one, too,' his mother replied. 'And you are right, I must wait until she gets to know me.'

'I hope your journey was uneventful,' he said.

'Compared to our arrival, it was very uneventful.' With a laugh, his mother stepped forward and patted his cheek. 'It's so wonderful to be here. To see you.' She turned to Clara. 'And to meet you, Clara. Alice's message said you've been a Godsend during her mishap. Thank you, and thank goodness you were here when the mishap occurred.'

'It's been a pleasure to help,' Clara said.

Roger noted how Clara kept her gaze from meeting his and how there was still a slight blush on her cheeks. He also noticed how she kept her hands clasped together to hide how they were trembling. It was all he could do to stand still and not put an arm around her, tell her that everything would be fine.

'Do tell, how is she doing?' his mother asked. 'She said her injury was minimal. Is that true?'

'She's doing well,' Roger replied. 'The doctor has been here several times. Nothing was broken and she's been resting the leg since it happened.'

'That's good. I must go see her, but first I must comment on how lovely the house looks,' she said.

'Did you expect otherwise?' he asked.

'Of course not, dear, it's just been so long since I've been home.'

Roger gestured for Aaron to see the guests up to their room, before he took a hold of Clara's arm. 'We'll allow you to get settled in your room and then have tea in the parlour. If that is satisfactory with you.'

'Certainly, dear. Whatever you say,' his mother said.

He gave both her and Stuart a nod, then led Clara down the hallway. 'Let's see how Sammy is doing after all that commotion.'

'Sammy?' Clara whispered as they walked. 'How are *you* doing? Are you sure you didn't hurt anything? You looked like you were diving into a body of water.'

'I'm fine. I wanted to save your flowers, which I did.'

'Yes, you did, and thank you, but please don't do that again. You scared the daylights out of me.' She let out a shaky breath. 'Oh, what your mother must think of me. Of the commotion that I've brought to your life.'

As Roger walked down the hallway beside her, carrying Abigail and thinking about the look on his mother's face when he said hello from the floor, he did the only natural thing he could do. He laughed. It felt so good, he laughed harder.

Clara glanced up at him with a frown, but then, she covered her mouth with one hand and giggled before giving him a playful slap on the chest. 'It's not funny.'

It was to him, and so far, today might very well have been the best day of his life.

* * *

While the rest of that afternoon and evening proceeded, Roger noted that the tension between him and his mother wasn't as strong as usual, and that night, after the others had retired, he sat alone in his study contemplating how it had been easier for both of them to look at each other, to speak to each other. He attributed some of that to Abigail, because his mother had spent a great deal of time attempting to make friends with the little girl. Clara was also part of the reason for the ease between everyone. She created conversations that were of interest to all, including Stuart, and more than idle chit-chat. Her knowledge of the plants in the growing room was evident, and her face shone as she spoke of the seeds and seedlings.

He also suspected the ease was there because of the way he felt. There was a happiness inside him that he'd never felt before. If he didn't know better, he might have said it was there because he knew the game his mother had played, and that he was going to call her bluff.

But that wasn't it.

No, he was happy, while being confused at the same time, because of the kiss he and Clara has shared.

He hadn't figured out what that kiss meant. Nor was he sure what he wanted it to mean. Clara was not the type of woman that he usually took his pleasure with, nor would he want her to be. He didn't want her to be anyone other than who she was, and that in itself was contrary to whom he knew himself to be.

He liked people to fit into expected categories, because then he knew who to interact with and who to consider nothing more than an associate. That made things easy.

Clara wasn't merely an associate.

There was nothing easy about her, either.

Except that she was very easy to like. Very easy to admire.

However, she was still in love with her husband, and she didn't want that to change. She'd said that liking him was a problem, and he now understood what she meant. She didn't want to like him because she would love her husband for ever.

He couldn't compete with a dead man. Didn't want to. That man was the father of her child. A man she'd loved with all her heart.

He had no intention of ever falling in love, of ever marrying anyone, but if he ever was to change his mind, he knew he'd want it all. He'd want his wife to love him with all her heart, mind, and body.

That wasn't likely to ever happen, so there was no reason to be sitting here thinking about it.

The knock on the door made his heart skip. Clara had taken Abigail up to bed some time ago. In the past, she'd never come back downstairs, but perhaps she had a question concerning their guests. Most likely she was wondering if he'd told his mother he was on to her scheme yet.

Odd, he had considered Clara a guest at one time, but now he was considering his mother a guest of *theirs*.

He crossed the room and opened the door. His mother gave a nod as she stepped forward and entered the room. 'I'd like to speak with you, if you don't mind.'

'I don't mind.' Nor would he mind calling her out on her trickery.

His mother walked to the buffet cabinet, poured herself a small amount of brandy and drank it in one swallow before setting the glass down and gesturing to the pair of matching chairs flanking the unlit fireplace. 'Shall we sit?'

With a nod of approval, he waited until she was seated before sitting across from her. He'd inherited her green eyes and black hair, but got his stature from his father. She was barely over five feet tall and as trim and petite as ever.

'You don't need my approval,' she said, 'and I'm not attempting to fool myself into thinking that you do, or that you will welcome it, but this house has become welcoming again. It's been brought back to life, and I want you to know that I approve. Clairmount deserves to be loved. It's an amazing home, and your father certainly loved it. I was hoping the day would come when you'd love being here again, too.' She twisted the embroidered handkerchief in her hands. 'You know now that it's people who make a house a home.'

Roger's spine stiffened. He didn't need her approval, never had, nor did he want her to think she'd won. 'Mother—'

She held up a hand. 'Let me finish, please. While I have the courage.' Touching the handkerchief to the corner of one eye, she continued, 'I know you blamed me for your father's death. You thought I told him he had to go to sea.'

Roger did blame her, and as she'd brought it up, he

told her the truth. 'I heard you tell him to go. He'd planned on staying home for the winter.'

She nodded. 'He had planned on that because I was pregnant. We both wanted more children. I'd lost two babies after you. Both times, Eldon had been at sea, and that time, he had insisted that he was staying home until I gave birth.'

Roger didn't remember a pregnancy, and he certainly didn't have a younger sibling. He didn't prompt her to say more, merely waited.

'When word arrived that there was no one to captain the ship, Eldon said it wouldn't sail. That the cargo could be put on other ships. But he was committed to his company, the ships, and the men who worked for him, and I knew he was torn. It was supposed to be a short trip and I told him to go, that we would be fine, that we'd be here when he got back, all of us. With luck, he'd be home before the baby was born.' She wiped at tears again. 'Luck wasn't on our side. A week out, the storm hit.' She swallowed, blinked. 'A week later, I lost the baby.'

Roger had never been an emotional man, and couldn't decipher if it was compassion or pity or remorse that struck first. They were all there. 'I don't remember that.' His statement sounded cold, even to his own ears.

'You never knew. I didn't want you to. You were too young to understand, and I was too full of grief to help you understand any of it. I should have been a better mother. I knew you blamed me and, well, I blamed myself. For letting him go. For his death. I was lost without him. He'd been my strength. With him, I could have got through anything, but without him, I...'

Roger swallowed at the lump in his throat.

She shrugged. 'My father, your grandfather, knew that, and he came and took you. I thought that might help you, but then I realised that I couldn't lose you, too. You would still be on one of his ships if I hadn't made you come back home after one trip. You were mad, said you'd run away, and I believed you, so I enrolled you in school. I kept visiting you there, hoping you'd eventually...' She shook her head. 'But you refused to see me. Refused to have anything to do with me.'

He remembered refusing to see her, but other things, he remembered differently. His young mind could have distorted things. Possibly, he wasn't sure.

'You refused to even come home, here to Clairmount, after I married Duane. You thought I was trying to replace your father.' She shook her head. 'No one could ever have replaced your father. Not in your heart or mine. But Duane had made me laugh. He taught me that I could be happy again, and I wanted that. After three years of crying, I wanted to laugh. Wanted to live again, to love again.'

Three years? In his mind, he'd thought she'd married Duane shortly after his father had died, within months, but now that he thought about it, it couldn't have been. That timeline didn't fit. He had gone sailing with his grandfather and had been at school for some time before she'd remarried.

'I didn't know what to do,' she said, 'other than hope that if I gave you enough time, you might come around to understand. That was wrong of me. I should have told you the truth, but at that time, when your father had died, I thought it would be better for you to hate me for asking him to leave, rather than hate him for leaving, because he'd loved you. Loved you with all his heart.'

Roger stood, crossed the room, and poured another splash of brandy in a glass for his mother, then more in a glass for himself. All she'd said was true. All of it. Deep down he knew that, yet he'd twisted it around in his mind. Had for years, so that he'd been the only one who had been hurt.

He hadn't been.

'Thank you,' she said as he handed her the glass.

'Why didn't you tell me any of this before now?'

'Because you wouldn't have listened,' she said. 'You would have come up with an excuse and left the room as soon as I walked into it.'

He had done that for years.

'I know I wasn't there for you after your father died, after I lost the baby, and by the time I was well enough to care for you, you hated me, and I didn't blame you.' She wiped at more tears. 'I just prayed that someday you'd be ready to listen to what I had to say. When I heard that you were bringing guests home, I hoped you had finally let go of the past and opened your heart.' She smiled. 'Upon arriving and seeing you save those flowers... It reminded me so much of your father. He would have done that. Save a vase of flowers because I'd picked them. I knew then that you'd changed.'

He opened his mouth to inform her that he hadn't changed, but the words wouldn't form. Some things had changed.

'I won't impose, but I've missed you so much. Missed so much of your life, and I'd like that to change. I'd like to be your mother again. Would like to see you and your family, regularly.'

Roger's hand froze with his glass halfway to his mouth. He'd almost bought into all she'd said. 'Mother, you are misunderstanding Clara and Abigail being here. We are not a family.'

'Not yet.' Her green eyes glistened as she took a sip from her glass. 'But you will be as soon as you ask her to marry you. Love left buried is a waste. Clara and Abigail deserve your love, and you deserve theirs.'

Roger heaved out a breath. 'Clara and I will not be getting married. I—we know what you did. How you contrived with Alice to fake an injury, for Aaron to suggest to others that Clara was my wife, the lady of the house.'

She didn't blink an eye, just stared at him.

He was a bit taken aback by her silence. Had figured that she'd attempt to deny it or to justify it. 'Why?'

'I'm your mother. I love you, and I don't want to see you go through your entire life alone.'

He finished his drink in one swallow and set his glass on the table. 'That is my choice to make.'

She nodded. 'It is.'

'I choose to remain unmarried, and Clara has chosen to return to America as soon as the war ends. I will take her there.'

Clara stood at the window in her bedroom staring at the stars and telling herself that she could not wish upon one of them. She wasn't sure which one she'd seen first, nor had she seen one shoot across the sky, therefore, none of them were wishing stars. Furthermore, there were far more practical reasons not to wish upon one. She was a grown woman, not a child. Grown women did not wish for things that could never be. The only wish she should ever have would be for Mark to not have died. No wishing in the world would change that, and it was wrong for her to wish for anything else. So wrong.

It had been wrong of her to kiss Roger the way she had. Wrong to feel the things she felt for him. Continued to feel for him. It went beyond being grateful, and that couldn't be.

She certainly couldn't ever kiss him again, either.

Never. Ever.

She was grateful that his mother had arrived when she had, and that she would be staying for a few days. Elaine Voss was not what Clara had expected. Roger had not only inherited his emerald-green eyes from his mother, he'd inherited her kindness.

Clara now fully understood why the household staff spoke so highly of Lady Elaine. She was sweet and caring, and Clara couldn't understand what could have caused friction between mother and son.

Nor could she imagine that Elaine would trick anyone.

Roger must be mistaken about that. There had to be a reason why he thought that, and Clara wondered if it was because he'd thought that his mother had never needed him.

That still hurt her, to think that was how he felt. That was also why she couldn't fully regret kissing him.

Clara shook her head, trying to clear her thoughts, but that wasn't about to happen. There was too much on her mind.

Stuart Voss was as tall as Roger, with dark hair that was streaked with grey and matching whiskers that covered the entire lower half of his face. He was a quiet, pleasant man who Elaine had married a couple of years ago, after her second husband had died from a long-time illness.

Knowing that—how Elaine had married two men since Roger's father had died—was making Clara think about things that she shouldn't be thinking about. Her father had never remarried after her mother died, and when Mark died, she'd known that's how it would be for her, too. But now, she was thinking about other widows she'd known who had remarried.

Movement in the yard below her window caught her attention, and recognition sent her heart thudding. It was Roger, and though it was dark in her room, and she was sure he couldn't see her, he stopped, turned, and stared directly at her.

She stepped backwards, let the curtain fall back in place and pressed a hand to the commotion going on inside her chest. Her mind was no better. It was getting harder and harder to think straight.

There was one thing she knew. She had to steer clear of Roger until she could get her mind in order, because she could not be falling in love with him.

Absolutely could not.

* * *

With Elaine and Stuart there, it was easy for Clara to keep her distance from Roger. Other than at mealtimes, she barely saw him. At first, she'd thought it was because he wanted to show Stuart the property, but after the second day, she wondered if Roger was avoiding her as much as she was him.

'I know Eldon is smiling down on this place right now,' Elaine said as they walked across the yard, following Abigail and Sammy. 'He loved children, and they loved him. I told him that Roger would never learn to walk because all he had to do was hold up his arms, and Eldon picked him up, carried him.'

Clara smiled as she nodded, thinking how much Roger was like his father in that aspect.

'We had a wonderful life together,' Elaine continued wistfully. 'I was engaged to another man when I met Eldon. I'd heard of him, everyone had, Eldon was very well known. And handsome. Roger looks just like him except he ended up with my green eyes. Eldon had dark brown eyes. He had a way of looking at me that made my heart melt. He came by to see my father one day, and I fell in love with him the moment he looked at me.'

'You did?' Clara asked.

'I did. He sent my heart racing and left me unable to think about anything except him, day and night. The same day that I met Eldon, I told Wallace Weston, the man I was supposed to marry, that I couldn't marry him. When Wallace asked why, I said because I was going to marry Eldon Hardgroves. Two weeks later, Eldon and I were married and we set sail for the Caribbean. When we returned, he brought me here, and I fell in love with Clairmount as quickly as I had him.'

Clara had to press a hand to her chest, against the quickening of her heart. Elaine's words had struck a chord within her. She, too, had fallen in love with Clairmount. Anyone who stayed here would. Not just because it was a lovely home, but because it felt like home. It provided all the safety and security that a home could. She'd never thought any place would feel that way to her again, and that was confusing. Frightening really, because she hadn't wanted to feel that way about anywhere but her farm back in Virginia.

Yet, it had happened. Deep down, the emotions that swirled inside her, were real. Very real. And they didn't just include Clairmount.

The breath she'd been holding escaped in a long, shaky sigh.

Roger had made her feel safe and secure even before they had arrived at Clairmount. She hadn't wanted to acknowledge the things that had been happening inside her, nor had she wanted to admit what they meant, but could no longer deny any of it.

She had started to live again. Live, not just exist, and her mind, those thoughts of what she believed was right, of how her life should be, hadn't been able to overrule her heart.

When had she fallen in love with Roger? How had it happened? Why?

It might have been when he'd taken care of her at the inn, or how he'd dedicated his attention to Abigail, or during the journey to Clairmount when he'd always seen that their needs were taken care of, or even after they'd arrived here, at his home, that he openly shared with them.

All she knew for sure was that she should have tried harder for it not to have happened. She'd planned on never loving again. Ever.

The scariest part wasn't that it had happened, it was the strength of how much she loved him. She knew the feeling of love, and what she felt for him went deep. Very deep.

'It was different when I fell in love with Duane,' Elaine said. 'He and I were friends, had been for years, and we gradually fell in love. It wasn't until I realised that he made me laugh again, something I hadn't done for a long time, that I knew I was in love with him.' She laughed slightly. 'With Stuart, it was because we were both lonely. Very lonely, and the companionship that we found with each other led to a gentler, older form of love. Love, nonetheless. He's a dear man, and I truly cherish our time together.'

Clara had never considered different types of love, yet could understand the way Elaine described them. However, it didn't help her situation. She couldn't be in love with Roger and still love Mark. That was impossible.

Chapter Fourteen

Clara woke feeling sad on Tuesday morning. Elaine and Stuart were leaving that day, going back to London, and during their short stay, Clara had experienced a kinship with Elaine. It had just been her and her father, so she'd never had the support or influence of an older woman. And though Mark's mother had been a wonderful woman and amazing help when Abigail had been born, they'd both been too busy to spend a lot of time just talking about things.

That had happened quite quickly with Elaine, mainly because of the growing room, the new drapes, and the few other changes that Clara had made to Clairmount. Elaine had been excited about everything and very complimentary. She was also knowledgeable, and Clara had enjoyed talking with her.

Abigail had enjoyed Elaine, too, as well as Stuart, once she'd warmed up to them.

As she finished getting herself and Abigail dressed and ready for the day, Clara had to admit there was also another reason she'd miss Elaine. She would no longer have a readily available excuse for either her or Roger to keep their distance from each other as they had the past few days. Ever since the kiss.

That memory was still alive inside her, and made her cheeks burn when Roger looked at her because she knew he was remembering it, too. She feared what he must think of her. Of how she'd kissed him. Really kissed him. Not just a simple peck on the cheek.

She didn't regret kissing him, and if he asked, she'd have to tell him that. And that it couldn't happen again.

With that thought, she smoothed the white collar of the pink and white dress that Abigail was wearing—one of those that Roger had recently bought—and picked up her daughter.

The dress she was wearing was a pale orange, with a layered skirt and squared neckline trimmed with cream coloured lace, and very lovely. She still wasn't used to having so many choices of what to wear, and wondered if she'd ever take clothes for granted again. Prior to the war, she'd never worried about not having something presentable to wear, yet she'd arrived in England looking like a ragamuffin. So had her daughter.

Kissing Abigail's nose, she said, 'I'll make sure it never happens again. You are far too beautiful to be wearing rags.'

Abigail giggled.

'You are,' Clara said. 'You are the cutest little girl ever, and Momma loves you so very much.'

'Momma,' Abigail said.

Clara's heart doubled. Despite all the things she had

to worry about, she never failed to find pure happiness because of Abigail.

Carrying Abigail, Clara left their bedroom and took the back set of stairs in order to stop in the kitchen first, to make sure everything was in order for breakfast. The layout of the house no longer overwhelmed her. Though large, it had become as familiar to her as the two-bedroom farmhouse had been back home.

She let Sammy outside to do his business and then entered the kitchen.

As always, Mrs Wells had the room full of delicious scents and Anita was filling serving dishes to be carried into the dining room. Because everyone knew how much Abigail liked to help, Anita gave her a silver sugar bowl to carry into the dining room. Clara knew that things would be different when she found a job, that many places might not be so welcoming to Abigail, may not let her have the run of the house like she had here—Sammy, either—and that was a great concern to Clara. She would not, ever, be parted from her child, not for anyone. If an employer didn't understand that, she'd keep looking until she found one that did.

Here they were treated like family, and she knew she couldn't expect that elsewhere, but she wouldn't give up hope that there had to be a family somewhere in England who would welcome a housekeeper and her daughter.

With Abigail walking beside her, carrying the lidded, silver bowl with both hands, Clara made her way into the dining room. Roger and Stuart were already there, and Abigail let out an excited squeal as she carried the dish to table.

Roger picked her up and let her set the dish on the table before he set her on the high stool and planted a tiny kiss on her forehead.

There were so many things that would be different for Abigail when they left here. Young as she was, Abigail wouldn't remember her life here, but for a time, she would miss it, and that was going to hurt. Clara could already feel the pain of seeing her daughter hurting. That's how it was. A mother hurt for her child, and with them.

Furthermore, Clara was already missing him herself. It seemed impossible that she could miss someone whom she saw every day, but she did. She saw Roger at mealtimes, and they spoke to each other, but it wasn't the same as the days prior to his mother's arrival, when they'd joked and laughed and talked.

'Good morning,' Roger greeted her.

'Good morning,' she said, including Stuart in her reply as she sat in the chair that Roger held for her.

'I dare say, both Elaine and I are going to miss the lovely company here at Clairmount,' Stuart said.

'You are welcome to stay longer,' Roger said. 'As long as you wish.'

Stuart chuckled slightly. 'We discussed that last night. If it was not for the things that we must see to before the ball that the Duke of Cambridge will be hosting prior to the exhibition, we would extend our stay. It's been a delightful visit.'

'It certainly has,' Elaine agreed as she walked

through the doorway. 'A delightful visit with delightful people.'

Elaine wore a lovely blue dress with a white underskirt that swished as she crossed the room to Abigail, who was seated between Roger and Clara, and placed a kiss on her cheek.

Clara greeted her and received a kiss on the cheek as well. So did Roger as Elaine made her way around the end of the table. He'd stood when she'd entered the room and had to lean down to receive the kiss on the cheek. He gave her one in return.

Clara watched all this with interest because, after that first day, when there had been a noticeable distance between mother and son, the two seemed to have grown closer. Others had noticed it, too, including Bertha, who proclaimed to be tickled pink that the two were getting along better than ever. Almost like old times, she'd declared.

Considering Roger had been a small child when his father had died, Clara wasn't sure that his and Elaine's relationship could be like old times, but she held her opinion to herself.

'Here, dear,' Elaine said, handing Roger an envelope. 'A messenger just delivered this. I told Aaron I would give it to you while he showed the man to the kitchen to eat before leaving again.'

'Thank you, Mother,' Roger said, laying the envelope on the table while he waited for his mother to sit down next to Stuart.

'I also bumped into Suzanne upstairs and she asked that we don't wait on her. She is putting together an envelope that I've agreed to deliver to a publisher that I know in London.' She nodded towards Roger. 'You know Henry Vogal, the Earl of Beaufort, dear.'

Roger nodded. 'Yes. Have for years. Henry's townhouse in London is next door to Drew's.'

Clara noticed an undertone in Roger's voice. Elaine had taken great interest in Suzanne's writing and had wanted to know all about the story. Roger had been supportive, too. Was he bothered by his mother's interest? That seemed unlikely.

'Henry has taken a far greater interest in his family's businesses than his father ever did,' Elaine said, 'and his publishing house might be interested in the story Suzanne is writing.'

Roger nodded, and Clara wished she could ask him what he truly thought, because there was something he wasn't saying.

Aaron appeared in the doorway and Roger gave him a nod, signalling for the food to be served.

While that was happening, Aaron whispered something to Roger, and with a nod, he lifted the envelope, opened it, and upon reading it, settled a gaze on Clara that caused a tiny shiver to ripple over her shoulders.

'Is something amiss?' she asked.

'No.' He set the message on the table. 'It's from Drew. They will arrive in London this week and would like us to meet them there.'

'Oh.' Clara should be ecstatic, shouldn't she? Then why wasn't she?

'You could travel with us to London,' Elaine said, clearly excited. 'Leave when we do, today.'

Roger's gaze had never left hers. 'That would be up to Clara.'

She swallowed, and knowing what she had to do, she said, 'That would be fine.' She managed to find an old fake smile. 'Wonderful, actually.'

'Very well.' Roger glanced at Aaron. 'Please send a note with the messenger for the Duke of Mansfield and another to let Garrison know we will be arriving at the townhouse sometime tomorrow.'

Aaron nodded, bowed, and left the room.

Clara then realised how wishes could change. At one time, it was her greatest wish for Annabelle to return. Though she still wanted to see her friend, she wasn't quite ready to leave Clairmount.

It was probably a good thing that she was, though, because leaving here was her first step in getting back to America.

Although two carriages left Clairmount for London, Roger chose to ride Smokey, because he needed something to be familiar, to be the way they'd always been.

Ever since that first night of his mother's visit, when she'd entered his study, told him things that hadn't matched with what he'd always known, always thought, he felt as if he'd been kicked in the stomach.

Had he been so miserable that he'd wanted everyone else to be as miserable? Had he created timelines and events in his mind to fit his emotions? If so, what else about his life wasn't true?

He'd thought about that a lot the past few days, and

found things, feelings and beliefs that were no longer there.

He no longer felt the need to avoid his mother at all costs.

For the first time in a very, very long time, Clairmount felt like home.

Working through those thoughts, he'd also discovered that he no longer considered bachelorhood to be the best life possible.

That was strange at first, until he realised that he no longer felt empty inside, hollow. He couldn't say exactly what he did feel, but knew who those feelings were for. Clara.

They were strong feelings, but it had been so long since he'd considered love, the meaning of it, or the feeling, that he wasn't overly sure if what he was feeling was indeed love.

Desire, lust, compassion, appreciation. The list went on. He desired to kiss her again, and again, and again. He lusted to do more than kiss her. He held great compassion for all she'd been through in the past, and appreciation for all she'd done to turn Clairmount into a home again, and so much more.

None of that meant what he felt was love. He'd told Clara that he'd never been needed, and that was true. He'd never been loved, either, or so he'd thought. His mother claimed she'd never stopped loving him, so where did that leave him? A man who had turned his back on love as a child couldn't just find it, understand it.

Above all else, Clara didn't want to like him, let alone

love him. She wanted to return to America, and he'd promised to get her there on one of his ships.

Clara knew what love was, and she would wish for ever that her husband hadn't died.

Being jealous of a dead man was ridiculous, but Roger wanted what Mark Walton had had—Clara's love. He also wanted Abigail as his daughter. To have her last name be Hardgroves instead of Walton, and that wasn't right.

None of that was right, but it didn't change the fact it was what he wanted. He also wanted more children with Clara. A son who would inherit his holdings and title.

It was a hell of thing when a man's life changed right before his eyes without him having a say in those changes.

But that was exactly what had happened, and Roger had to figure out what he was going to do about it all.

Their first day of travel went without mishap, but the weather on the second day chose not to cooperate and it was pushing into the evening hours when they finally arrived at his townhouse. Although not nearly as large as Clairmount, he'd always considered his house here of adequate size. However, it had never hosted two women, a child, a dog, and three extra servants. Bertha had come along to look after Abigail as needed, Loren had driven the coach and would remain in London with them, and Anita, a kitchen helper, had come along so that Garrison wouldn't be expected to cook and clean for so many additional people.

The gloomy, drizzly weather they'd travelled through

all day turned into a drenching rain near the outskirts of in London, and by the time they arrived at his house, Roger was soaked.

He quickly dismounted when Garrison opened the door of the house with an umbrella in hand. 'No sense in both of us getting soaked,' Roger shouted to the servant as he hurried up the walkway to get the umbrella. 'I'll escort the women inside. You can show them their accommodations.'

'Yes, sir,' Garrison replied, as he handed over the umbrella. 'Everything is prepared.'

Roger made two trips, getting Clara, Abigail, Suzanne, as well as Bertha and Anita, and Sammy, from the carriage into the house.

Clara met him with a towel as he entered after the second trip.

'Thank you,' he said and sopped the water off his face.

'You are soaked through. Garrison has set out dry clothes in your room. Go change before you catch cold. Supper will be served as soon as you're ready.'

Roger didn't attempt to hide his grin. He didn't mind how she'd taken charge. Nor was he surprised.

Once he had changed, he joined the others in the dining room and realised he couldn't remember a time where he'd ever had guests for a meal. He also realised his townhouse was not fitted to Abigail's needs as there was no tall stool for her to sit upon at the table, nor was there a crib upstairs.

If any of those things had been here when he'd been little, they'd long ago been thrown out. That made him think about his mother. How thrilled she'd been with the prospect of being a grandmother. He liked the idea of Abigail having a grandmother—and a grandfather, as Stuart had also gained the little girl's trust.

He liked a lot of the ideas he was having these days about Abigail and Clara. But all of those ideas involved them becoming his family. The very thing that he'd never wanted.

Later that night, after the storm had ended, the luggage had all been hauled in, and everyone was settled in their bedrooms, Roger sat in his study, contemplating all the things his mother had told him. She'd said that she'd failed him, but the truth was, he'd failed her. He'd failed his father, too. He should have stepped up, become the man of the family. Instead, he'd thought only about himself, how he'd felt, and he'd continued that long after he'd grown up.

Lost in thought, he wasn't sure if he'd heard a knock on the door until it came a second time. 'Come in,' he instructed.

The door opened slowly, and only wide enough for Clara to peer around the edge. 'I don't mean to disturb you.'

He stood, walked towards her. 'You aren't. Is something amiss?'

'No, everything is fine. Your home is lovely and everyone is settled into their rooms. I just would like to ask you a question.'

'Of course, come in.' He gestured to the sofa, and as he watched her walk, he silently admitted just how much he desired her. He'd desired women for years and knew the feeling. He also recognised just how different that desire was this time. It went deeper.

She sat and folded her hands together. 'At Clairmount,' she started, 'when your mother mentioned a publisher who might be interested in Suzanne's story, you seemed concerned.'

Roger walked to the fireplace and rested a hand on the mantel. Henry Vogal was a good chap. It was the gossip circulating around about him that concerned Roger. It wasn't worth repeating because it wasn't true, and that had been what he would have told his mother had she brought it up. But other things he knew about Henry were true. Roger's childhood and family life seemed like a walk in the park compared to what Henry had lived through.

'I ask only because I don't want to see Suzanne's dreams crushed,' Clara said. 'She's very excited about the possibility of turning her story over to a publisher, and if you have concerns about the owner, I'd appreciate if you mentioned it.'

Of course Clara would be concerned for Suzanne. 'I wouldn't want to see Suzanne's dreams crushed, either,' Roger said. 'I have no idea how much involvement Henry has in his publishing house, but I could make inquiries if you'd like.'

'No, I don't want any special favours, and Suzanne wouldn't, either. I never mentioned to her that you knew him. I was only concerned for her sake.'

He nodded. 'Rest assured, I do know Henry and can vouch for his character, but I know nothing about the publishing house he owns.'

'Thank you. Suzanne hopes to deliver the story to the publishing house herself before we leave London with Annabelle.'

He moved away from the fireplace and sat in the chair across from her. 'She'll have time for that. The ball isn't until Saturday night.'

'Ball?'

'The Duke of Cambridge is having a ball this Saturday in honour of the exhibition. Drew and Annabelle will attend to honour Prince Albert. He and Drew's father were best friends, and Albert watched out for Drew after his father had died. Albert died in December, but he'd been a driving force behind the International Exhibition. He also organised the Great Exhibition ten years ago that people still talk about.'

'Will you go?'

'To the ball or the exhibition?'

She shrugged. 'Both?'

'Yes, I'm interested in seeing the industrial exhibitions, and I believe you would be interested in the horticultural exhibits. We will also attend the ball in honour of Prince Albert.' Though he hadn't been as close to the prince as Drew had been, he'd known him well, and had respected him a great deal.

'We?'

He nodded. 'You, me, and Suzanne.'

She grimaced. 'I have Abigail.'

'Bertha will be here with her the entire time.'

'Yes, well, I've never been that far away from her.'

'We will merely be across town.'

'Oh, well, I'm not really ball material,' she said.

He chuckled at her description. 'Oh? How do you know? Have you been to a ball?'

'No, but I've dreamed about them.'

'You dreamed about them?'

She nodded.

He wondered what she would say if he told her that he dreamed about her quite regularly. For he did, every night. Dreams that lived inside him each and every day, too.

He leaned forward in his chair. 'Annabelle will want you to attend I'm sure of that.'

She nodded again, and glanced down at her hands clasped in her lap. 'Did you speak to your mother about…'

'Her scheme? Yes, I did.'

Clara lifted her head. 'What did she say?'

'She admitted to it.'

'She did?'

'Yes. I told her it was wrong of her to involve the servants and wrong of her to involve you, to put you in that position to take over the running of the household.'

'I didn't mind that,' Clara said, quickly. 'I appreciated it, actually.'

'Appreciated it?'

'Yes,' she said. 'It allowed me to learn what I would need to know in order to get a housekeeping job.'

A quiver raced over his shoulders. 'A housekeeping job? Where?'

She stood, walked to the window, fluffed the curtain. 'I don't have one yet. I'm hoping Annabelle will be able to help me with that part. Help me find a place who needs a housekeeper so I can earn money, enough to rebuild the farm when the war is over.'

Roger's spine stiffened as her words sank in. He'd failed his mother by never giving her want she wanted, but he wouldn't fail Clara. He'd make sure that she got exactly what she wanted.

Chapter Fifteen

Clara was beside herself with excitement at seeing Annabelle, and triple-checked that everything was in order one last time. The table was set, complete with two bouquets of flowers from a shop that she had visited that morning. Anita had a meal prepared that would start with a chicken and vegetable soup, followed by roasted pork along with potatoes and rice, carrots and peas, rolls with butter and jelly in individual dishes, and sweet pickles. Dessert was a custard pie.

Children normally ate prior to others in the household and often in the kitchen. Clara had learned that while at Clairmount, but Abigail still needed assistance with some foods, and she much preferred to assist her daughter herself. She couldn't believe that Annabelle would mind. Furthermore, Roger approved of Abigail at the table.

This evening was his idea, after all. He'd said that they would be arriving back from Scotland sometime today, and knowing that Annabelle would want to see her and Suzanne as soon as possible, he had invited her and Drew to dinner.

Clara had spent the day preparing for the event. Though the house was clean and neat, Garrison—a short, older man, with dark hair and blue eyes that twinkled beneath his bushy brows, did an excellent job of managing the house—had said this morning that Roger had never hosted a dinner party in the townhouse before. She'd told him not to worry, that she would handle everything.

Mostly everything.

Suzanne had gone to the market with Garrison to get the items that Anita had requested, and Anita had done the majority of the cooking. And Roger had bought the high chair that now sat at the table for Abigail to sit in.

Clara's heart was in the midst of sinking low, already dreading the day when she and her daughter would no longer have Roger in their lives, when he appeared in the doorway with a grin on his face.

Her heart shot into a fast beat at the sight of him.

'Drew's carriage just pulled up out front,' he said.

'It did? Oh, my.' She gave herself a once-over by smoothing the dress over her stomach and patting her hair to assure herself that the pins were all still in place.

'You look beautiful,' he said. 'Not a hair out of place.'

'She's been my best friend for years, so there no reason to be nervous,' Clara said. 'Yet, I am.'

He took a hold of her hands. 'Because you haven't seen her for a long time.'

Clara knew she should pull her hands away from his, step away from him, but for the life of her, she didn't have the ability to do that, not with the way he was looking straight into her eyes.

When he leaned forward, her entire being leaped into life, remembering their one and only kiss. The kiss she'd wanted to experience again ever since. She remembered exactly how wonderful it had been, how she'd wanted to go on kissing him and never have it end.

Her heart was thudding, her lips tingling…and the frown that tugged on her brows when he merely brushed his lips lightly on her forehead was nearly painful.

'Go find Suzanne,' he said. 'I'll see Drew and Annabelle into the front parlour.'

He was looking at her, waiting for her to move first. She didn't want to move, but couldn't stand here staring at him like some statue. His hands still had hold of hers, and she felt the hold tightening, felt his body leaning towards hers again.

She was growing dizzy, light-headed, but knew one thing. The longing inside her would not stand for a simple brush of his lips.

Quickly, before she lost her nerve, she rose on her toes and pressed her lips to his. Softly at first, but then more firmly when she felt his lips move in response.

He was kissing her back then, with as much fire as she felt inside her. The kiss didn't last long, but it gave birth to the heat of passion that she hadn't felt in a very long time, and when it ended, it was because Roger stopped it, not her.

She was speechless and unable to move for a long moment, but knew, deep down inside her, if things were different, she would take Roger by the hand and lead him upstairs to one of the bedrooms whether or not company was arriving at the door.

Things weren't different, though, and they never would be.

With a sigh that held both satisfaction and regret, she drew her hands from his and stepped back. 'I'll go find Suzanne.'

He grinned. 'I don't think that's necessary.'

She frowned. 'Why not?'

With a chuckle, he looped her arm through his and escorted her out of the room. 'I believe we'll find Suzanne and Annabelle and Drew in the parlour.'

She instantly knew that Annabelle had arrived while she'd been kissing him. There wasn't time to be embarrassed, though, because Annabelle rushed around the corner and engulfed her in a hug.

Their reunion was heartfelt, and tearful, and full of happiness all wrapped together and lasted well beyond the dinner hour. All three women had so many questions to ask and answers to share, and Clara was most shocked to learn that Arlo was actually Annabelle's stepfather. Her real father had been a duke who had betrothed her to Drew when she'd been a baby.

The tale was complex, even confusing at times, but had a happy ending, and Clara gave Roger a playful punch in the arm. 'Why didn't you tell us all this?'

He shrugged. 'It wasn't my story to tell. It's Annabelle's, and Drew's.'

That answer, along with the way he looked at her, was enough to make Clara fall in love with him. If she hadn't already been in love with him, that is. She'd hoped that he'd tell her more last night, when she'd asked him about his mother, but he hadn't, and it had been foolish of her to even consider that he might change his mind about marriage. Foolish because it didn't matter.

'How about you and I walk down to Pall Mall Street?' Drew asked Roger. 'Give these women a couple of hours to visit.'

They all rose from the table, and while the men took their leave of the house, Bertha arrived to take Abigail up to bed. The women then proceeded into the parlour, where Annabelle hugged them each again.

'I can't believe you are here, truly can't,' Annabelle said. 'Even though I knew it would happen. Roger promised he'd find you.'

'We are very grateful that he did,' Clara said. 'We had no money, no place to go, and would have starved to death had we remained living in the root cellar.'

'Root cellar?' Annabelle's brilliant blue eyes were as big as saucers as Clara proceeded to tell her about the life they'd lived since the night of the fire.

They shared hugs, and tears, and even a few laughs while the story was told, and silence ensued when Clara stated that she would be returning to America as soon as the war ended.

'Drew and I will visit America, too,' Annabelle said, frowning. 'Someday.'

'I will be moving back home,' Clara clarified. 'To the farm, to rebuild it.'

Annabelle glanced at Suzanne.

'Of course, Suzanne doesn't need to return if she doesn't want to,' Clara said. 'But I do.'

'Why do you need to return?' Annabelle asked.

'Because the farm was Mark's dream. My dream. One we created together, and I need to rebuild it for Abigail, so she has a way to remember her father.' Clara hoped repeating it would revive the passion for the dream inside her, because lately she hadn't been longing for it as she had before she started feeling differently about Roger. 'I'm hoping you can help me, Annabelle.'

'Of course, how?'

'I need a job as a housekeeper so I can earn enough money to rebuild the farm. Roger has promised that Abigail and I can travel on one of his ships.'

'I can believe he has,' Annabelle said. 'The reason he is the most sought-after bachelor in London is because he has a heart of gold.'

Clara didn't have the heart to respond to that. The idea of leaving was already twisting hers in a very painful way. 'Do you know of anyone in need of a housekeeper?'

'I'll think about it,' Annabelle said. 'In the meantime, do you two have your dresses picked out for the ball? We have to attend. Drew was very close with Prince Albert and will attend in his honour.'

Clara stared at herself in the mirror while listening for footsteps in the hallway. Someone was sure to come along, knock on her door, ask if she was ready.

She wasn't ready. Would never be ready.

The dark burgundy gown, one of the many that Roger

had bought, had a fitted waist, with a white and burgundy floral print overdress that was open in the front and had three-quarter-length sleeves and a high collar in the back. The front had a square neckline and the dress had come with a matching choker necklace and ribbons that Bertha had woven into her up-styled hair.

The satin slippers on her feet matched the gown.

Wearing this, her dream of having patched clothing and holes in her shoes couldn't come true, but that didn't ease the nerves that were jittering inside her, threatening that her stomach could erupt at any moment.

A ball, hosted by the cousin of the Queen, was not a place she belonged. She had tried everything she could think of to get out of going, but not a single one of her excuses had worked.

Not with Roger or Annabelle, or even Suzanne and Bertha.

Therefore, she was going.

She just knew it wasn't going to turn out well.

Knew it couldn't.

The footsteps finally sounded, the knock happened, and Clara pressed a hand to her mouth, willing herself not to be sick.

Roger met Drew's gaze, and as they'd done for years, they read each other's minds. The three women standing before them were exceptionally beautiful. Dressed in their ball finery, each one of them stood out in her own special way. One with dark brown hair, one with blond hair, and one with black hair.

'You might be in trouble tonight, my friend,' Drew said beneath his breath.

Roger was already in trouble. He'd fallen head over heels in love with a woman who would never love him in return. Pulling up a grin, he asked, 'Why do you say that?'

'Women are not going to be happy about losing the most eligible bachelor in London.'

Roger laughed, but then swallowed hard. 'How did I get here, Drew?'

'I told you, it just happens.' Drew elbowed him. 'I gave you my advice last night—don't fight it. What's on the other side is far better than bachelorhood.'

Roger hadn't said a word to start their conversation at the gentleman's club last night; Drew had known what had happened the moment he'd met Clara and saw the blush on her face. Roger hadn't denied kissing her, nor did he deny having fallen in love with her. He couldn't deny the truth.

The women stepped forward, and he and Drew parted, making way for the three to exit the house. Drew and Annabelle had arrived a short time ago, so that Annabelle could help Clara and Suzanne get ready for the ball.

Because the gowns took up room, they took two coaches, and Roger didn't mind when Annabelle asked Suzanne to please ride with them. He enjoyed any time he had to be alone with Clara, and knew that wouldn't happen at the ball. Though he attended them, and had for years because that was a duty of his title, he had never enjoyed them. Balls, to his way of thinking, were little more than mating rituals, where, like birds, people preened and showed off their feathers in an attempt to impress the other sex into choosing them.

He'd never wanted to be chosen.

Not up until he'd met an American widow.

'You look lovely,' he told Clara as they sat across from each other with the clip-clop of the horse's hooves echoing inside the coach. It reminded him of their first coach ride. That seemed years ago now, rather than weeks.

'Thank you. You look quite handsome,' she replied, not meeting his gaze.

He leaned forward, reached out, and touched her hand. The sun was slowly setting, but still provided enough light for him to see the worry on her face. 'There is nothing to fear.' A pang struck him, because she did have cause to fear. A ball was unknown to her, as unknown as England had been, and sailing across the ocean. But she'd faced each challenge admirably, despite the obstacles thrown in her way. He was proud of her. Very proud of her.

Lifting her hand, he held it between both of his. 'That was a stupid thing for me to say.'

She frowned.

'This is all unknown for you, and it's natural for you to be nervous. What I should have said is this—a ball is nothing compared to what you've already faced. You are an amazing woman. The most amazing woman I've ever met, in fact, and I have one wish for you.'

'One wish for me?'

There was confusion on her face, but he knew that

inside she was feeling a whole lot more than confusion, or even worry about the ball. She was afraid. Afraid to hope because her hopes had been crushed in the past. So had her dreams.

He nodded. 'My wish would be for you to forget the past, just for tonight, and live like you've never been hurt. It sounds impossible, but it's not. I've done it for years.'

She lifted her chin, looked at him. 'I wish you'd never been hurt.'

'I believe it's part of life.'

'I believe you are right,' she said.

'I've done a lot of other things for years, too,' he said, hoping to dispel the solemnity. 'Some good, some not so good.'

She shook her head as a full-fledged grin came through. 'I believe there was more good than not so good.'

'Others would disagree with you.'

She shrugged. 'Others don't know you as well as I do.'

He stared at her for a moment, taking in her beauty and the truth of her comment. She might know him better than most, for he had told her more than he'd ever told others.

Her cheeks took on a blush, and she looked away, and that made him realise another truth. His desires for her continued to grow, and he knew his limits. Knew that sooner or later, they'd break.

Needing to get his mind on a different route, he said, 'You are going to meet a lot of people tonight, so let me help you with a few so you don't have to waste your time.'

'Waste my time?'

'Yes. Waste your time figuring out if they are worth knowing or not. Take Henry Vogal, the sixth Earl of Beaufort, who owns the publishing company. He's a good guy, but Viscount Tom Mahler is someone even Sammy would bite. To make it easier, when you are introduced to someone decent, I'll nod once, like this.' He nodded a slow, yet slight nod. 'But, when you are introduced to someone not worth your time, I won't nod.'

Giving a thoughtful nod herself, she asked, 'What about the women?'

He shrugged. 'The same.'

She grinned. 'You seem to hold an insurmountable degree of confidence that your opinions of people are correct.'

'They are.' He was very sure of that, including his opinion of himself.

Chapter Sixteen

The ball would have been overwhelming if Clara hadn't had two things. Roger and Annabelle. Roger was never far away, and she knew that he had one eye on her at all times, if not both.

And Annabelle was the Annabelle that Clara had always known. She might be a duchess now, married to a duke, but that hadn't changed her. She was herself. That allowed Clara to let go some of the worries that had been dragging her down. She had been certain that she would fall short on the rules of society—mainly because there were so many they'd made her head spin when Bertha had listed them while styling her hair.

If she hadn't lived at Clairmount for the past few weeks, she would have been overwhelmed by the beauty and expanse of the home where the ball was being held, but in all honesty, it didn't hold a candle to Clairmount.

The walls of the massive ballroom were papered dark gold and the ceiling had a mural painted on it of cupids with bows and arrows, and fluffy white clouds. Roger saw her looking at it, and whispered, 'I've always thought those cupids look a little evil, like miniature devils.'

She giggled to herself, because she agreed.

He took a hold of her elbow. 'Come, let's dance.'

When they had arrived, and had been handed small booklets, Annabelle had explained that if they wanted to dance, they could use the dance cards, otherwise, they could simply scribble names on each line and say their card was full.

Clara had scribbled names.

Suzanne hadn't. Her card had been filled within minutes.

'My dance card is full,' Clara said.

Roger winked at her. 'I know.'

He led her onto the dance floor that was filled with women wearing gowns that she would have been in awe of if she wasn't wearing one that, to her, rivalled all the others. The men were dressed in suits and some wore top hats, but not a one compared to Roger's handsomeness. She'd noticed right away that his long-tailed burgundy waistcoat was of the same shade of burgundy as her dress. His pants, boots, and double-breasted waistcoat were all black, and his shirt a bright white.

As he took her into a loose embrace for the song, her heartbeat increased. It had been a long time since she'd danced, and never to a full band.

He easily guided her through the first steps, allowing her to learn the rhythm, and then led her across the dance floor with a flair that made her giggle.

From that moment on, the evening was dreamlike. Dancing with him, eating with him from a buffet that could have fed half the country, and mingling with people that he would either nod his head for or not, which made her giggle at times. Especially when they'd encountered his mother and Stuart, and Roger had shaken his head and whispered, 'Stay clear of these two. They might steal your daughter.'

He did that several more times, made teasing, secretive comments that only she could hear, and they danced. Danced again and again.

When the band took a short break, Annabelle approached her, stating she was going to use the facilities, and asked Clara joined her.

It was down a long hallway with red floral wallpaper.

There was also a line of women in waiting.

'Let's step in here,' Annabelle said. 'We can sit while we are waiting.'

The room was full of woman, all with the same plan, no doubt.

'How badly do you have to go?' Annabelle asked, noting the room. 'We can sneak out the side door and find a bush.'

Clara laughed, because that was proof that Annabelle had not changed. 'Not bad. I've avoided drinking anything, just for this reason.'

'You know all the tricks already.'

'They are the same around the world,' Clara replied.

'Let's just get some fresh air then,' Annabelle suggested. 'Have you seen Suzanne recently?'

'On the dance floor,' Clara replied as they walked across the room. 'She loves the adventure of all this.'

'I wish I was more like her at times. She is so carefree. But I wouldn't change my life for anything. Drew is amazing. I swear I love that man more every day.'

'And he loves you,' Clara said, happy for her friend. At the same time, she wished that she, too, could be more like Suzanne. Their old life was over, and Suzanne had fully accepted that and was embracing what she referred to as an adventure of a lifetime.

'I know, I'm so lucky,' Annabelle said. 'I didn't accept that in the beginning, but I do now and wouldn't change a thing.'

As they arrived at the door to the balcony, a woman stopped Annabelle. The two began a discussion and Clara discreetly slipped outside. The balcony wasn't very large, but no one else was on it, and Clara walked to the edge to catch a breeze and to consider if she should be accepting of what had become of her life.

'And she a widow!' a woman's voice said from below the balcony.

'No!' gasped another.

'Yes,' the first one said.

'An American and a widow!' a third voice said.

Clara felt her spine quiver. She was an American and a widow. It had to be her they were talking about.

'What is this world coming to?'

'Yes, well, the Duke of Mansfield married an American. Being his best friend, maybe the marquess is following suit.'

'The duke's wife was born in England. Her mother was the lost duchess, not a penniless widow.'

'I'd always heard that Hardgroves claimed that all

widows were looking for was their next husband, and that wasn't going to be him.'

'That's true, and I know first-hand that it was because of his mother. Her being married three times put him off marriage. Perhaps he's getting his due. Getting saddled with another man's child. And an American's at that.'

Clara had heard all she'd needed to hear. As she spun about, she ran into Annabelle.

Clara's heart sank, and she grasped Annabelle's arm.

Her hold didn't stop Annabelle from moving to the edge and glancing downward. 'Nothing comes to those who gossip except trouble.'

There was silence below, other than the rustling of leaves.

Clara tugged on Annabelle's arm. 'Come on.'

'That, too, is the same around the world,' Annabelle said. 'Gossips.' Over her shoulder, she continued, 'Only those who are miserable in their own lives talk about others.'

Clara tugged harder. She knew that no good came from gossip or eavesdropping, yet she couldn't unhear what she'd heard.

The ball had lost its dreamlike quality, and when Annabelle suggested that it was time to leave, no one complained. Not even Suzanne, who rode home with Clara and Roger.

Once there, Clara went straight to her room, and started packing her trunks. Thank goodness that Abigail was sleeping in Bertha's room tonight, because she… She sniffled and forced the tears to remain at bay.

There was no use crying. It wasn't as if she'd expected things to be different.

They weren't and never would be.

The knock on her door didn't come as a surprise. She'd seen Drew talking to Roger, and knew that Annabelle had shared what they'd overheard with her husband.

'Come in.'

Roger glanced from her to her trunks, and nodded. 'We can leave for Clairmount first thing in the morning.'

Clara pinched her lips together to keep a sob inside before she said, 'I'm not returning to Clairmount. I'm going to ask Annabelle if I can stay at their townhouse until I find a job.'

'You don't need a job. I will provide—'

'No,' she interrupted. 'I've already allowed you to do too much. It's time for—'

'Then marry me.'

Clara sank to her knees, pretending that she was merely pushing the clothes down deeper into the trunk, when in reality, her legs had given out.

He knelt down on the other side of the trunk. 'I'm serious, Clara. Marry me.'

Tears formed as she shook her head. 'I can't.'

Her entire being shook from the silence that echoed in the room. She felt as if the entire world was crashing down on her all over again.

'I'm not asking you to love me, Clara,' he said.

That was the problem. She already loved him, and couldn't. Shouldn't. She had Abigail to consider.

'The war in America may not be over for years,' he

said. 'You can't put your life on hold until it is. Nor can you let a few scandalmongers who have nothing better to do with their time than spread idle gossip, affect your future.'

She lifted her chin, stared at him. 'Is it gossip when it's true? Because I am an American, and I'm a widow. A penniless widow, and you are Drew's best friend.' She refused to repeat more, because it didn't matter. None of it mattered. She'd known she'd never belong here. In this world of aristocrats living in palaces.

If it had just been about her, she would have tried, but this was about him. If he married her, the gossip would be damaging, and she couldn't let that happen.

'Clara—'

She shook her head. 'Thank you for all you've done for us. I'll never forget you, but right now, I'd like you to leave so I can finish packing.'

He stayed still, stared at her for what seemed like an eternity. 'Is that what you want? What you really want?'

To say yes would be a lie, but to say no would also be a lie. 'It's how it needs to be, Roger.'

He nodded, stood, and walked out of the room.

She could easily have collapsed into a pile on the floor, but that wouldn't do anyone any good, so she continued sorting through the dresses and packing only the ones that were suitable for a housekeeper. The rest she'd leave and hope that he'd find someone who wanted them. Perhaps even Suzanne.

Other than the burgundy one that she was wearing. She would keep that one because someday she would be able to cherish the memories of the night she'd worn it. The night she'd danced in a palace with a man who was not only noble, but also the man who had completely stolen her heart.

Hours later, after a sleepless night, Roger could have remained in his bedroom, or his study, while Clara, Abigail, Suzanne and Sammy moved out of his house, but he chose not to. Instead, he helped carry the trunks, bags, and even the high chair that he'd purchased for Abigail.

Then he bid them all a farewell, told them if they ever needed anything, they knew where to find him, and watched as Loren pulled the carriage away and drove it down the street.

He watched until it disappeared around the corner and then stood there a bit longer, as if that might change things. It wouldn't. He knew that.

Clara had looked as if she was made of glass this morning. So vulnerable, so fragile, that if he'd touched her, she would have shattered into a thousand pieces.

He hadn't meant to blurt out a marriage proposal, but as soon as he'd asked, his hopes that she'd say yes had shot up. But she hadn't said yes, and he knew why.

Feeling about as downtrodden as Sammy had after being scolded for chasing Ports, Roger turned, kept putting one foot in front of the other until he was at the door, and then entered his house.

He could go down to Pall Mall Street, burying the pain with drinks. Or he could leave town, go to Southampton, or even Clairmount.

No, not Clairmount. He doubted he'd ever be able to step foot inside that house again.

Without the energy, or want, to put the effort into going anywhere, Roger walked into his study and closed the door. What those gossips had said had been true. He had stayed away from widows because of his mother. He'd thought that she had been trying to find him a new father, when in reality, she'd merely been looking for a bit of happiness.

Something she deserved.

So did Clara.

If moving in with Drew and Annabelle would make her happy, then fine, but what if that wouldn't make her happy? What would she do then?

What would he do then?

Not worry about it. That's what he had to do. He'd offered her all he had to offer and she didn't want it. Why would she? He'd lived his entire life thinking about no one but himself.

It was an hour—or it could have been three hours, he had no way of knowing—later when someone knocked on his door. He wasn't hungry so he ignored the knock, figuring it was Garrison telling him lunch was ready.

The door opened and Drew walked into the room. He closed the door behind him and took a seat on the sofa before he said a single word. Two words actually. 'They're settled.'

Roger nodded. 'That's good.'

They sat in silence for a few moments, before Drew said, 'We had a good run, you and I. We thought we had it all figured out. Then, along came a couple of American women who turned our lives upside down and inside out.' Drew sighed. 'That's what happens when it's the right woman. She changes what a man wants.'

Roger shook his head. 'I don't have the finesse that you had. The only thing that Clara wants is to return to America.'

'That's what Annabelle had wanted, too, and the truth is, if she hadn't changed her mind about that, I would have gone with her. Moved to America.'

Roger had already come to that conclusion for himself, but things were different. Clara didn't want anything to do with him. 'Annabelle didn't have a dead husband in America. Clara is still in love with her husband. Will always be in love with her husband. I can't compete with that.'

'Is it a competition?' Drew asked. 'Or are you afraid of what loving her will do to you? I was. Both you and I thought we could live without it. I held on to that belief until Annabelle showed me that a loveless life wasn't what I wanted.'

Roger huffed out a breath. The same could be said about Clara, but it was more complicated. 'I had love and chose to ignore it. I was too stubborn, too selfish to even consider that what I believed might not be true.' Shaking his head, he continued, 'I failed my mother, Drew, completely. I can't do that again. Clara deserves better. So does Abigail. I'm not what they need.'

Something dark and cold filled him, but it wasn't new. He'd lived with it most of his life and would continue to. 'I trust you'll take care of them until the war is over.'

'Of course.'

'Clara thinks she needs a job, but...'

'I'll provide for them,' Drew said.

Roger nodded. 'Thank you.' Then, because he knew he had to get away, he slapped the arm of his chair and stood.

'Where are you going?' Drew asked.

'To sea.'

Chapter Seventeen

A full blaze of warm sunshine filled the parlour at Annabelle's London townhouse, yet a shiver trickled over Clara as she crossed the room, laid her hands on the shorter, older woman's shoulders. 'Bertha, what are you talking about?'

'It was me, all me. I told Mrs Mills to send a message to Lady Elaine, saying that His Lordship had brought home the perfect woman, and I suggested that we should find a way for you to take over the running of the house, so he would know what it was like to have a home again. A real home. I convinced the others to help me. Aaron to tell the doctor and the pedlar that you were the lady of the house. I suggested that the shelf be pulled away from the wall and made sure that you were in the growing room when Aaron and Mrs Wells laid the shelf down on Alice.' Bertha shrugged slightly. 'I didn't convince Sammy to find her—he did that on his own.'

It had been two days since she'd moved into Annabelle's house. Two days since she'd seen Roger. 'Who sent you here? To tell me all this?'

'No one,' Bertha said. 'Loren, Anita, and I are leaving for Clairmount tomorrow morning, and I wanted you to know the truth before I left.'

'Have you told Roger?'

Bertha's shoulders slumped. 'Yes, he said it doesn't matter.'

'And Elaine?'

Bertha shook her head sorrowfully. 'She's known since her visit to Clairmount. Roger had confronted her, and she told all of us to let him believe it was her and not me. I just wanted to see him happy, and after seeing how he cared for the little miss that first morning…' She gave a quick curtsy. 'Forgive me, I shouldn't have meddled, but I did, and I wanted you to know the truth, before you moved to Mansfield.'

Clara didn't know what to do with the information, because, like Roger had said, it didn't matter.

'I would be fired if I worked anywhere else, and rightfully so. I'd deserved that for my meddling and deceit, but His Lordship said that I could go back home, remain there, unless…'

'Unless what?'

'You wanted me to help with Miss Abigail,' Bertha said, with a hopeful shine in her eyes. 'I could move to Mansfield with you. If they don't already have a nanny in residence. Or I could stay here, for when you visit London.'

Clara couldn't afford to pay her and Abigail's way, let alone that of a nanny. 'Bertha, I'm sorry, but—' She sighed, shook her head.

'That's all right. I understand,' Bertha said. 'And I'm sorry. I do hope you can forgive me for what I did.'

'I forgive you, Bertha.' Clara did forgive her. 'In fact, I'm honoured that you thought so highly of me. Thought that a penniless widow could become a marchioness.'

'I knew you could, and you did,' Bertha said. 'You brought Clairmount back to life just like you did those seeds. We all saw it. That's why everyone agreed to my plan. It's been a lonely place, but like you said about the seeds, it wasn't dead, just dormant, and needed a little coaxing to come back to life.' Bertha waved to the window. 'I'll leave you be now. Loren's waiting on me. I already miss you, and Miss Abigail, and suspect I will for some time.'

Before Clara could respond, Bertha spun about and rushed through the doorway.

Clara followed, all the way to the front door, where she arrived in time to watch Bertha climb in the coach. Loren waved, and she waved back.

Tears prickled the backs of her eyes as she pulled the door shut, and knowing she couldn't hold them back, she turned and hurried up the staircase, into the bedroom where Abigail was taking her afternoon nap on the bed the two of them had shared last night.

Clara walked to the dresser and opened the top drawer, pulled out the wooden box that she'd brought with her from America. There were two things inside it. The Bible her father had given her upon her marriage, where Mark had noted Abigail's birth the night she'd been born, and the wedding ring he'd given her.

She slid the ring on her finger. It fit again. Months

ago, she'd taken it off, fearful she'd lose it because she'd lost so much weight it had been too loose to safely wear.

The simple gold band felt cold and uncomfortable, like it no longer belonged on her finger. She closed her eyes as tears escaped. Her hands shook as she removed the ring, put it back in the box and the box back in the drawer.

Then she turned, looked at her sleeping daughter.

As she had when he'd been gone from Clairmount, Abigail had been looking for Roger the past two days. Saying his name over and over and running to the door each time it opened.

Clara knew the feeling. The emptiness she'd felt since moving into Annabelle's house was encompassing. Could she live with that emptiness the rest of her life? Did she have to? Did she truly have to?

No, she didn't, or did she?

A soft knock sounded and she walked to the door, opened it.

'Come out here,' Annabelle whispered, while waving a hand.

Clara stepped into the hallway and closed the door.

'I was just reading the newspaper,' Annabelle said. 'Look at this advertisement. It's perfect for you.'

Clara took the paper Annabelle held out and read the advertisement requesting a housekeeper. 'Did you read this?' Clara asked, reading it again.

'Yes, I read it—that's why I said it would be perfect for you.'

'It says they must know how to care for plants and

flowers, children and pets.' Clara frowned. 'Doesn't that seem odd to put in the advertisement?'

'No, it's describing what they want.' Annabelle took the paper back. 'It's fine if you aren't interested. You can live here as long as you want.'

It was exactly what she was interested in, a job. An opportunity to earn money for her return to America. 'I am interested. You don't need a housekeeper here or at Mansfield. No one knows how long the war will last and I need to find a job. A way to provide for Abigail and me.'

Annabelle took a hold of Clara's hand. 'I can't imagine how hard life has been on you since Mark's death, but I understand your desire to return home. I wanted that, too, until I recognised that there was nothing for me back there. No one knows how long the war will last, or if there will be anything left of your farm to return to. I know that was your dream, Mark's dream, but maybe it's time for a new dream. Maybe a whole new life.'

Clara rubbed her finger, the very one where the ring had felt so foreign. 'I loved him. Planned on spending the rest of my life with him, and it made me so mad that he died. So mad that he left me and Abigail on our own.'

'He didn't mean to,' Annabelle said.

'I know that. I know it wasn't fair of me to be mad about it, but I was because—' She pinched her lips together as her throat swelled, stopping her from saying that she'd needed something to stop her from falling in love with Roger. It hadn't worked, though. Shaking her head, she continued, 'It's not right. Mark's only been dead less than a year.'

'A year of hell, that you lived through,' Annabelle said. 'You survived, and you deserve to love again. To be loved. I've seen the way you look at Roger, the way he looks at you. There is love there.'

Clara wasn't surprised that Annabelle had seen that, but it didn't make it right. 'That makes it worse.'

'How can love make anything worse?'

'Because it's not the same. I fell in love with Mark over time—years—but with Roger, it just happened. I didn't have time to stop it.' It felt like a tremendous relief to say that aloud. To admit that she was in love with Roger. Loved him deeply, completely.

'You couldn't have stopped it,' Annabelle said. 'And there was no reason to.'

'I vowed to love Mark for ever.'

'You vowed to love him until death parted you,' Annabelle said softly. 'You are still very much alive.'

That was true, but it didn't solve everything. 'Yes, I am, but I'll never fit in this life. You heard those gossips.'

Annabelle huffed out a mock laugh. 'Who were gossiping because they were jealous. Furthermore, do you think that I fit in when I arrived here? No. I was determined not to, either. My mother didn't have a happy life here, and I was afraid to follow in her shoes, until I realised I was walking in my own shoes and could make my own path.' She sighed. 'I'd do anything, become anyone, as long as Drew was by my side.'

Any hope that might have grown inside Clara, had one more hurdle. 'You don't know what I did.'

'Then tell me, because I don't believe it's as bad as you make it sound.'

'Roger asked me to marry him, and I refused.'

The gleam in Annabelle's expressive blue eyes made Clara's spine quiver. 'You already knew that. What else do you know that I don't?'

Annabelle waved the newspaper. 'Let's go find you a housekeeper's dress, and I'll tell you all I know.'

Clara began to follow, but then stopped and turned about, looked at the door to where Abigail slept. A bout of happiness rose up inside her. This was their new life, and she would do whatever she had to, for both of them.

Roger looked out the window for the twentieth time in the last two minutes. Time had never moved so excruciatingly slow. The message had said Clara would be here at four. It was now... He moved closer to the clock, so he could hear the tick. Three fifty-five. She wasn't late.

This was either going to work well, or blow up in his face, at which point he'd have to come up with another plan, because he wouldn't give up.

Drew's carriage rolled past the window, stopped near the walkway in front of the house, and Roger jogged out of his study to wait for a knock to sound on the door.

Maybe he should have had Garrison answer the door, or Anita or Bertha, rather than him, but he'd sent them all away. The house was empty. Silent, except for the clip of Clara's heels on the doorstep.

He balled his hand into a fist as he waited for the knock that finally came. Opening the door, he nodded. 'Hello, Clara.'

She held up a newspaper. 'I'm here in response to your ad for a housekeeper.'

She was wearing a grey and white dress, much like the staff at Clairmount wore. He waved a hand, inviting her in. 'This way, please. I would like to ask a few questions.'

'As would I.' Chin up in her dignified way, she stiffly walked inside the house.

He gestured in the direction of his study. 'This way.'

Following as she moved down the hallway, every part of him throbbed and ached to touch her. Just even her hand. He'd missed her. Tremendously.

'How is Abigail?' he asked.

'Fine, thank you.'

'And Sammy?'

She entered the study and turned about to face him. 'He, too, is doing well.'

'No cats in the neighbourhood?' He gestured for her to sit on the sofa.

'Not that we've seen so far.' Back straight, perched on the edge of the cushion, she asked, 'Where exactly are you looking to staff a housekeeper?'

'My country estate.' He sat opposite her.

'Clairmount? What about Mrs Mills?'

'She is currently still there, but I'm considering asking her to move to Southampton, to oversee my place there, because I'll be spending more time there going forward.'

'May I enquire as to why?'

'I plan on becoming more involved in sailing, captaining a ship, and will use Southampton as my home base.'

'You will?'

'Yes.'

'Why?'

'It's time.'

The past few days had been hell and he was already tired of this game. All he wanted to do was hold her, kiss her, tell her that he'd do anything for her, everything. He was no longer a man who despised marriage. He wanted to be married to her more than anything he'd ever wanted. He wanted a family. A home. All the things he'd told himself that he didn't want, he did want. Had always wanted them. He'd just been afraid to admit it because he had been afraid to love, afraid to need someone.

She pinched her lips together, and laid the newspaper down on the cushion beside her. 'How many other people have inquired about the job?'

'None,' he answered. 'I only had them print one copy of the newspaper and gave it to Drew, to give to you.'

She didn't appear to be surprised by that. 'So I can set my terms?' she asked, 'My demands?'

'You can request, I may choose to negotiate.'

'What if part of my demands includes your home base being Clairmount, not Southampton?'

His heart skipped a beat. 'I would consider that.'

She looked him straight in the eye. 'Would you consider asking me to marry you again?'

Roger had a fair idea of how much that cost her emotionally to ask, but questioned if she truly was ready for that. 'Are you sure you'd want that?'

She nodded. 'Yes, I am.' Her smile grew slowly. 'That is if you want to ask it again.'

He fought against a full-blown smile, but lost. He also lost the battle to sit still. He stood, but only enough to take one step and kneel in front of her. 'I asked you to marry me the other night because I love you. Before I met you, I didn't think it was possible for me to love someone, nor can I say exactly when that happened. I'd guess at some point between Southampton and Clairmount, because by the time we arrived, I knew there was something different inside me.' He took a hold of her hands. 'I understand that you are scared about living here, in England, but we don't have to. We can live anywhere you want. Anywhere in the world.'

She wrapped her fingers tighter around his. 'I'm not afraid of living here. I was afraid of leaving here, leaving England and never feeling the way I feel when I'm with you, ever again. I love you, Roger. It happened so fast, came on so strongly, I didn't know what to do. I didn't think it could happen, and when it did, I didn't know how to accept it. I didn't think I deserved to be happy again, but you...' She shook her head. 'You make me so happy. I want that. I want you.'

'I want you, too. You make me happy. So happy. I understand you loved Mark, and I accept that. I will never compare your love for him to how you feel about me, but I swear to you that I will love you with all my heart, now and for ever.'

She held his gaze, and he noticed there was a new

clarity in her eyes. One that hadn't been there before. 'I love you with all my heart,' she whispered. 'Every part of it. Abigail will know who her father was, but it is you who she already loves.'

'I love her, too,' he said. 'As strongly as I will any child we may produce.' He cupped her cheek. 'And I vow that our children will know how deeply I love their mother every single day.'

'I know you will.' A tear trickled down her cheek.

Holding her chin, he kissed her, a soft, gentle kiss, showing how much he cherished her.

'You make my head spin,' she whispered. 'There's one more thing I need to say.'

He nodded, waited as she swallowed, blinked.

'I have a lot to learn about becoming a marchioness.'

Leaning his head against her forehead. 'No, you don't. You've already mastered that.'

She shook her head. 'No, I haven't. There are so many rules.'

Understanding her concerns, he leaned back, met her gaze. 'The only thing a marchioness has to do is love her husband.'

She laughed. 'That I can to. I already do.'

'I'm so glad.' He chuckled. 'I was prepared to hire you as a housekeeper, you know. To keep you here until I could convince you to stay for ever.'

'You'd already convinced me,' she said. 'Hold me, kiss me, so I know that I'm not dreaming.'

He wrapped his arms around her and kissed her like he'd been wanting to do for days. So thoroughly, so completely, that they both knew they weren't dreaming.

The want to carry her upstairs, to his room and ease the ache in his body was powerful, but he could wait, would wait, until she was his wife.

Clara, however, had other plans. 'I told Annabelle that I won't be back until tomorrow to pick up Abigail.'

He grinned. 'You did?'

She nodded.

'Why is that?' he asked, kissing the side of her neck.

'Because you are now stuck with me, for ever.'

There was nothing he could say to that, except to silently thank his lucky stars. Roger stood and lifted her off the sofa. Kissing her soundly, he then carried her out of the room and up the stairs.

In his bedroom, with the afternoon sun still filling the sky, Clara trembled with anticipation as she unbuttoned the grey dress and let it slide off her shoulders, then drop to the floor. Her underclothes followed.

Roger's gaze roamed over her, affecting her as strongly as if it were his hands touching her breasts, stomach, and thighs. Her flesh tingled, her nipples pebbled, and her eyes met his, her lips smiling.

'You are beyond beautiful, Clara,' he said huskily. 'Beyond beautiful.'

The confidence inside her was unimaginable. She had become a new woman. The old one, who had lived through hell and back, was gone, replaced by a stronger, bolder, version who knew what she wanted, now and for ever.

Clara stepped closer to Roger, who had removed his

boots, but had then stopped undressing to watch her. She looped her arms around his neck and kissed him.

Kissed him until the anticipation of having his hard, firm body pleasuring her became more than she could take. 'I want you,' she said, not afraid in the least for him to know that. 'Now.'

He removed the pins from her hair, let the tresses fall down her back. 'I want you, too.'

She was busy with the buttons on his shirt, and as soon as the last one was done, he pulled it off and tossed it aside. Then he lifted her by the waist so their faces were even and kissed her again.

Locking her arms around his neck and her legs around his hips, she clung on as his kisses nearly drove her insane. 'I said I wanted you five minutes ago. I'm dying now.'

Chuckling, Roger carried her to the bed, laid her down on it and got rid of his pants. He crawled onto the bed, and starting near her feet, he kissed his way up her body.

He took his time, and was confident and purposeful in every touch, every caress. He worked his way along both of her legs, across her stomach, and paid a lavish amount of special attention to her breasts before his face was even with hers.

Clara's entire body was not only throbbing with the deepest need, it was burning with the sweetest fiery heat.

As Roger's skin merged with hers, his weight settled upon her, and he slid deeply inside her, he looked at her in such a way that she'd never felt more beautiful, or loved, or wanted.

Clara had thought that, as a married woman, she'd known it all, but Roger proved she hadn't, by loving her so thoroughly, so intently, that when her time came, it wasn't just a release of the wild pressure that had built inside her, it was a celebration. One of love and life, and sharing, and freedom. Loving him had given her freedom from the past and hope for the future.

Roger's lips left hers, for he'd kissed her solidly while her body had been celebrating the sharing of their love, and he gave her nose a soft peck before he smiled down at her.

After that release, and his kisses, she was still gasping for air, yet Clara met his gaze, smiled, and flung an arm above her head. 'That was amazing.'

'Was?' Roger laughed. Planted a fast kiss on her lips. 'Clara, we've only just begun.'

Lord but she loved this man.

Epilogue

The shorter days were a clear sign that autumn was on its way and Clara was looking forward to it. Not because she was tired of summer, but because she liked the changing of seasons. Change was good. It gave a person room to grow.

Smiling, she rubbed her stomach. That too would soon be growing.

Sammy let out a bark from where he lay near her feet.

'Behave,' Clara said.

'He is behaving,' Roger said, carrying Abigail on his shoulders.

Clara lifted her face for her husband to kiss. He did so, and then set Abigail down on the deck of the ship.

'We'll be docked in Southampton by this time tomorrow,' he said, putting one arm around her shoulders and resting his other hand on her stomach.

'I know. I was standing here, watching the sun drop lower and thinking about Clairmount. I've missed it.' She leaned her head against him. 'This has been wonderful, though. Seeing such beautiful islands and eating bananas. I do wish we could find a way to make them last long enough to ship home.'

'Perhaps we will, once we get those new engines installed on our ships as well as those refrigerators.'

They'd seen them at the International Exposition , and Roger had invested a great deal of money in trying both new inventions. In her mind, it would be worth the money if they could figure out a way to ship bananas. They were delicious.

'Or maybe you'll make that tree grow tall enough to produce all the bananas you can eat,' he said.

'Maybe?' She glanced at the little tree that he had dug up for her, and that she planned to plant in the growing house as soon as they got home. 'I'll definitely make that tree grow.'

He chuckled. 'I know you will.'

Stretching on her toes, she kissed his cheek.

He hugged her tighter, kissed the top of her head. 'Maybe by the time we take our next trip, the war will be over and we can stop in Virginia.'

She twisted and looped her arms around his neck. This man. This wonderful, amazing man, who had given her everything when she had nothing, who had changed her life when she'd thought that wasn't possible, was always thinking of her first and foremost. 'Virginia was my home once, but England is my home now. It has all I'll ever want. All I'll ever need.'

'I love you.'

She never tired of hearing him say that. 'I love you, too,' she whispered against his lips. 'More and more every day.'

His mouth covered hers, consumed hers, and they

would have gone on kissing, standing there on the deck, if a growling meow, a bark, and a little girl's squeal hadn't sounded.

Breaking apart, Roger quickly scooped up Abigail, but there was no chase happening.

The big yellow deck cat was sitting atop a barrel and Sammy had leaped upon another one, both of them looking at the water.

Clara wrapped a hand around Roger's arm. 'Look!' There were several dolphins swimming along the side of the boat.

He chuckled. 'That's a good omen.'

Clara turned her gaze from the huge, graceful mammals, to her husband. 'So are you. I've been lucky since the moment I met you.'

Clearly.

She'd gone from a penniless widow to a marchioness. That took luck.

And a few wonderful household staff members.

* * * * *

If you enjoyed this story, be sure to check out the first book in Lauri Robinson's Southern Belles in London miniseries

The Return of His Promised Duchess

And whilst you're waiting for her next book, why not have a read of The Osterlund Saga duology?

Marriage or Ruin for the Heiress
The Heiress and the Baby Boom

◆ HARLEQUIN
HISTORICAL

Your romantic escape to the past.

Be seduced by the grandeur, drama and sumptuous detail of romances set in long-ago eras!

Six new books available every month!

HARLEQUIN
PLUS

Try the best multimedia subscription service for romance readers like you!

Read, Watch and Play.

Experience the easiest way to get the romance content you crave.

Start your **FREE TRIAL** at
www.harlequinplus.com/freetrial.